Bay Roses

Tom Richmond &
Susan Bandy

PUBLISHED BY FIDELI PUBLISHING, INC.

Bay Roses

Copyright © 2019 Tom Richmond & Susan Bandy

Certain characters in this work are historical figures, and certain events portrayed did take place. However, this is a work of fiction. All of the other characters, names, and events as well as all places, incidents, organizations, and dialogue in this novel are either the products of the author's imagination or are used fictitiously.

Books may be ordered through booksellers or by contacting:

Fideli Publishing, Inc.
119 W Morgan St.
Martinsville, IN 46151
888-343-3542
www.FideliPublishing.com

ISBN: 978-1-948638-66-1 (soft cover)
ISBN: 978-1-948638-69-2 (eBook)

Library of Congress Control Number: 2019932257

Printed in the United States of America.

1

My name is Frank Barrett. In the late fifties, I remember riding home from church with my family in Tampa, Florida. We skirted Hillsborough Bay on Bay Shore Drive, and that bay stunk! Foul odor emanated from algae rotting in industrially polluted water. Oxygen depleted marine life added to the inescapable zephyrs.

My sisters cried plaintively in an un-air-conditioned car. My brother and I tried to "buck-up" as Dad used to say.

He offered no excuses, "Come now, kids. It's only the 'Bay Roses' you're smellin'."

Years later, I watched across that same bay. I was a jet pilot stationed at MacDill Air Force Base in Tampa. Looking across the bay, I wondered what had happened since I'd been gone. It doesn't matter now, I told myself. Let God sort it out. I've been through it all, yet *still* I wondered what more was in store for me.

I had learned to confront my demons and put hollow vengeance behind me. There was only one concern — put vengeance behind me and justice before me. A lot of that came from unexpected sources.

When I left the U S Air Force another door opened. I was discovered in a vexing sort of way by an intriguing man. His name was Curtis Selway. He stood barely six feet with a narrow waist and broad shoulders. With crew-cut reddish hair and wire-rim glasses, he looked more like a professor than an insurance sleuth. Yet, nature abhors a vacuum and fills niches with experts all the time.

Curtis needed a pilot in a hurry; and I was his man. Since then, I've teamed up with Curtis on several insurance fraud investigations after leaving the U S Air Force in 1974. He operates in a quasi-nebulous, covert world of high-end insurance claims resolution. In other words, when he is involved, the bad guys don't get the money.

We always fly on *Company Business,* his private Gulfstream II jet. Our relationship requires my services as bodyguard on occasion. So, I always carry my standard service pistol.

Curtis was currently on an assignment that was sure to require a lot of flying in days ahead. That's why I was tagging along with him in Ybor City, Florida. Presently seated in "Rough Riders Bar" I had just ordered a Sam Adams Beer. Curtis had his usual shot of Chivas neat in front of him. He seemed deep in thought, so I kept to myself looking around at memorabilia on the walls. Rough Riders Bar was a quarter of a mile from the original point of debarkation of Teddy Roosevelt's Rough Riders on their way to their famous encounter charging up Kettle Hill in Cuba in the Spanish American War in 1898. I wondered how many really knew that. Due to limited space on transports, their horses were left behind. In fact, the First Volunteer Cavalry became Wood's Weary Walkers, after their commander, General Leonard Wood, whose second in command was Col. Theodore Roosevelt.

Curtis lifted his scotch quickly draining it. Then, as he tapped it down, a tremendous explosion rocked the bar shattering every window. Splintered glass was flying all around us as we instinctively jumped for the floor. U.S. Phosphoric Chemical Plant was erupting a half mile away. The shock was felt all over East Tampa blowing windows out in every direction. The former site of the plant was belching thirty years of accumulated polluted waste into the air as it imploded, pushing a tower of yellowish smoke half mile into the air.

When the initial tremors settled, I looked up from my prone position seeing Curtis sprawled in front of me with his hands still cupped over his ears. With wire rimmed glasses askew on his face underneath his favorite Irish flat-cap (the one he bought in Galway), he appeared almost comical. Rising cautiously, dusting off our jackets, we started assessing the immediate situation. I noticed none of the patrons were too worse for the wear. Mainly, their faces bore looks of panic and bewilderment as they bustled out the door. Curtis regained some composure walking and weaving over shattered glass. He peered through the empty frame of the bar's front window. Looking up and down the street, he said nothing. He made no attempt to go out with the crowd. He only pointed east, stoically saying, "It's U.S. Phosphoric."

He was right. In place of the three 300-foot smoke stacks above the plant there was only a giant pall of yellow smoke billowing thousands of feet above the nearby small town of Riverview. Sirens began to wail plaintively as they drove toward the scene of complete devastation.

It used to be the Lust Brothers' primary site for manufacturing fertilizer from raw phosphate. Now, it was a huge fireball on the ground pulsing black smoke columns into the air. Now, it was a boiling cauldron. I had not witnessed anything like it since the all-out bombing campaigns conducted over North Vietnam. I had not been back one year, and it seemed as if I was being followed. Curtis interrupted my thoughts.

"They're going to be calling me soon enough. Let's get going."

Still numb, I parroted, "Right boss, let's get going."

We jumped into the candy-apple metallic red '66 Shelby Cobra — the former pilot's car I received by default. Curtis fired him for running me and my girl, Sandy, off the road back in St Petersburg. Now, the 427 cubic inch, fuel injected engine purred only for me. Preoccupied in his thoughts, Curtis hardly noticed the smooth powerful ride I was delivering straight across the Howard Franklin Bridge over Tampa Bay toward St. Pete/Clearwater International Airport.

As we neared Pilot's Cove (the little base of operations bars he owned), also home away from home for many of his pilot friends, we took the sudden turn off onto the twisting oyster shell road, leaving a cloud of dust behind. Taking time to clean up, we then drove over to Curtis' hangar. It was my job, of course, to get the aircraft pre-flighted, although Curtis was fully checked out in the Gulfstream II only a week after he purchased it, the year before.

A commercial/instrument pilot, I trusted him completely at the controls of his 40,000-lb. twin-engine biz-jet. Yet, piloting a jet was the least of his skills. After graduating with a J.D. in Law from Notre Dame with Honors, he accepted a position in the U.S. Government Services Agency. As assistant to the Inspector General, he soon became disenchanted with government waste and left for a position as Insurance Council/ Inspector with a top legal firm in Chicago. The gifted Irish-American often operated on the periphery of legal authority establishing a reputation for relentless, irresistible, dogged determination. He reveled in exposing the duplicity and deceit of the rich in their endless attempts to defraud the insurance industry. Only in his late thirties, he was already known as one of, if not *the* best, in his game. He dressed nattily and abided in the form of good breeding and manners. In short, he was a most affable man, unless he found good reason to despise the nature of people's undertakings.

While I warmed up his jet, *Company Business,* Curtis went to the lounge and then got on the phone. He spoke with his client, who had vested insurance interests with U.S. Phosphoric.

"Yes, Greg, it's Curtis. I'm in my plane on the ground at St. Petersburg ramp. We are now warmed-up and ready for takeoff."

There was a pause while Curtis listened patiently to a distraught man on the other end, whose company stood to lose millions of dollars in loss claims. No small figure in 1974.

"I will take a full roll of aerial photos shortly. I promise you that. Of course, it will take at least a month before any real inspection results will be ready from the fire department. As soon as they are published, I'll obtain a release of records and stay on top of it until we've got something. What's more Greg, I've already got a feeling about this one and I want to get a head start by going up to Ontario to follow-up on some leads."

"What? Why Canada? We have no interests there related to this disaster."

"No, you don't. However, your clients, the Lust Brothers do."

"Just let me do some preliminary work up there, while they're sifting through the ashes in Riverview. I think I've got an angle on who's responsible for this entire debacle. Anyway, I want to develop a lead I've been working on. I'll see you first thing when I get back. Your camera boys should have enough to keep them busy for at least a week. I'll be back before they're done, trust me."

The dejected V.P. of J.E. Chairs Insurance replied, "Right now, it seems you're the only guy in town I can trust. Have a good trip, Curtis. I'll be anxious to see what you've found in Ontario. By the way, where is it you're going exactly?"

"It's a little town about 30 miles west of Niagara Falls."

"Well, alright. Get back as soon as you can and good luck."

"Thanks, we'll probably just make our own though. See you later. Goodbye."

Curtis came forward, taking up the co-pilot's position next to me.

"Will this be a long stay in Canada? I didn't pack my long johns."

"That depends on what I find there. Don't worry, I'm sure you'll have enough to do to keep you warm."

"I was afraid you'd say that. Would you like to fill me in as to why we are heading for Canada when the demolished chemical plant is here? I thought U.S. Phosphoric, alias the Lust Brothers, were the bad guys."

"They still are. Sometimes you have to look in a few dark corners before you find all your rats."

"Whatever you say, boss."

"Yes, and please stop calling me boss. Curtis will do, you know that. Sometimes I think you just call me that to annoy me."

"Why heaven-for-fend, Curtis, why would I ever do that?"

Curtis caught sight of the corner of my mouth leaving my impish smile behind.

"Just taxi now."

"Yes, sir", I replied, smartly steering the whining jet to the active runway. Then, with a shimmering jet blast on the tarmac, we were on the take-roll.

"St. Petersburg/Clearwater Tower, this is Whiskey Tango 1331 on runway 35 right, requesting a straight-out departure."

The tower replied, "Roger, Whiskey Tango, you are cleared for a straight-out departure, contact departure control on frequency 119.2 and have a good day."

"Roger, tower. *Company Business,* is on the roll."

Frank knew, technically, his jet should be referred to as Whiskey Tango 1331 in all communications with the F.A.A. Yet, he knew the boys in the tower realized his plane was the only Gulfstream II based there. In seconds, *Company Business* was steaming down Runway 35. Frank scanned all gauges for any sign of required emergency action. Curtis kept his eye on the airspeed indicator. As the plane approached 100 knots he called, "rotation V1", that meant the jet's nose was lifting off. Seconds later, he called out, "*V2*" for lift-off. This meant, once again, the sleek jet slipped the surly bonds of earth. The 78-foot-long, 80-foot wing span jet was now climbing out at 3,800 feet/minute.

Frank keyed his microphone, "St. Pete departure we are requesting flight instructions we are leaving your area on a northbound heading 350."

"Roger, Whiskey Tango 1331, we have you. Continue heading of 350. Ascend to 25,000 and have a good day, sir. This is St. Pete departure out."

Frank responded, "Roger, St. Pete departure out."

Company Business continued its climb uneventfully reaching 25,000 ft. leveling off. On course northward, Frank eased back in his seat turning to Curtis. Both men were more relaxed now that the busy part of the flight was over, for the time being.

Frank asked, "Now are you going to tell me why we're flying to little ole' Dunville?"

"It's a long story, fortunately, on this trip we've got time. Ever since the creation of the Environmental Protection Agency in December of 1970, large chemical plants, which for the time being I will call fluoride emitters, have been under the gun. They have been feeling the pressure of litigation from many quarters for the damage they have done to their local environments. For instance, our 'friends,' the Lust Brothers, have acted with impunity when they allowed their phosphate fertilizer conversion operations to pollute the air and water with emissions from their plants.

"The process of making fertilizer out of phosphate leaves behind airborne fluorides which enter the atmosphere surrounding plants poisoning the land for miles around. Many farmers in the area began to complain of stunted growth in their vegetables and other crops.

"For years, the huge operations like U.S. Phosphoric got away with it by bribing local authorities and other business interests. The farmers had little to show for their case, as they really did not know what exactly was causing the problem. Finally, when the fluorides got into the water in quantities large enough to affect livestock, the pressure increased. The litigation for damaged herds of livestock of all kinds, finally, became an issue for them. Gradually, their response was to contain the drain-off from their overheated water in their conversion plants. Then, some enterprising group, which must publicly remain nameless for the time being, hit upon the idea they could purchase storage from remote areas to hide their unwanted export from the E.P.A. Dunville is one such area."

"Curtis, you sure know how to cut to the quick when you explain things. What are we going to do in Dunville?"

"I want to go out and talk to the farmers affected and see how it is first hand. I think it will strengthen my case against a corporation that blew-up their own plants and will try to collect on the damages."

"So, you really do believe the Lust Brothers destroyed their own plant?"

Curtis' face took on that dogged look he was known for in court, replying, "Sure as a heart attack, Frank. They did it."

The flight was going smoothly as the two Rolls-Royce Spey turbo-fan engines drove *Company Biz* along at 500 mph. At that rate, Curtis knew it would be hours before they reached their destination.

"I'm going back to the lounge and take a nap. Hold on to things up here. Okay?"

"Sure boss."

Curtis winced behind his steel rims as he left the cabin.

2

As we flared out on landing, Curtis reappeared. It was an uneventful flight. I chose not to disturb him, as I knew he would be concentrating on this case. Too bad he missed the scenery passing over Niagara Falls on a clear fall morning. Witnessing the billowing mist thousands of feet below was inspirational. Only angels could have dreamt-up something so breathtaking. I could almost feel the chill spray on my face as I banked west for Hamilton Municipal Airport 30 miles away. On the taxi roll, Curtis appeared in the cockpit with his Irish plaid flat-cap, his ubiquitous Moleskine note pad poking out of his vest-pocket. It was the ever-present nomadic object on every assignment, ultimately becoming an integral part of his personality. It was an 8x5 inch ruled notebook. To Curtis, it was a ubiquitous extension of his investigations. A trusted, worthy traveling companion rarely left behind.

As we walked away from the aircraft, I turned looking over my shoulder as several men accompanied a tug pushing *Company Business* into the dark hangar behind us. Now, my responsibility shifted. Curtis and I were on our way to a farm outside of Dunville. I felt uncomfortable rocking around in the huge interior of the ponderous Checker Cab, as we rolled up and down bumpy country roads. The land was dotted with cattle and sheep and small white buildings clustered around tall red barns with black roofs shadowed by an occasional shiny blue silo.

Eventually, we rolled up a long, gravel drive amidst a flock of skittering Guiney hens. As I stepped from the cavernous dinosaur of a taxi, I felt out of place. Before me bordering the drive, was a long row of holly hawks in bloom. Behind it, two beautiful peacocks displayed their wondrous rainbow of feathers. I was reminded of days on our farm amongst the beauty of nature.

I was taken back to where I spent every summer of my youth on our family farm in Central Illinois. My ancestors settled there in 1828 when land was twenty-five cents an acre. My privilege was to grow-up and learn there, gaining a healthy respect for the land and nature's gifts. I allowed myself to daydream about a time when I was truly happy. My older brother by four years stood next to me in a seemingly ancient I.G.A. store with wooden floors. It was founded in 1872. My brother, John, and I were being introduced by our grandfather to the mayor of Armington, Illinois (population 300). His name escapes me now. Though, his daughter enchanted me, amidst the scent of new leather gloves my grandfather just bought me.

I was proud. I looked like a farmhand. Thanks to Granddad my outfit was complete. I wore new Levi's, white T-shirt, and sturdy work boots. I stood there in front of Donna, almost a mirror image of my brother, except I was the husky one. *Always the husky one I thought.* Later, I got to know Donna better. At the age of fourteen, I was thrilled to be seen with that blond haired, blue-eyed girl anywhere. There were always happy memories of our relationship, which renewed every summer.

Sadly, I also recalled a farm crisis that arose during that time. Once, our Black Angus grazed in some poison snakeroot. It brought down and killed thirteen cattle and their calves, before it was discovered. I was about to learn something much worse was plaguing this poor Canadian farmer.

When Curtis stepped up to shake the farmer's hand, he could see crusts of spent tears in the corners of his reddened eyes. The farmer held back his misery as he deftly explained what he knew of events past. It was a tale of ecological devastation.

"We first noticed something mysterious on some garden plants. We found burned peppers; then we found burned fruit. He once had beautiful Bartlett pears, now all were shriveled. Likewise, shriveled grains drooped over the ground. It seems everything that grew was damaged. Around these parts, it broke the farmers' hearts.

He told us, "Our cattle started to fall. One day, I was on my tractor bringing out some hay, and I saw one of my prized Hereford's down on her forelegs. She was stumbling along, on her forelegs, no foolin'. As I got to lookin' at the rest of my herd, I found cases of swollen joints. I called the vet right away. When he got out here, we rounded them for inspection. We found falling teeth and sore jointed cattle lying down just out of plain misery."

The problem was clear. Curtis was learning, from the veterinarian's written report, a source of raw phosphate ore containing high concentrations of fluoride, plus hydrogen fluoride, had been introduced into the animals' feeding area. Fluoride contamination was clearly present in the area and Curtis knew why. He remembered seeing something like this as a child in Polk County on his father's cattle ranch. His father noticed the same change. He watched his cattle become gaunt and starved looking. Their legs became deformed, reproduction fell off, and when a cow did have a calf, it was stillborn. The blight continued to affect his cattle. Some lay in the pasture, barely able to move. Others limped and staggered on swollen legs or painfully sank down and tried to graze on their knees. Their fate was dehydration, starvation, and death.

Curtis asked, "Have other farmers reported the same kind of losses in the area?"

"Oh yeah, several of my neighbors have. We are holding a town meeting tomorrow night about all this."

Curtis asked, "May we attend that meeting?"

"Of course, you can. It's open to the public. Do you think you know something about all this?

"Yes, but I'd rather wait until the meeting and share my findings with everyone."

"Okay, I expect that's the best way to do it. Fellas, I got a lot of cleanin' up to do yet, so if you don't mind."

"Sure, we understand. I've got all I need for now. I'll see you at the meeting, Mr. Bogar."

The middle-aged farmer turned his back and waved as he headed for the cattle barn. Curtis and I took our lumbering, yellow Checker Cab back to our motel. When we arrived, Curtis suggested we find a place to eat lunch. There wasn't much to choose from. On the main drag, which was appropriately named Main Street, we spied two dubious prospects. One was more modern looking than its competitor and, hopefully, cleaner. It was the Red Barn, also appropriately sided with faded red barn wood. As we stepped to its porch, there were a couple of hanging signs to greet us. One read, "We don't save your money or offer credit, but the bank doesn't make our biscuits either." Another read, "Spend generously, we wanna see ya again."

Curtis quipped, "I hope their biscuits survive their humor."

I just smiled as we entered. Looking about, I could see they did a fair amount of trade in farm implements and antiques. For instance, there were old coffee grinders of different manufacture affixed to the walls along with an assortment of worn out washboards, galvanized wash tubs, twin handled ice saws (seven feet long), meat grinders etc. One item caught my eye. It was an old carom board. It was refinished and coated with a modern polyurethane finish. Someone spent a lot time restoring that old game board. I hadn't seen one since I was child on the farm in Illinois. Next to it was an open box attached to the wall with all the red and green carom rings in it.

My grandmother would let my brother and me play that old game on stormy nights. I remember it took some skill, yet after my granddad instructed us, I caught the hang of it mighty quickly, much to my brother's chagrin. I seemed better at it than him, which was quite pleasing for a brother four year his junior. When it got late, Grandma made us put up the board, but Grandpa would take us up to bed. Once we were tucked-in, he would peek down the stairwell making sure the coast was clear, then he would tell us what he used to call "tall timber stories." There was always a young buck in the stories named Frank. Obviously, from the background and nature of his stories, he was a young woodsman who trapped, hunted, and lived off the land. Grandpa never revealed the true nature of his character. Yet, he reminded me of him when he was young. Sometimes, I wonder if I wasn't named for that young boy who lived off the land.

Clarence Darby, short-order-cook, interrupted my daydreaming. He was an erstwhile new employee hoping to curry favor with his boss, the owner.

"Now, what can I get you gents for lunch today? You seem new in town? Maybe you'd both like the Country Fried Steak Lunch Special? I can fixer-up special for ya in a jiffy. Whadda ya say?"

Curtis raised a finger drolly replying, "A grilled cheese sandwich will do." Immediately, Clarence started his spiel.

"Oh, come now. A finely dressed gentleman like yourself surely deserves more than that."

"You're right. I'll have a Diet Coke, as well."

Clarence blurted, "We just don't have that drink here."

Looking up through steel rims Curtis replied, "Perhaps a Pepsi, please."

Clarence returned, "We've got Royal Crown Cola?"

Never looking up Curtis simply said, "It's a deal."

Just then, Clarence's boss entered from the back. Looking across at Clarence expectantly, Clarence reacted with renewed vigor.

Turning to me, he asked, "Would you like the lunch special today, sir?

"No, I think I'll just have a garden salad with blue cheese dressing, thank you."

Deflated Clarence retreated to the kitchen where he could be heard explaining to his boss how hard he tried.

Unbelievably, after lunch, I found myself seated in a pew of the Dunville Christian Church. The meeting had been going on over an hour. Because I only accompanied Curtis, I lost interest rapidly.

I found myself doing something I hadn't done in years. In North Vietnamese prison camp, they attempted to re-educate us. They harangued us until we learned to sit bolt upright, daydreaming about anything else, other places, anything. My favorite escape was back to elementary school days when I was carefree.

I was in second grade in Mrs. Walker's class. When she entered the class one day, she planted her colossal derrière on her chair, launching a pile of chalk dust I left in anticipation of a grand turbid eruption. Results were better than anticipated. The resultant mushroom cloud rising above her, left every child laughing, and chanting deliriously – "duck and cover, duck and cover…"

Calamity was only the beginning of my school career. I was wrestled from my seat and summarily marched to the principal's office. Apparently, that little weasel-squeezer, Mike Royal, sitting behind me finked. I was interrogated, then, turned over to my mother where the real punishment began. I was, in turn, remanded to the custody of my father when he returned home.

It never worked. Soon, I was back at it. Next time, the class ant farm received a liberal dose of honey. I must admit it seemed educational as the class looked on eagerly that morning. We learned the strict societal structure of worker ants suddenly deteriorated into a sugar frenzied, claim jumping, honey fueled, winner-takes-all, psychotic maze of malevolent ants gone wild. Before our eyes, we realized the farm became a miniature of our own world where only the strong survive. Older than my years, I recognized something eerily familiar with the whole scene. Soon, I advanced to the principal's office, where the cycle only repeated itself.

Then came third grade. Despite the paddling, I finally made it. Nevertheless, I did discover Ms. Sail, my third-grade teacher. I was immediately smitten. She was agile, beautiful, witty, and dark-haired. Of course, it was instant love.

She inspired me to apply myself to greater heights. I wanted to excel just for her. Soon, I soared to the pinnacle of my academic career. I was leading the class in long division. All was right with the world with Ms. Sail in it. The following summer, most startling of all, it was decided I would skip a grade, from fourth to fifth.

Principal Bagley, clinging on for a thirty-year retirement, possessed the face of a losing boxer, bless her heart. She even seemed to like me. I developed a propensity for solving mathematical word problems; something no one of my ancestry would have predicted.

Suddenly, it was summer again. No school, no Ms. Sail. So, resigning myself to model airplane building and baseball, I got on until fall. When that day arrived, I was ready. First in the hallway outside Ms. Sail's classroom, I waited with my new Roy Rodger's lunchbox.

Suddenly, disaster struck. Ms. Sail transformed over summer into Mrs. Wilson. Even the name on her door was changed. I was devastated. I felt so betrayed.

Some older girl said, "She's married now, so you better watch out or her husband will beat you up if he finds out you like her."

I slid down against the wall by her door in disbelief. Opening my lunch box, I decided to take the apple I saved for her and smash it against her door. Just then, Mr. Jenkins, the custodian, turned the corner with his extra-wide dust mop, so I slowly closed the lid.

Forlornly, I trudged home promising myself I would never love again. In the kitchen, I mixed up a quart of cherry Kool-Aid with extra sugar and proceeded to drown my sorrows. Then, things got worse. Over dinner, Dad explained he was being transferred to Sidi Slamain, Morocco.

I asked, "Where's that Dad?"

"It's in Africa, son."

He patiently explained it was best for us to stay in America, because the standard of living wasn't good there and the country was presently unstable.

I asked, "How long will you be gone?"

He remained silent so long I thought it was a U. S. Air Force secret he couldn't divulge. Then, he looked around at us speaking slowly.

"Kids, your dad may have to be away as long as three years."

Three years! I thought, *No, Dad, no way, for three years!* Even at my tender age, I thought, *this is total bullshit!*

Then, I felt a churning coming from my stomach. Kool-Aid was rising, along with meatloaf and mashed potatoes. Mom noticed. Standing up like a shot, she snatched her dishtowel off the back of her chair. I tried holding everything down as she came at me with the towel.

Dad warned, "Frankie, don't you do it!"

It was too late. Mom never did get that cherry colored stain out of her tablecloth. It was a total loss, as was the meat loaf dinner I ruined for my family. Mom was kind assuring me all would be okay, only this time I knew better.

That night, lying in bed, I heard Dad reassuring Mom, between her sobs, how this time he would surely make Colonel when he got back. His pep talk wasn't working. It was little consolation for me and my brother, John, either. Though he was taking it better than me, at least he didn't barf over the news.

He said, "I'll be in charge around the house while Dad's gone, so you better do what I say."

"I will as long as you don't make me pick-up dog doo and stuff like that."

He chuckled, "Oh, all right", he replied, grinning down mischievously from his upper bunk.

"Only on Saturdays."

Suddenly, I felt a poke in my ribs.

Curtis whispered, "Would you please stand up so I can get out? It's my turn to speak."

With a rude awakening, my attention focused on the town hall meeting in progress. Curtis strode to the podium with Moleskine note pad in hand.

"Good afternoon, folks. My name is Curtis Selway. Simply put, I am an insurance investigator from Florida. The heart of your problem is the reason I'm here. You have a severe pollution problem on your hands here, and I can tell you why. I know the chemical agent that's causing your crops to fail and your livestock to die."

The meeting house immediately erupted in a cacophony of questions, and comments all directed at Curtis. Patiently, he waited for the unrest to die down before he chose to address the good folk of Dunville again. He tried announcing his explanation to the agitated town folk. With his hand up-raised, he attempted to quiet down the crowd. Mayor Blount arose and raised his strong voice.

"Now folks, we've had our say. This man's come a long way, possibly, with some answers to our problem. We owe him the sensibility to hear him out."

The hall seemed to get quiet enough, so the Mayor re-introduced Curtis.

Curtis began, "Ladies and gentlemen, the problem at hand is somewhat complicated. I have background in this sort of pollution first hand. I can make this as simple as stick figures, if you'll just hear me out. A chemical called fluorine has polluted your crops and livestock. It did not previously exist here, but was shipped here by a local businessman. He's dumped thousands of gallons of this stuff in your river. My preliminary investigation has determined the source of this fluorine is Tampa, Florida."

3

ayor Blount jumped to his feet addressing the town folk.
"Why, this is an outrage! How can we believe some so-called outside *expert* is right about all this? We have no proof. So far, all we have are reports from our county agents. The toxicology reports from the vet's blood tests haven't even been completed yet."

He drew up his sagging middle-aged paunch, standing erect at his full 5'6" height. The easy years appeared on his mottled, jowly face, as he regarded Curtis (the interloper) with increasing ambivalence.

"You, Curtis Selway, *mister insurance investigator,* are guilty of inciting these fine folks here without real proof or cause."

Curtis replied, "You are partly right, Mayor Blount. I am expressly here to establish a link between U.S. Phosphoric Corporation and Westlake Industrial Storage here in Dunville. I strongly suspect U.S. Phosphoric shipped thousands of gallons of fluorine-contaminated water intentionally mislabeled as something less toxic. Since the primary owner's own their shipping line, I contend they shipped 55-gallon drums deliberately placarded with the hazard symbol Xn/Harmful; X Irritant instead of N/ Environmental Hazard."

"In so doing, they could ship their hazardous effluent here; then truck it 3 miles to Mr. Wesley Westlake's warehouse by the river. All this could be done, at a price for rental of Westlake Warehouses, Inc. space. This has been done before in South America, and even in Garrett, Montana. Federal agents discovered their ploy there. That is how I've come by my information and recent suspicions. I only work on behalf of my clients in Florida who wish to protect their interests against exorbitant illegal claims being made by their insured. You see, ever since the inception of the E.P.A., huge fertilizer manufacturers like U.S. Phosphoric are seeking ways to hide their useless, poisonous by-products. If my remarks have incited the good towns' folk, I assure you it was not my intention. I simply wanted to inform them what is happening here in Dunville. Certainly, I will include the local vet's lab findings in my report.

In the meantime, I intend to continue my investigation, legally, of course, and will be happy to inform the authorities of my findings before I leave. Thank you for your time."

Curtis strode toward the door with me in tow.

"I want you to rent us a car. We can't go around in that monstrosity of a cab any longer. We're going to have to get a closer look at Westgate's Warehouse, and it won't be through the front door. I'm sure someone at that meeting will let him know he's a person of interest in this whole thing, so we'll have to hurry before a cover-up gets underway. I'll meet you back at the motel.

Back in his room, Curtis unpacked his Nikon DSLR with telephoto lens. Looking it over, he cleaned the lenses and checked battery power, then returned it to its carrying case. With a slight bit of hesitation, he slowly reached into his suitcase pocket taking out his Walther PPK/S 9mm pistol. Picking up his shoulder holster, he strapped it on underneath his tweed sport coat with leather-padded elbows. Sitting on the edge of the bed, he contemplated his next moves. *If Frank and I can just get close enough to that warehouse, I'm sure I can get some revealing shots. Pictures won't be enough, though. I've got to get some samples of what's in those drums and have it analyzed.*

Frank rapped on the door lightly before turning the knob.

"Come in, Frank. I'm almost ready to go."

Curtis went to the desk and picked up the phone to call Mr. Bogar at the farm. His wife answered.

"Hello, Bogar's."

"Yes, Mrs. Bogar, this is Curtis Selway. My associate and I were out to see your husband yesterday."

"Oh, yeah. Well, he's down to the cattle barn with the vet, again. Do you want me to call him up to the house?"

"No, don't bother. I just needed directions to the Westlake Warehouse."

"Oh, that's easy. You just go west out of town and take Shady Maple to the right, about a mile out, then, go to the crossroads where Highway 3 goes through. After you turn left, take that all the way along the river and you'll come to it in about two and a half miles. Okay?"

"I'm sure that will be fine, Mrs. Bogar. Thank you very much." Curtis hung-up and said, "All right, let's get going, if you're ready."

I quipped, "I stay ready, just to keep from getting ready."

A slight frown showed on his face as he picked up his camera and opened the door. His frown deepened when he saw our rental waiting outside.

"Really, Frank, a red Renault?"

"I'm sorry, boss. It was all they had left."

He winced, shaking his head with dismay. Curtis put his camera case on the miniscule back seat and starting stuffing himself slowly into the brutishly small car. Once in, our knees were up higher than our waist. I cranked the faithful little engine and took to the road.

Curtis grumbled, "I hope there are no sizeable hills on the way. We only have so much time before sundown."

I just kept my eyes forward not venturing a guess. At least the road was paved, although very curvy in places. Twice we had to wait for cattle being crossed on the road to another pasture. Curtis seemed a bit nervous, then I noticed him looking out the window. As he turned, part of his shoulder holster was revealed. I thought, *well I'm glad I brought my piece. Maybe he knows something I don't.* I decided to pry.

"Curtis, is there something about this warehouse or its owner I should know about before we get there?"

Turning from the window, he gave me a half smile.

"I don't know for sure, to be honest, Frank. It's just some of the background on this Westlake guy tells me he's in a desperate situation. The banks are after his house and business, which could cause him to act desperately, if cornered. I just want to get all I need on this case before he knows exactly what I can do to him."

"Is that why you're wearing your gun?"

"Oh, you noticed."

"I'm paid to notice. Besides, that's my job."

"I'm sorry Frank. I guess I should be more trusting in you."

Just then, I had to swerve abruptly to miss a squirrel dashing across the road.

"That was close. I thought I almost had him."

"In a Renault, are you kidding? That squirrel doesn't know how lucky he is."

We both started laughing and were still chuckling when we reached the turn-off for the river road. Beneath us, we could see below from our highpoint on a ridge the warehouse situated close to the riverside. It appeared clear with a steady current. The fall sunset reflecting off its surface made it sparkle. Curtis thought, *what a place for toxic waste.* He wanted to take pictures of the warehouse and what could be seen stored outdoors on acres of concrete paddock surrounded by chain-link fence.

The entire warehouse area and more was once an R.A.F. bomber training base. After military cut backs, they closed the facility. It was offered by the government on the military surplus market at ten cents on the dollar. An astute businessman, Leslie Westlake, bought the base after getting an inside tip from a friend. Since then, it served to store almost anything, but was mainly used farm implements. When a more lucrative opportunity came along, those were evicted.

Westlake learned from some chemical production journals about U.S. Phosphoric and its generous proposal for renting storage space for its *non-hazardous chemicals*. Soon every available square foot was occupied with their chemicals. Then, Leslie had a brainstorm. Why not get rid of some of the existing stock to make room for more? It soon became easy to increase his income by renting additional space. Using his expected projected income in advance from the treasury of his real income soon led to disaster when some new ventures went south. In desperation to save his property, he signed contracts for additional storage for which he had no space.

Pressure to make room for incoming chemicals led to stepping-up his schedule of illegal dumping. The obvious results were haunting him now. One of his employees sat in the Red Barn Café informing him about Curtis Selway's announcement at the town hall meeting the previous evening. Leslie was feeling the need to get out of town in a hurry.

Meanwhile, Curtis sat on a guardrail at a curve in the road about a quarter mile above the sprawling outdoor storage area of Westlake Industrial Storage taking pictures. As I stood by his side, he looked through his telephoto lens while speaking to me.

"We need to get down there and sample some of those 55 gallon drums. Then, we can test our samples for proof of the toxicity of that stuff he's dumping."

"You probably mean *I* need to get down there and get the lids off a few drums and get samples. I'm also guessing we'll want *me* to do this after dark, too."

Curtis looked away from his camera lens momentarily.

"Frank, sometimes you are so prescient, it just amazes me."

Later that night, Curtis drove me up to the warehouse storage yard where he waited and watched. Appropriately dressed in dark clothing, I stealthily crouch walked along the long line of barrels on the back perimeter of the warehouse on the riverbank parallel to the chain-link fence. About twenty feet along, I picked a spot to use my wire cutters and cut away a portion of fence large enough for me to crawl through.

With three vials in one pocket and a battery tester bulb in the other, I was prepared to remove the bungholes from the top of the barrels with a pair of vice-grips. Curtis suggested the barrels be several feet from each other to get a valid sampling. To me, hazardous was hazardous, but he's the boss. The whole operation went off without a hitch, and soon we were back in our hotel room with three vials of hazardous waste. I was even sure to put the lids back on, so none would be the wiser.

The next day, we sent the vials to a local lab for testing marked URGENT. When we arrived at the motel, there was the local sheriff's car parked in front of our room.

"Well, Curtis, that's not a good sign," I remarked.

"No, indeed, what have you been up to lately?"

The Sherriff got out of his car to greet us. "Good morning, gentlemen. I wonder if I might have a word with you."

Curtis replied, "Certainly, Sherriff, what can we do for you on this fine day?"

"Well, I just spoke to Jeff Stevens, the security guard at the Westlake Warehouse. He reports finding a hole cut into the fence behind the warehouse. Would you gentlemen know anything about that?"

Curtis lied, "Why no, Sherriff, I don't."

"Well, it seems kind of curious. After all, there's nothing but thousands of 55 gallon drums back there, and Jeff didn't see any of them missing."

Curtis replied, "Well, that certainly does sound curious. We'll let you know if anything turns up, Sherriff."

"Well, since you two are the only strangers in town, I figured I might ask you first, know what I mean."

The Sherriff stared hard at each of us before turning toward his car. Walking away, he mentioned something else unusual.

"Well, since Mr. Westlake isn't in town right now, I guess there'll be no charges filed yet. Maybe it was just vandals."

Curtis raised his eyebrows and turned for the motel room. Once inside, he told the obvious.

"I'll call the lab and have them forward those results to my office. We gotta pack our bags, Frank."

As I checked in with Air Traffic Control coming across the U.S. border, my thoughts turned to Sandy back home. I knew she would be surprised I was home so early. I decided to surprise her. I thought I would drop in on Howie Gardenes in Safety Harbor first and ask him a favor. The flight was going well and Curtis even slept as we passed through a thunderstorm over West Virginia. By the time I was lining up on final, he came into the cabin changed and ready to go again. He wore his jacket with all the pockets, which told me he was headed out to fish and think. I knew him well, and I was glad of it. When it came to a man like Curtis, you didn't want to disappoint. I'd learned that. He reminded me of my first C/O in Nam, a no nonsense straight talker who demanded the best. I asked no less of him or myself.

I wanted to see Howie first, when I got back, because I wanted to borrow his 30 ft. Chris Craft, perfect for plying the waters of the Gulf of Mexico. It was just the boat to take me and Sandy down the coast to Sanibel Island. I was planning a getaway for us because I knew there would be more to this case with U.S. Phosphoric. *It's only the beginning,* I was thinking. We touched down without incident and I stayed behind checking details after grounding the aircraft. Curtis met with a driver in a Mercedes. He piped in saying, "An improvement over a red Renault, wouldn't you say?"

Before I could answer, he ordered, "Stay by the phone Frank, we're bound to hear something on the case again soon."

I smiled, "Right, boss."

He winced disappearing into the back seat.

I took in a deep breath of sea air standing on the tarmac at St Pete/Clearwater International thinking. *I'm on my way, Sandy.*

First order of business was securing that boat from Howie, then I would make reservations at our favorite place. After all, Sanibel was the place to stay, play, dine and, yes, rest…According to *USA Today* it was one of the Top 10 Beach Towns in which to stay away. Though, I truly wish they had kept that a secret.

When I drove in to Safety Harbor, it was nearly dusk. I was just in time to catch Howie and his dog Jack closing the realty shop. The noise of my deep-throated, barely muzzled Cobra exhausts perked Jack's ears.

"Hey, Howie, how's it going? Howdy, Jack, mind if I scratch your ears?"

"Well, just fine now, Frank. It's going like the end of the day. What can I do for ya?"

"Well, I'm home for a spell, and I wanted to surprise Sandy with a little cruise down to Sanibel, that is, if I had a nice boat to take her there."

"Sure, Frank, same deal as usual. You have the fun and leave me the fuel. Oh, and, ah, make sure she's clean when you get back. Okay?"

"That's my kind of deal, Howie. I'll try and bring you back something special."

"Make it a mess of Snook, and you're on."

"You got it, Howie. I'll be back around eight."

"I know you mean eight tonight, too, you old romantic. There's nothing like a moonlight cruise down the coast on a night like this."

When I got home, I could see Sandy was in the front of the house watching TV, so I walked in thinking I'd sneak up behind her. She foiled my surprise by standing behind the door as I walked through.

"I saw your headlights. It's too easy. Cobra lights are low as a snake."

I turned grabbing her, kissing her full on the mouth — hard. Drawing away quickly, I said, "God, I love you Sandy", before kissing her again.

"Jeez, Frank, you haven't been away that long. Did something happen?"

"Oh, I just want to be near you again. Me, I'm such a lucky guy. I love to hear you say you love me, too."

"Wow, what's gotten into you?"

"I don't know. It's just you. I just wanna be near you."

"Well, you didn't have to say it that loud. I already made you potato salad the way you like it with olives, red onions, and mustard."

"Well, you can just put that in the cooler, 'cause I'm shipping you to Sanibel."

"No, really? That sounds great. Maybe I should go to town and pick up some of that lobster bisque?"

"Better yet, I've got Howie's Chris Craft and we're sailing down to fish for Snook."

"The evening is definitely improving."

"So, my lady, if you will get your blue-eyed, blonde-haired butt in the shower, we'll sail at eight bells."

"So, the captain's getting rough with the crew."

"Well, I am the captain, so be reasonable, do it my way."

I slapped her on the butt for emphasis, thinking it might have been better received.

I'd really hoped I'd put out to sea with Sandy this way. Though, I never really saw what was coming either. Some things just work out in a different way than planned. We were under power along the coast, nearing Sanibel, when we rolled up on a sandbar. Drudgingly, I sat pulling off my Dockers.

"I guess it's time for me to go swimming."

I slid over the side putting my shoulder to the hull pushing with all I had. I started sinking into the ooze of the sand under pressure, and I felt the hull slowly giving way, sliding off the sandbar. As she came off, walking alongside her, I felt something disturbing. It was the sandpaper skin of a Nurse Shark bumping against me in the darkness. It was testing, determining if I was edible. Quickly, heaving myself aboard with one adrenalin-fueled thrust, I, at once, landed on deck.

"Well, that's one way to get on board," Sandy remarked. "Something down there bothering you?"

"I don't think I like the company down there. It's time to bait-up. Just let me get the boom rigged with hubcaps."

"Hub-caps, what are you talking about? Are we driving these fish to town?"

"Oh, that's right, you've never fished for Snook at night. Here's how you do it. First, you take ordinary hubcaps you'd find on the roadside. This might be a bum's delight, if he only had a boat. After all, the ingredients are easy. So, first you tie a length of nylon cord as you see here."

Holding his bag of tricks proudly for his lady's approval, he proceeded to educate.

"You take the nylon cord, run it through the hole in the middle of the hubcap, and knot it on the other side. This allows us to suspend the hubcap above the water attached to our fishing poles. Which do you prefer, Chevy or Buick?"

She rolled her eyes, "Buick, of course, you know I always fish with class. Though, I still don't get it Frank."

"Patience, Love, patience is a virtue you know and I know you to be a vitreous woman."

"Please, Frank, I think you've had too many Coronas."

Frank raised his hand as if to still the night, restoring order to his mutinous crew.

"Watch and be amazed." Frank quickly tied a sheepshank knot behind the hubcap, raised it up running his fishing line through the hole, suspending the hubcap at the end of his line. He collected his arrangement moving aft to the boom suspending it over the sea.

Looking over his bared shoulders he explained, "Snook are sport fish, spawned in tropical waters. They migrate north in fall to escape heating waters of the tropics.

"Tonight, we should bring in 15 to 20 pounders, just drift fishing. We'll chum the water with live bait, some call Pilchards. You'll see; they look like sardines. I have a cooler full. They will swim to the flashlight's halo cast by suspending the light under the hubcap. Light attracts even more fingerlings. Snook can't help themselves. The popping sound their mouths make when sucking down the little Pilchards gives them away. Then, the fun begins. With our hooks baited with our darling little fingerlings, we hook the Snook. They will fight and grapple, but we will win in the end because we are smarter and stronger. Sound like fun?"

"As long as I don't bait the hook, I guess I'll celebrate the victory."

4

All the popping sounds, amidst shouts of joy, as two anglers reveling in luck or victory, be that as it may, attract attention. Dropping our ninth fifteen pound plus Snook into our cool box, I heard an ahoy. Jealously, I thought, great just when you find that perfect spot, someone else wants to share your joy.

Again, "Ahoy! May I come alongside?"

The light from his cabin silhouetted a sturdy looking young man. I thought he might be with Fish and Game Patrol. We already selfishly exceeded our limit of two per person. Then I reasoned, *why would he be alone, don't they come in pairs?*

Graciously, I returned his hail. "Ahoy, yourself. What can I do for ya?"

He was under power closing quickly. Now, I could hear him clearly without speaker.

"You seem to be having quite a night with the Snook, I hear."

I replied coyly, "Yes, we've been lucky so far. So, what brings you here?"

Sandy seemed oblivious to the goings on. She was seated under her Buick hubcap with another fighting Snook on the line, a Corona in her hand, and having the time of her life. She slammed the last of her Corona into the cup holder, shouting without turning to see our visitor. "Got another one for the cool box, baby. This one's a real fighter. Must go twenty pounds, easy."

I didn't reply. I was facing a trader. Sometimes, anglers share. This was his intent.

Pleasantly, he introduced himself from alongside. "Hi. I'm Randy White. I live over there on Pine Island. I fish these waters. Sometimes, I take out charters. I couldn't help hearing the Snook running over here and you guys. You know, sound travels far over water."

"Yes, so you came over to introduce yourself?"

At first, my comment took him off balance. Then, he laughed genuinely. "No, really, tonight I've been lucky, too. I just thought you might want to trade."

I felt more at ease knowing his intentions happily thinking, *At least he's not with Fish and Game.*

He continued, "I have a full box of Bonita and I'd be willing to trade for some of those Snook. My thoughts trailed back to what I'd told Howie in Safety Harbor. As I hesitated, he asked, "How many have you brought in tonight?"

Before I answered, he interjected, "You're not from around here are you? I see by your boat number you're from up coast. You do know there is a limit here. Right? So, maybe I could take some off your hands and no one knows. Right? I mean, that way we both come out to the good, since you'll get your share and have some variety in your catch, as well."

I was thinking, *I'm not sure I like the way this fellow does business,* when my mind was suddenly made up.

This time it *was* the Florida Fish and Game Commission Patrol and they were making speed in our direction with their lights on us. Thinking fast, I made Randy an offer. "Okay. We've caught ten. Give us two for one and the rest are released. Deal?"

Randy quickly nodded his assent, just as the Fish and Game Patrol arrived. One uniformed officer shone his flashlight in my eyes, then over the deck and back. "Nice to see you're complying with our catch and release program folks. Is that you, Randy?"

Randy sarcastically replied, "Yep, it's me, Steve, looking through your flashlight at your lovely, bright, brown eyes."

Steve knew Randy's ploys. They often met on the waters of the Gulf, not always on the right side of the law as Steve saw it.

"So, who got the best trade tonight, Randy?"

I thought, *Great we got a young smartass on our hands.*

The Game Commission boat bobbed alongside as two officers dressed in tan discussed our fate. Quickly reaching a decision, they moved to their stations before Steve called out to us again. "Yawl be mindful of the law, folks, so's other fishermen can share in our state's bounty. Ya hear?"

We all dumbly nodded as they motored off. Feeling foolish, I thought Sandy must have been disappointed in me after taking her out on such a jaunt. I'd let my wish to satisfy a promise to a friend cloud my judgment. I felt we'd better be shoving off. We each said our goodbyes to our fish-trading partner and headed south along the coast.

The next morning, I had new plans. "Sandy, why don't we go ashore and lie on the beach or go bicycling?"

"Okay, that sounds fun."

"Also, I could drop off these Snook at the Marina Pier. They could clean one for us and we could freeze the rest for Howie."

"Sure, I guess our plan for plundering the Gulf wasn't so bright after all, was it?

"Wait until you've had that fresh Snook for lunch. You might be wishing we'd kept them all. Anyway, I'm sure Howie will like the Bonita almost as much."

I turned the boat for the outline of the dock lights near shore. I was surprised how far we had drifted in the night. It took longer than I thought to get back to shore. In the night, things appear closer than they truly are. Sandy and I stood together with our arms around each other as we made way toward the sun just beginning to shed its soft pink rays into the heavens. It looked like it would be one of those cloudless late October days; perfect weather for a bike ride.

After getting changed into our bathing suits, Sandy and I took a long stroll down the beach stopping to look for shells now and then. We went for an hour headed northward until we ran out of Sanibel Island. Since we didn't feel like crossing the bridge to Captiva Island, we just turned around and started back again. It was great to be headed no place special for a change. After a while, we each agreed we should stop and rest.

"I hope you remembered to bring along some suntan lotion, with this sun were going to need it."

"It's right here in my bag with our little blanket, Frank."

"Oh, you're just too wonderful, you know it. You think of everything."

Sandy shook her hair in the breeze, then let her hand slip into mine. She whispered in my ear.

"I even thought of letting you come along." For that, she received a quick tap on the butt, since there was no one looking. When I got situated on the blanket, suddenly, I felt very tired. I barely remember Sandy finishing with the sun tan lotion on my back. I drifted off asleep. I dreamt I was a child again. It was the time in 1960 just after Dad was transferred to Sidi Slamain, Northern Morocco. In my dream, I recalled how I compensated for his three-year absence. I choose a surrogate father figure. He appeared regularly on TV. It was the actor, Richard Boone, star of the series *Have Gun Will Travel,* who played the part of a restless, roving, bounty hunter in the Old West. He happened to look like my dad, with the same build and mustache. Every Sunday night, he would appear faithfully, dressed in black and ready for a new adventure. In my dream, I heard my mother calling me as I lay on my stomach in front of the T.V.

"Frankie, there's something on the news we have to watch; turn to channel 8."

"Why, Mom? I'll miss my show."

"It's important, do it now."

I reluctantly changed channels to see what I thought were boring newsmen named Chet Huntley and David Brinkley talking earnestly and looking grim as they spoke.

"What's this supposed to be?" I complained bitterly.

"Hush, this is important, our base must go on full alert."

I remembered hearing about such a condition, but as a child I gave it little consideration. Little did I know, we were entering the toughest phase of the 1962 Cuban Missile Crisis. The situation was more than tense; it was electric. All in my neighborhood were rushing out to the stores clearing the shelves, buying bottled water, and anything they thought might help them survive a nuclear exchange. Some were climbing into their bomb-shelters. This was it! To me this was what "duck and cover" was all about. I dreamt, *I hope I get it right when the time comes.*

"Mom, do I have to go to school tomorrow?"

Hanging on every word of the news bulletin, she replied distractedly. "Yes."

In my dream, it was all too clear. It was so real all over again. The next day, I was forced to walk three miles home in a driving rainstorm. At least there were others from school with me. My mom had to do some work with a group of Air Force wives and couldn't pick me up. The schools sent everyone home and the time for brinksmanship was neigh. President Kennedy would not back down and the rest is history. My dream went on though taking me to another place in time. Dad was telling about the time he met Charles A. Lindbergh.

"I was just eight years old on the farm in Illinois when my dad got a call on the partyline. Someone said, "Quick, come see. There's a flyer down in the corn stubble just off Stringtown Road." He grabbed me up and whoosh, out the door we went. In his truck, we arrived on the scene to see an aviator down in corn stubble surrounded by a bunch of gawking farmers watching him try to repair a busted oil line. It was November 3rd 1926. After a while, he gave up on the downed U.S.

Mail plane and asked if someone could give him lift twenty miles into Bloomington to the airport. My dad's hand shot up and we took him to town. I must have asked a million questions, but he patiently answered. It was then I knew I wanted wings. You know, that was more than a year before he crossed the Atlantic. After he did, they called him Lucky Lindy. He won the $10,000 prize offered by the New York Times for being the first to do so. Moreover, he left from a muddy field that day in May 1927 with only a periscope arrangement to see forward, then with an overload of fuel he lifted his tiny single engine craft, narrowly clearing power lines at the end of the strip with inches to spare. Some veteran pilot observers thought him fool hearty. Few knew he hadn't slept for twenty hours before takeoff. Some shook their heads at the feat thinking, he was lucky and it stuck.

In my daydream Dad asked, "Well, do you think he was lucky?"

I said, "Yes."

He laughed saying, "Hell, son, he had angels on his shoulders."

Suddenly, I awoke. Everywhere people were jammed together on the beach. It was like a circus. I wondered, *How did I sleep through all this?* Bicycles crossed paths left and right behind. The beach was abuzz with tourists strolling in their leisurely ways. It seemed I was a modern-day Gulliver suddenly awakened to a new day. Then, I felt the sting on my calves as I flexed them. I'd been too long in the sun. With sun tan lotion worn out, wishing I felt better, I called out to Sandy, but she was not there. *Why am I alone on the beach? I could do better than this.*

Sandy showed up almost as soon as I missed her. She was on a beach bike with wide white tires. "I went to the boat to get us some long pants. Do you want to rent a bike?"

I smiled good-naturedly. "Sure, but soon I'd like some of that Snook for lunch."

"Okay. But first, we ride. I need to pick up a few things from the store. Then, we can grill on the boat away from the crowd, all right?"

"Sure, that sounds great."

After a short ride along the island bike paths in the balmy breeze, we steered back to the marina. Sandy bought some hash browns and a few good-sized navel oranges. I took the Snook from the small fridge aboard and gave them a light dusting of sea salt and placed them on the grill. Soon, their aroma was tantalizing alongside their golden-brown counter parts. As they were finishing I sliced one orange and squeezed all its juices over the fish.

Just then Sandy asked me a question about work. Normally, she didn't pry, but I knew she did get a bit curious about our next moves.

"Frank, what do you think will happen in the aftermath of the explosion at U.S. Phosphoric?"

Truly, not knowing what course of action the giant fertilizer corporation would take next; I felt no need to be coy with her.

"I have no idea. I suppose they'll try and rebuild. A lot depends on the outcome of the investigation and their damage claims."

Sandy speculated, "There's got to be a lot of money involved in that claim, most likely millions. Do you think they did it to themselves? I mean had the plant blown-up on purpose?"

"Now, wait a minute there, girl. That would be quite presumptuous; especially considering the investigation is still ongoing."

"But, isn't that why Curtis is on this case. I mean, that's his specialty, isn't it? I mean, he works for the insurance companies that don't want to take a loss."

"Let's just refer to them as the good guys, since my boss works for them."

Sandy persisted, "Yes, but he wouldn't be on this case if it didn't involve so much loss, right?"

"Is there somewhere all this is going, Sandy? What's your point?"

Hesitantly, she began.

"I just want to know, since you are involved. Please don't tell me all you do is fly him around. I wash the clothes when you come home, and I see your service revolver gone from its holster perch in the closet every time you leave. So, I want an answer. Are you in danger when you go out to work with him? Don't even tell me about the inherent danger of flight. I got all that."

Sandy stood close by on the deck. She also stood with arms folded across her chest giving me that come clean look. So, I decided to give it to her straight.

"Sandy, I've already been in some danger on this case. If I figure this correctly, a lot of people will try to get in the way of a decent investigation. There's just too much at stake. The Lust Brothers are bad actors on the scene. They stop at nothing to make a better bottom line. They lie, cheat, steal, bribe, and are cohorts of underworld figures. For Christ's sake, they pollute other people's water, crops, and livestock just so they can continue their illegal operations in this country. So, in answer to your question, yes, there will be risks, but for all the right reasons. Okay?"

Sandy lowered her eyes and let her hand slip into mine. For a moment, she remained silent, then raised her head giving me the look of confidence I needed to go on.

"All right, Captain, how about some Shook?"

The meal went well as we drifted there on Dinkins's Bay. Several bays away, a more important board meeting was taking place. Atop the corporate building of the Lust Brothers overlooking Tampa Bay, the eldest brother of seven and CEO Big Jim was announcing a nefarious plan.

5

S eated at a mahogany table, six of the Lust brothers listened intently as Big Jim described a plan that would change the landscape of Tampa and their futures forever.

"Brothers, this may come as a shock to you. I have a plan to once and for all divest us completely of our fertilizer operations."

The news did shock and dismay his brothers as expected. At first, there was no sound in the room only an electric current of foreboding connected them. Apprehension in the room rose to a palpable level. Looks in their eyes held daggers of unrest as each in their own way struggled to make sense of his emboldened statement. Then, out of the disturbing atmosphere of disbelief, Jim maintained a sense of decorum raising his hand slowly to still a raging tide of resentment. Taking his seat at the head of the immense, glossy, mahogany surface he recited his plan.

"My brothers, I propose a plan that will make a tabula rasa of our entire U. S. Phosphate works wiping away in one explosion years of corporate enmity and bureaucratic struggle with endless environmental red-tape. When the litigation over our loss claims ends, our battery of experts and attorneys will bring us the victory. I will insist we sell short all our controlling interest in what is left of U.S. Phosphoric in Florida. By offering rock bottom prices, our holdings overseas will go to their knees. They will have no choice but to capitulate and get the hell out. Then another foreign phosphate/fertilizer magnate, (with whom we've already aligned), will step in taking over the old U.S. Phosphoric overseas operations. This, in turn, will free us to pursue our newest venture in real estate development."

Suddenly, Jim's younger brother, Sam, rose from his chair as if propelled by some unseen hand.

He blurted, "So, what you are suggesting is a complete one hundred and eighty degree turn about, leaving U. S. Phosphoric to others while we pursue interests completely different than anything we've endeavored all financed with our insurance loss claims?"

Sam possessed a cunning, astute, adroitness no other attorney could rival. He quickly saw a novel opportunity unfolding. It was an approach to real estate evolving out of an energetic penchant for larceny. His own business dealings left him with a reputation. Tenacious as a praying mantis with the charm of a black widow, he saw this plan his brother was suggesting as doable.

He enthused, "We can do this, brothers. For once, this mighty explosion will give us the chance to rid ourselves of these unmanageable, costly, environmental albatrosses. These so-called gypsum stacks have been a thorn in our collective sides for years. Finally, in one stroke, we could get the E.P. A. off our backs. Jim is a genius and this is our exit strategy."

Jim made his final argument encouraged by Sam's unexpected support.

"You see, brothers, by transforming these gypsum stacks into prime real estate before the E.P.A. regulates everything in sight, we can create condominium towers that will return ten times what anyone would pay for this useless blown-up property now. Simultaneously, we slip the environmental noose from around our necks before the feds spring the trap."

The second oldest brother, Joe, spoke out defiantly.

"Do you honestly believe you can pull this off, Jim?"

"Indeed, I do," he said with extraordinary grit.

"There's a judge in our employ that can get our property rezoned through the help of his associates on the rezoning committee, thereby rendering the stacks commercially viable. All we need do is run an aggressive ad campaign touting our *convincing* environmental cleanup to the public. Finally, we culminate our campaign with one of the most extensive real estate developments in the history of the Tampa Bay area. I envision the most prestigious, high-end condominium developments. They will be called the "Bay View Towers" and will rise high atop our former gypsum stacks. Their fifty story twin towers will overlook the bay with room for only the highest paying owners. It will be the talk of the town and everybody who is anybody will want to live there."

Immediately, the office suite was filled with commentary from all the brothers. Some sounded skeptical, while others spoke excitedly over the bold, even dangerous, venture. Some were almost giddy over the prospect of leaving their old industrial ball and chains behind them for such a high states investment opportunity. None of the brothers had reached the age of fifty; Jim, being the oldest at 49. The rest followed like stairs steps. There was Joe, second in line, then came Charles, Peter, Michael, Martin, and, of course, the youngest, Sam.

Charles remained one of the skeptics of the grandiose plan to sweep the giants of heavy industry into the glamorous world of high priced, waterfront real estate. He stayed behind writing on a yellow legal tablet after the others had filed out for lunch.

His notes revealed, "You've always used violence to protect your word. Why should it be different? Who will be the boy beat down? This time you go too far…"

On the Gulf that same day, Frank and Sandy made their way homeward to Safety Harbor aboard Howie's boat. They motored into the sleepy little harbor late Sunday afternoon.

"I'll drop you off at our dock so you can clean up, Sandy. I won't be long in returning the boat. Is there anything you want from the store?"

"No, I think were set. I'll see you soon."

Frank backed away from the single dock leading to their back door taking the boat across the tiny harbor toward Howie's place. He passed the Paleolithic Indian Oyster Shell Burial Mound laid down by the Calusa Indian tribe 10,000 years earlier. As he slipped up into the narrow waterway leading to Howie's dock, he saw Howie's faithful miniature black and tan dachshund trundling down the dock.

"Oh, you never miss a trick do you, Jack? Where's Howie? Is this all the greeting I get?"

Just then, I heard a clattering down the dock. It was Howie, after all. It seemed by his stumble he and Messrs. Paul & Mason were enjoying a previous engagement. Brandy in hand, he spoke with blurred alacrity. Come ashore, come ashore, my friend, we await your return with great anticipation. Sandy has called ahead."

After tying up, I proffered the cooler with its bounty of cleaned Snook and Bonita. Howie seemed overjoyed to receive his new guests. While listening to his small talk, I tied down the craft with the best of intentions of cleaning her up ship shape in the morning. Howie gregariously offered me a ride home, which I graciously refused knowing she would be along shortly in my Cobra to collect me after my conversation with Howie. It didn't take long before our snake's eyes were back in the drive. The first thing I did when I arrived home was play back my messages on my answering machine. There were three waiting, all from Curtis.

I listened to his voice playback. "Frank, I received the results back from the lab on our three drum samples. All three are highly contaminated with fluorine. Working backward from the parts per million of our samples, it looks like it came from approximately 27,000 pounds of phosphate and 3,000 pounds of nitrate barreled and shipped in one day. Recent E.P.A records show Phosphoric has been warned about dumping at these levels, but it seems they still hold sway with local officials and the Tampa Mafia. Get back to me as soon as you can. I'm on my way to a Tampa Fire Department Advisory Committee Meeting, call me."

Five days earlier, Tampa Fire Marshall, George Fox, ran out in the rain joined by Lieutenant Investigator Bill Mitchell. Despite their slick, heavy, yellow raincoats, they were bound to get wet this day. The last of the torrential rainfalls of the hurricane season were pummeling the Tampa Bay area. Bill was, as some say, on the up and come. He made his bones with a great firehouse. He reckoned there was more, so he studied diligently. His two sons and beautiful wife might have to wait, but it would all be worth it someday, he reckoned.

"You're sure about this. Right, Bill?"

Bill spoke unequivocally, "Chief, I'd stake my reputation on this one."

George shook a little, as much to bead the rain from his cap as to shake loose fear that's never supposed to show on the outside of a true firefighter. In his heart of hearts, he sometimes wished Bill wasn't always so damn good at what he did. When they arrived at the scene, he had visited too much in the past week, he ordered the fireman/driver to take them as far back as their truck would permit. Nobody wanted to walk through the twisted metal and charred remains of brick collected in a crater of mud and ash the size of two football fields.

Their entry upon the scene was always overwhelming. To say it was like a war zone would be an understatement. Rain always made things worse except in an active fire. George stepped down from the cab of his personnel command unit surveying all about. Nothing had really changed. It was once a fertilizer production factory, now it was no more.

Why? How did it really take place? Was there arson involved? That's what they paid Bill Mitchell and him the big bucks to find out.

Bill walked beside his boss explaining, "I've been up and down all over this demolished plant trying to discover a reason for such cataclysmic explosions. Using the last set of plans drawn up for this plant was about all I had to go on. Looking for an accelerant as my source, I noticed when they upgraded their plant back in '63, they added on two separate rooms. One was a lacquer spraying area where workers spray coated the insides of 55-gallon drums. This is done to reduce corrosion inside the barrels. Lacquer, of course, has an alcohol base to speed up evaporation causing the lacquer to dry quickly. The chief raised his eyebrows.

"Where's all this heading Lieutenant?"

"Well, you see, I learned the second room added on was for an entirely different purpose. Management decided it would be better for their foreman to have electric golf carts to get around the plant more easily. This room was where the carts were parked to recharge their batteries at the end of the day.

Consequently, since no one was in the plant over the Labor Day weekend, except one, unfortunate Pinkerton Guard, every cart was in the charging room the day of the explosion. When I examined the remains of one cart, I found a piece of the console where the on/off switch is located just under the driver's side of the seat. I think that is the reason that part was still partially intact. What I noticed on that thin piece of aluminum was the imprinted outline of the on/off switch. They are made of hard plastic and the telltale outline of the switch showed it was left in the *on* position. I was also able to find the manufacture date on the metal plate located on the underside of the cart on the driver's side."

George was tapping his foot impatiently listening to Bill's lengthy explanation. Noticing, Bill commented, "I know this is drawn out, but, Chief, I want you to be sure of what I found and how I reached my conclusion. The cart's manufacture date told me it was an older model that did not have an automatic shutdown circuit to protect against overcharging and overheating. Therefore, I contend because the switch was left on the batteries overheated and, eventually, they exploded. There are eight of them in those carts, you know. That would create an explosion large enough to quickly spread to other carts. Then, the flames reached the lacquer room next door and all hell broke loose. What's more, the forklifts in the plant operated on liquid propane. They were left scattered about the plant after their drivers refueled them and parked them in their work areas. I did some calculating and figured the explosive force of each of those propane tanks would be equivalent to a 500-lb. bomb! Finally, when the propane storage area was reached the explosion was cataclysmic. The entire plant smoke stacks and all just imploded!"

"So, what you're telling me is some employee left a golf cart charging with the switch left on?"

"That's certainly what it looks like, Chief."

George shook his head in dismay. Now we can't label that arson, can we?"

"Not for sure, sir. I can continue to comb the plant with my crew, but so far that's all the hard evidence we have as to what happened here. We found no trace of the Pinkerton guard's body except for his scorched badge, gun, and shield off his cap. It's as if he vaporized in the explosion."

"Well, Bill, I think you and your men have done a fine job so far. I think we should wrap this investigation up and submit our preliminary reports to the district. They and the attorney's will have to wrestle with who's at fault. As it stands, I can't even tell the police I have a suspect. This is going to be one hell of a litigation battle. The Lust Brothers are claiming a total loss of $150 million. They just may be awarded that, too, since the only possible witness has vanished or vaporized, as you say."

"I'll have my report on your desk first thing tomorrow, Chief. I don't blame you for wanting to put this thing behind us. At least, for all the destruction, there was only one victim, *I think.*"

The chief turned toward his truck muttering as he went.

"I wish this damn rain would let up. Oh, by the way, see if you can find out who the foreman was that drove that cart. If you do, tell him I want to ask him a few questions."

"You got it, Chief. I'll see you tomorrow."

The following day Chief Fox had a visitor. It was the foreman who drove the golf cart.

"Come in, sir. What was your name? I'm sorry they didn't tell me you were coming."

"I'm Carl Perkins. When your Lieutenant told me you wanted to see me, I decided to come over right away."

"Well, thank you for your cooperation, Mr. Perkins. I just wanted to clear up a few things before I submit my report."

"Anything I can do to help?"

"There is this, Carl. Did you drive the cart every day?"

"Yes, I was assigned that cart. Why do you ask?"

George hesitated before answering, choosing instead to ask if he also put the charger on his cart every day."

"Yes, that's part of my job. Look, you're not trying to connect me in any way with that explosion, are you? If you are I think I'll see my attorney before I answer any more questions."

George persisted, "When did you leave the plant on Friday?"

Carl replied tersely, "Five p.m., same as any day."

"Just one more question, Carl, and I think we'll be finished here. Have you ever discovered you'd left the switch in your cart in the on position by mistake?"

Carl answered indignantly, "No, I've never done that. That cart was my responsibility and I take my job seriously."

"Would you be willing to state that just for the record on an affidavit?"

"I don't care if I have to swear on a stack of bibles. I'll stand by my word any day, no matter what you say."

"All right, Carl, calm down. Nobody's accusing you of anything. It's just we've found evidence of your cart being the one that caught fire which led to all the rest. So, I hope you can understand my line of questioning. I must submit my report to the District Fire Chief tomorrow, and I can't leave a stone unturned in this investigation. The stakes are very high for your bosses and the insurance companies that bear the liability. It's tragic that there was a life lost in the fire. But, I'm not connecting you with that because you might have made a simple mistake. Anyway, I do appreciate you coming here. I hope I haven't offended you with my questions, but it's all part of my job. I hope you understand."

"I've worked for the Lust Brothers for eighteen years now, and I've never been written up for anything. As I said before, I take my job seriously. So, I'll say good day to you, sir."

Carl got up and left George's office. George watched him leave and muttered under his breath.

"Go your way and sin no more."

It was two weeks after the District Chief submitted the department's findings to the hearing committee that litigation began. Curtis was seated in an office in City Hall waiting with his insurance clients and their attorneys. In all, there were six men and a female stenographer. Soon, the three arbitration judges entered the room and sat at a small table facing Curtis, the attorneys, and his clients. The atmosphere was tense. With all that at stake, it didn't help matters that the Lust Brothers and attorneys arrived a half hour late. Curtis watched them all file in to the small room. He leaned over and whispered to his clients.

"Ten attorneys to our three. What a crowd."

One client whispered back, "I've instructed our attorneys to stick with the pollution angle. I think you've dug up enough evidence to cast some doubt on the veracity of their claim."

Every brother filed in behind the battery of attorneys. Extra chairs had to be brought in to seat them. Once again, they sat according to age with Big Jim then the others like stair steps demonstrating their solidarity.

One arbiter began immediately, "Gentlemen, we are here to listen to the report from the District Fire Chief regarding the damages to U.S. Phosphoric phosphate & fertilizer plant in Riverview, Florida. I will now ask the District Fire Chief to make his findings known regarding the arson investigation completed on October 15, 1974. Once the report is completed, all interested parties may speak in their own turn. Any decisions made here today by this arbitration panel will be final. Before we proceed, is there any one here who does not understand the terms of the agreement of arbitration in this matter?"

No one spoke. The arbitrator's spokesman told the District Chief he could then proceed with his investigation report. As he read his report, the Lust Brothers sat stone faced hanging on every word. Big Jim's premature balding forehead revealed small beads of perspiration as the Chief gave a thorough explanation of every step taken by Lieutenant Mitchell in discovering the cause of the conflagration. The other brothers seemed nervous of the outcome, as well. Jim thought he saw their loss claim slipping away as the Chief described the fire reaching the lacquer room. He leaned forward and whispered to one of the attorneys closest to him.

"Could they prove negligence for us storing flammable chemicals next to the battery charging room?"

He leaned back saying, "They might try, but I'm going to wait and see what else transpires. Don't worry, we'll have our opportunity to rebut some of these statements."

When the Chief got to the part about the cart switch being left in the on position, several Lust Brothers' attorneys smirked with little smiles. Now, they were hearing the testimony they wanted to hear. They could see the way to win this arbitration case. When the Chief finally finished and sat down, the arbiter's spokesman gave the Lust Brothers' attorneys their chance to speak. At first, there was quite a bit of chatter back and forth amongst themselves until they agreed on their approach. The head of the law firm stood and approached the arbiter's table confidently.

"Gentlemen, according to the District Chief's report, a switch was apparently left in the on position and he cites this as cause of the catastrophe that destroyed our client's valuable property and deprived them of their livelihood, not to speak of the hundreds of loyal workers who are now having to seek workman's compensation. Clearly, this investigation reports a switch was left on accidently. Gentleman, this proves the entire conflagration was due to negligence, not arson. So, I contend that no real intent to commit arson ever existed. Therefore, our clients should be fully entitled under the provisions of their insurance policy to be awarded the full amount to compensate their loss and the livelihoods of hundreds of loyal workers. I leave it to you, gentlemen, to do what is good and decent and help restore this industry that is so vital to our county's economy.

Curtis began to feel a sinking in the pit of his stomach. Every instinct he had about the Brothers told him there was something very wrong about this entire case. Even though he had irrefutable evidence that they were engaged in acts of industrial level pollution, there was no defense against someone making a mistake. Jim and his brothers found it difficult not to smile like seven Cheshire cats. Of course, they never told their attorneys what they planned to do with their award, should they win the case. In a matter of minutes, the arbitration judges discussed the case amongst themselves. Then, they called upon the insurance parties' attorney to make his case. Despite a valiant attempt to shed light on the low value the Brothers placed upon others and their property, he was unsuccessful in convincing the arbiters that despite their dismal record of polluting the environment by the terms of their insurance policy, they were awarded the full amount of $150 million.

Plans for surveying the property began the following week. Soon the Brothers would engage in a gigantic cleanup project followed by the start of construction of the "Bay View Towers" atop a three hundred-foot high gypsum stack spread out over 600 acres overlooking Hillsboro Bay. For Curtis, it was a stunning blow that he took personally. He thought *Once again the bad guys win. I'll be seeing you again you sons of bitches.*

6

When I got the call from Curtis, I sensed frustration in his voice. He was trying to sound professional about it, but I could tell he was full of get-back about the decision on the Lust Brothers' claim. I ought to know; I've been in that revenge spot before. I told him I'd meet him at Pilot's Cove as soon as I could get there. Sandy was still sleeping, so I left her a note.

When I arrived, there were no other cars in the lot. I wondered *why not?* As soon as I opened the front door, I had my answer. There was Curtis draped across the bar, while some country blues tune blared away on the jukebox. I just smiled.

"Well, hello there, Curtis. It's a little early for happy hour, ain't it?"

Curtis lifted his head enough to reply, "Hell, you know damn well it's five o'clock somewhere."

I thought, *Yep you can't argue with that logic. I'm not about to argue with a drunk either.*

"Come on in, Frank. Join the party. Say, that reminds me of that joke about the burly Scotsman who asked the frail little man, 'Are ya comin' to my party? There'll be drinkin' and dancin' and wild sex.'" The little man replied, 'Oh my, who will be there? What shall I wear?' The Scot replied, 'Ach, cum as ya are. It's just you and me.'

"Oh, Curtis, you got quite drunk, didn't you?"

"Yeah, and you are my pilot. But, by morning I'll be sober and you'll still be my pilot. Then, I want you to fly me over the Lust Brothers' private enclave so's I can drop a load of bull-shit on each of their seven little mansions."

"Well, we'll just consider that tomorrow. Where have you been anyway? The hearing was supposed to be over by yesterday morning."

"Oh, I've been here and there. I took a cab from the hearing and somehow I ended up here this morning."

"Ouch, an all-nighter, huh? We are getting too old for this Curtis."

"Whadda ya mean we? You gotta mouse in your pocket?"

At that, I just put my arm around him and guided him carefully out the door to my car. I decided it was best to take him home and let him sleep it off before the regular staff came in and found him there. I know he'd do the same for me. He was too good a man to be embarrassed that way. Once I poured him into the front seat, he sat with his head tilted all the way back with his eyes closed.

"Are we going for a ride?"

"Yes, we are Curtis."

"Where are we going?"

"We're going to your place."

"Is the party there?"

"Sure, Curtis. You bet. You'll really like it there. You can get some rest."

"Yes, I think I'd like to rest."

He was soon asleep. I thought, *Poor Curtis. They sure put you through the ringer this time. We gotta get some justice out of this case somehow.*

I stayed at Curtis' home that day. He slept until eight p.m. He was very confused at first, since it was dark outside. He knew he arrived at Pilot's Cove sometime during the day when the taxi driver retrieved him from his last stop at Applebee's. Apparently, the driver got his business card and took him there.

I was watching T.V. when Curtis entered the room. He didn't look half bad. He'd managed to find a robe and had already shaved.

I hailed, "There he is, man of the hour."

"Oh, please, Frank, I've had enough. Did you bring me here?"

"Yes, I felt it was better than sleeping at the Cove."

"Oh, no. How did I get there? Never mind, I don't even want to know. How long have you been here?"

"Ever since I brought you over here this morning from the Cove. Remember?"

"Are you kidding? The thing I remember is having a few drinks at Rough Riders with my clients. They were none too happy. I guess I felt guilty about the whole outcome, but I promised them I would keep investigating as long as they wished. When their CEO told me, he'd get back to me I started drinking double scotches. After, we went to Applebee's and everything else is a blank."

"I'm sure it was a little drunk out that night for more than a few. So, do you think we're off the case?"

"I dunno yet. I didn't see any messages on my machine, so I guess no news is good news so far."

"Good because I had some thoughts about how we should progress."

"You *do?*"

"*Yes,* I do.*"*

Curtis sat on the other end of the couch folding his arms.

"Well, pray tell, mister insurance investigator, I guess your ideas couldn't be any worse than what I've come up with so far."

"I thought we could keep an eye on what their next moves might be by taking over flights of their entire property. We could take pictures for evidence to submit to your clients."

"What would you expect to see in these photographs?"

"I know it's a bit of a stretch, but I've got a hunch they're going to do something different with that property, especially those phospho-gypsum-stacks."

A slight smile crossed Curtis's lips as he asked, *"Why?"*

"Think about this angle, Curtis. If you were the Lust Brothers engaged as purveyors of death on water and air from phosphate fertilizer production, every day creating noxious smog choking employees who breathe the pollution until they sicken and die and if you had the E.P.A. so far up your ass you could read their name badges, don't you think, if you had the money and no plant left, you might just consider another means of livelihood?"

Curtis seemed genuinely intrigued. He leaned forward, his face appearing animated.

"Frank, I think you may have something there. For all these years, they felt they were exempt from the law. When the E.P.A. began tightening the noose, they probably started looking for a way to escape millions of dollars in settlements over hazardous waste complaints. So, why would they build another plant and start the whole fight over again? They may be greedy, but there sure as hell are not stupid."

I interjected, "With occasional over flights and photos, we might just catch a glimpse of what they'll try next."

Curtis countered, "Although, they might try some foreign venture and just get out altogether."

"I don't think so. They are homegrown Florida boys. I don't think they have the stomach for living overseas, especially, with their seven cozy mansions right here in Tampa in their private exclusive compound."

"Have you seen their property yourself, Frank?"

"Yes, one day, years ago, Ramsay and I slipped down that little private lane leading to their homes. We were house hunting at the time and our curiosity got the best of us. Anyway, we took the risk one Saturday. I've always wanted to see what was behind those big stone walls. I remember the single lane into the property was very narrow, just wide enough for one car. I knew then that meant one way in and one way out. We drove right past a large "No Trespassing" sign and continued with dense foliage on either side. We couldn't see anything around the next bend. I guess, at the time, it was a little exciting moving along, meandering through groves of dense, moss laden, live oak which naturally lent an air of mystique to the reclusive lair of the Brothers' compound. Several turns later, we caught a view of an imposing three-story Georgian style mansion with a circular drive. There were several Mercedes Daimler's and a black Porsche parked there. At the time, I remember just wanting to get out of there before we were caught trespassing. Soon, I realized we couldn't get out until we'd passed all seven mansions. They were all palatial estates with pool and tennis courts surrounded by gardens and fountains along with Grecian statuary. I was quite impressed, until we encountered two men standing in the road beside their parked Mercedes with another man inside. They were not small men. We were stopped, of course, questioned closely, threatened with arrest, then finally released. It's not something you forget. At the time, I could just see us in jail on a weekend without bail. Ah, yes, I remember the Lust Brothers' lovely compound. What about you? Have you ever been there?"

"Yes, oddly enough, I saw it as a young man. I worked for a Studebaker dealer. I went on a repair call with the head mechanic. He seemed to like me. He had me come along as his assistant. I didn't know it at the time, but thought he would get a kick out of showing how the very rich live. So, after the repair, we went up that same circuitous drive. He was right. I did keep my face glued to the window of our repair truck marveling at the opulent style the rich live in. It was memorable for me, as well as I was just a working lad then with little to my name. Sidney, the mechanic, was a black man who would never realize such wealth in four lifetimes.

As we left, he turned to me and said, "Now do see what can happen when you get rich?

I just replied, "Sure, that's okay, but I'd rather be lucky than rich."

I can still hear old Sidney saying, "Son, you're enough to make a dog laugh."

"Right now, I don't feel very lucky. But, if I wanna stay rich, I've got to win this case. Let's do this. We'll get a good set of pictures of the property now to form a base line. We can use for comparisons later. That way, we'll easily detect any changes in the lay of the land. With that kind of operation, you just can't blow up the plant and walk away.

Not with two ponds full of 1.5 billion gallons of acid and two mountains of toxic radioactive waste. They can't just blow it all up and walk away. The state, my clients, and the taxpayers could be stuck with the cleanup for years. There's a natural connection between phosphate mining and radioactive material. That, my friend, is because phosphate and uranium were laid down at the same time in the same place by geological processes millions of years ago. They go together. Mine phosphate; you get uranium! You can't turn the earth upside down and get less. For every pound of commercial fertilizer they create, they render 5 pounds of contaminated phosphogypsum slurry. That slurry is piped right from the plant to the acidic waste water ponds that sit within those mountainous gypsum stacks. God as my witness, we're gonna be there to see what the hell those brothers are gonna do with it!"

The following week Curtis and I were ready. Curtis found a suitable aerial photography camera we attached to the underside of *Company Business*. With some help from the local avionics shop, we got it connected to the instrument panel so we could activate the shutter over areas of interest. With enough film in the can for one-half hour, we felt ready to give it a try. Curtis suggested we fly over the demolished plant in a crisscross pattern to get different angles of the subject below. We were both new at this, but it seemed like a place to start. Anxious to see how things went, Curtis stayed in the cockpit with me as we did our first over-flight. We soon realized we'd have to fly the aircraft at near stall speed to get anything that wasn't a blur, because we lacked a high-speed shutter. Also, I learned to anticipate a target so I could line up with it exactly underneath, so the pictures were framed properly. With a half-hour complete, we landed and hurried our film off to the developer.

Curtis seemed nervous as a mother hen waiting for that film to be processed.

"Frank, do you think we should get a bigger canister so we could stay and film longer?"

"Let's just see how this run turns out first. Then, we'll know if were getting somewhere."

Curtis paced the hangar. "I guess you're right, Frank, this seems to be the only alternative to get information on what these guys are up to. I mean, it's not like you can walk up to the guard and ask permission to come in and get some candid shots of our favorite industry."

"I know, Curtis, I'm just as concerned as you are. I want this to be our ace in the hole."

An hour later, we finally got the call. The film was processed and ready for viewing. Curtis sat in my car tapping his pen incessantly on the fire extinguisher between us. It made a metallic tink, tink, tink, sound which was driving me nuts. I looked at him sideways several times, but he didn't get it. So, I just lived with it until we got to the film lab. We used the Coast Guard's lab at the airport. We arranged, if they weren't busy and the price was right, usually one quart of Chivas Regal was enough. When I pulled up, Curtis jumped out of the car and went in first.

"Do you have the film we dropped off this morning ready?"

"Why, yes, I called and said as much. I'll go get it."

Now, Curtis stood at the metal-topped counter tapping his pen incessantly.

"I sure hope this works out. I'd sure hate to see you get drunk again."

Curtis turned and gave me a healthy look of distain. I decided to take a seat.

"Here you are, sir. One hundred feet of exposed 35mm film, no guarantees."

Curtis winced behind his steel rims, as he took the film from the Coast Guard technician.

Back in the Cobra, we whisked the film back to Pilot's Cove, where Curtis had a projector set up. He seemed so nervous I decided to load the film on the reels. Soon, the lights went out and the screen lit up. Without sound or any reference points, it was difficult at first to keep track of what exactly we were looking at. Then, the outline of Port Tampa came into view.

Curtis exclaimed, "Look, there are two Lust Brothers' tankers leaving port. We should get another angle on them when we make our next crisscross pass. Yes, there they are again, the same ones. Now, let's see where they're headed just to get a notion of how we're getting all this photographed."

On the following pass, the two ships could be seen hugging the Peninsula that juts into Tampa Bay where MacDill A.F.B. is located. They were headed from West to East.

Curtis remarked, "That's curious. Why aren't they headed out to sea?"

The last pass revealed they left the peninsula and were heading southeast back toward the Florida coast. Then, the film ran out. Curtis seemed curious and exasperated all at once.

"Now, where could they be going? They're empty except for those containers on deck. You can see by the bow markings they're empty. Right?"

"Yes, Curtis, I agree. I guess we'll have to figure on filming later to see where they go. That is, if they repeat that trip."

Curtis looked concerned. "Yes, if they repeat the trip," he said absentmindedly. "Let's look at it from a timing point of view. If we captured them at that point in time, we should try and film them later to see what progress they've made, right?"

"It seems logical to me. Let's try it."

"Yes, but before we fly again, we need to do some ground work. We need to get over to Port Tampa and sniff around a bit. I don't want to attract attention, so we should wear some dock workers' clothes and take a different car. We'll go tomorrow evening. Frank, find us a nondescript car for the docks and meet me at the Cove at seven."

"Okay, boss." Curtis winced as he left the Cove.

The following night I showed up at the Cove, driving Howie's old Mercury station wagon. Curtis approached the car cautiously trying to look in to see if it was me driving. When he did, he came forward and opened the passenger door.

"Good job, Frank. Where did you get this clunker?"

"Oh, I borrowed it from a neighbor friend of mine."

"Well, let's get over to Port Tampa. We should make it there by eight."

"What exactly do you expect to learn there, Curtis? I'll just wait and see, but I think I should be able to learn why empty containers are going to sea don't you?"

"Sure, I hope so anyway. If we talk to the right people, we might learn something. If we talk to the wrong people, the Lust Brothers might learn something, too."

"Yes, we'll need to be careful who it is we are speaking to, if anyone. These longshoremen can be pretty tightlipped about shipping and cargo going in and out of their docks."

We arrived at Port Tampa at half past eight. Many ships were lined up in their slips. Some were Lust Brothers' ships, so we headed down the dock to see if anyone would speak to us. The first people we saw were a group of young men who appeared to be in a hurry to get ashore. They breezed by us talking amongst themselves, never giving us a look. Then, we saw one older seaman trundling along slowly on the dock headed towards the exit gates. Curtis took a chance and stopped him to talk.

"Excuse me, sir. Are you off one of the Lust Brothers' ships?"

"Hell, no, I've been to sea. Their boats ain't goin' to sea."

"I'm sorry. What do you mean?"

"I mean, they quit goin' overseas. All they do is paddle around the point in the bay."

"Do you know why they aren't going to sea?"

"They say it's somethin' about their plant being shut down. That's all I know. Say, can you spare a cigarette?"

"Sorry, I don't smoke."

"Well, how's about five dollars for my information?"

Curtis opened his wallet discreetly and pulled out a ten. Here's a tip. You've been most helpful."

"Thank you, commodore, don't mention it."

Curtis asked, "What do you make of that information?"

"To me, it sounds like the Brothers aren't doing any shipping because of the plant closure. I'm not sure what he meant by paddling around the point in the bay though."

"We know this much, their ships aren't going overseas right now, but they're not all here right now either. I can tell they have more than what's here tonight."

"So, where are they docked?"

"That's what I want to find out. We're going back in the air tomorrow, Frank."

The next day, I met Curtis at the Cove and we took the short drive to the tarmac where *Company Business* was already rolled out and washed for the day. I stepped aboard and started getting her warmed up while Curtis loaded the camera. This time, we figured to abandon the criss-cross pattern in favor of going looking for Lust ships, as far out as we could find one. Our suspicions were confirmed when we discovered another one hugging the coastline of the Tampa Bay Peninsula.

"Frank, take a course along the other end of the peninsula. See if there are any ships up that way."

After flying a few miles north, I spotted another near Gandy Bridge.

"Wait just a minute. The other day, I read an article about the Nuccio brothers winning the contract for scrapping the old Gandy Bridge. I thought, at the time, that was rich since they got the contract to build the old Gandy Bridge years ago, but it didn't hold up to traffic as expected. There was some talk from seasoned engineers about saltwater being used in the concrete batches, but they couldn't prove it. You know, the Nuccio brothers have a long shady past and some say they have been with the local mafia. No one's ever proved a thing though. Fly over the bridge project, Frank. I want to have a look see."

As we passed over, I could clearly see a Lust Brothers' ship parallel to the bridge, about two hundred yards out. The wrecking crew had reached this point in the mile-long bridge. The ship was riding low in the water by the numbers on her bow. It was obvious she was taking on some of the broken-up bridge pieces. Cranes on the bridge could be seen lowering a huge chunk of debris on the deck in front of an open container. Then, when it was clear, a forklift would push the chunk of concrete through the container doors.

"Now what do you suppose the Lust Brothers would want with used concrete rubble?"

I added, "Where do you suppose they are shipping it to?"

"I figure it can't be far. Number one, it's nearly worthless. Two, it isn't leaving port according to that old sailor we spoke to. So, where could it go logically? There must be a need somewhere."

From his home in Clearwater, Florida, Curtis could not see the gypsum stacks looming over Hillsborough Bay, but that never diminished his desire to set the wrongs committed right.

7

The third day we flew out over the bay, we got a lucky break. We spotted a Lust Brothers' ship riding low in the water on the east side of the peninsula headed for shore.

Curtis snapped his fingers, as it all came clear.

"Port Sutton, I'd bet that's where they're headed. Take some time, Frank. Loiter for a while. I want to watch this play out."

"I flew over the Gulf for a joy ride while we waited for the ship to make more progress toward its port. By the time we got close enough, we could both see she was lining up for Port Sutton.

"Now what, exactly?" Curtis wondered.

"Keep watching, Curtis. This has got to be interesting."

I took another long pass out over the bay. By the time I returned, we could see the containers being off loaded on the dock. Further away, we could also see trucks lining up with cranes placing one container on each flat bed. The containers were standard shipping containers each 48 feet long by 8 feet wide.

"Frank, we're going to need to be on the ground to get the rest of this story. Take her back to the barn."

As ordered, I banked *Company Business* over and headed for home."

When we were taxing in, I saw a black Mercedes parked near our hangar. Two men in the front were not familiar to me. One had a camera pointed in our direction.

"Curtis, we've got company. You see that black car over there with two guys in front? They're takin' pictures."

"Oh, really? I suppose I shouldn't be surprised. We watch them, now they watch us. The stakes are getting higher, Frank. Make sure the ground crew locks up the hangar tight tonight and put two guards on it, also. That is, armed guards, if you please."

I nodded and steered our craft toward the fuel pumps. When we came to a full stop, the Mercedes backed out of its position and headed for the exit gate. I wondered, *how did they get on the airfield?*

It was too late in the day to do any more surveilling of the container loaded trucks, so we called it a day. I was glad to get Howie's old Mercury returned without mishap.

Handing him the keys, he asked, "What would you want with an old man's car like that?"

"Oh, you'd be surprised Howie. Mostly, dirty work, but you can see I had her washed before I came back."

"Well good, that should be done twice a year, whether she needs it or not."

Across the bay, the Brothers convened atop their twenty-story office building in a suite. The building was just south of Jefferson Street in downtown Tampa. From their penthouse, they could clearly see the gypsum stacks on the coast in Riverview, Florida. They were the topic of their current discussion.

Big Jim dominated the conversation, as usual, with his self-confident, in charge manner.

"I just got word from some of my men that the insurance investigator we tangled with in arbitration is still snooping around. He's using his company plane to spy on our operation."

Peter, who was also self-assured and aggressive by nature, addressed Jim's statement.

"So, what, he's flyin' around, probably takin' pictures, too. He can't prove a thing. The most he'll figure out is we're filling in the slurry pits on the gypsum stacks. The E.P.A. would probably give us a medal."

Sam spoke out, "Not quite, if they knew right now that we were dumping metal containers full of concrete into those pits, they might have a case against us. Nothing corrosive should be put in those pits, according to them. The only loop hole that protects us is we are dumping on our own property. I wouldn't put it past them to be drafting new legislation to prevent us from doing it, even on our own property.

Always the schemer, Martin replied, "They won't be able to argue with a smooth, graded, level piece of ground one hundred and fifty acres square, now will they? If our ships and trucks stay on schedule, we should have those stacks filled in a month. Then, let the E.P.A. find something wrong with that. They'll never catch up with our plans. They're bogged down by their own bureaucracy."

Michael, the trusting one, voiced his opinion.

"I think Martin is right. With our fleet of ships and trucks, we have them all out classed. We only need to stick to our schedule. I'm confident we can fill these stacks, smooth them over, and move on to Phase Two."

Joe had his turn and made it clear he suspected more trouble from Curtis Selway.

"I think we should put a tail on him to make sure he doesn't get too close to our operation."

Jim seemed to settle the matter for good, when he agreed.

"We'll put a tail on him and see where he wants to go with his so-called evidence. If it's the E.P. A., I say let him knock himself out. We're way ahead of those guys."

The rest of the meeting was concerned with details of Phase Two, once the pits were covered over. The rest of the plans were all subject to the Brothers' scrutiny, yet one overriding factor would determine the fate of the project. The pace at which the Brothers set upon was dangerous, at best. Joe was always wary about that aspect of their planning.

When Curtis arrived home, there was a phone message waiting. He stood by the machine, and turned it on. It was the chairman of the board of his clients.

"Curtis, it has come to my attention that you have not submitted your final report on the Lust Brothers' case. If you are still working this case, as I suspect you are, I order you to cease and desist. We cannot risk a counter-suit. We certainly don't wish to underwrite an investigation that has been closed and paid in full. Call me if you don't understand any of this."

Curtis slowly slid down on the sofa as if he'd been pushed down under the weight of the world. He sat staring into the darkness of his living room contemplating his next move. If he went on alone, the expense could be prohibitive. If the evidence he presented wasn't strong enough to persuade the E.P.A. to step in, then he would have nothing to show his clients. He knew in the pit of his stomach, with all his being, something was terribly wrong with this project undertaken by the Lust Brothers. Now, he must decide if it was worth pursuing on his own.

It didn't take much soul searching to reach a decision. Curtis spent a good portion of his life watching the Lust Brothers run rough shod over anyone who got in their way. Their way of life was not just affected by greed; it was the embodiment of it. He knew he had one shot at bringing down this family of Lust. One shot was good enough for him.

The next day, Curtis was looking over a map of the Tampa Bay area when I walked in the Cove. It was clear that he wanted to get an early start. He looked up from his scrutiny of the map.

"Good, I'm glad you are here on time. I need you to call Enterprise and arrange for a car. Also, be sure to get the good binoculars out of the plane and see if you can find us some bush hats. You'll need to get some dark colored coveralls from the mechanics for both of us. Then, beat it back here as quick as you can. Are you armed?

"Yes sir."

"All right, then get going, please. I want to get there early."

I wasn't for sure where there was, but I had a pretty good idea. I knew Curtis wanted to complete the chain of delivery from boat to shore then beyond. I knew that would mean the ground transport link in the Lust Brothers' delivery of shipping containers full of concrete. The transport of such a cargo seemed ludicrous. Obviously, there could be no profit in it, at least the way I saw it. Maybe Curtis had a different angle. I'd learned some time ago not to question his logic. He had proven many times over he knew what investigating was all about.

By the time I gathered up the gear, the rental vehicle Curtis wanted arrived. I thought to ask for a Jeep, but not a black one. When I spoke to the rental rep, he assured me it was the last one. Curtis wasn't going to like this; I just knew it. When he came out the door, he spotted the Jeep and started shaking his head.

"Frank, this won't do. Did you know we're going to Port Sutton?"

"I had some idea Curtis, but I wasn't entirely sure."

"There's nothing but weeds and sand and oil transfer pipes out there. It's like a desert and a jungle in one place."

Port Sutton was little more than a transfer port where ships put in to off load oil and molten asphalt. It was cut out of the east coast of Tampa Bay with little thought for amenities. Only one road led to and from the port. It was a gravel access road for tractor trailers to pick up fuel oil. The rest of the property was rolling mounds of sand and gravel with a dense area of foliage at the exit site along U.S. Highway 41.

"Frank, with a black Jeep, we're going to stick out like a bug in a jar. I guess we'll have to hide it in the brush and walk the rest of the way to the access road. I don't want any of those truckers to see us spying on them."

So, Curtis gathered up his maps and put on his coveralls and joined me in the Jeep. We got off early at eight a.m. and made our way down Highway 41 south, close to Riverview. When we reached the road sign that read Port Sutton, Curtis ordered me off road. I got along okay for about a quarter mile on a dirt road used to access the telephone poles, then, it ran out. Curtis decided we could camouflage the truck by driving into the brush and walking from there. Once we were out of the Jeep, we found the going tough since the brush, small trees, and palmetto bushes were thick. I found myself wishing I had a machete. Curtis boldly led the way pushing aside brush and trees oblivious to the threat of rattlesnakes in the palmettos. I was soon covered with any type of plant seed that could cling to cloth. My face was getting raw from scratching brush. I could feel the cool sweat sticking my shirt to my back as we pressed on for at least two hundred yards. Finally, we broke out on to the sand hills and oyster shell dredged up to form the man-made port facility. Covered with burrs and stickers, we now trudged along for several hundred more yards until we could hear trucks on the road. Curtis fell on a sand hill and immediately pulled out his binoculars to get a view of the road.

"I can just make out the door sign on one truck. This dust is making it difficult. Now, I see, they're using Nuccio Brothers' trucks. I don't know what they're hauling in those containers, but I'll bet its concrete. The only other thing would be petroleum products in a tanker truck. We've got to see where these containers are being delivered and I've got a great idea on where to start looking."

Now, it was another long trek back across the sand hills and through the brambles and brush to the Jeep. When we arrived, we looked like we had been on safari for a week.

"We need to hustle up the road and watch for these containers."

After we got our coveralls off, we each felt a lot cooler. We drove up the highway to a place where we'd wait for the next container load. Soon enough, one appeared and we fell in behind it. Sure enough, the truck made its last turn into the gates of the phosphogypsum compound of U.S. Phosphoric. Seeing that, Curtis nailed an essential truth.

"Frank, they're using those shipping containers full of concrete to fill in the pits of the two gypsum stacks."

"Wouldn't that take a lot of containers?" I asked.

"Yes, but if anyone can afford them it's the largest privately-owned shipping line in the nation, the Lust Brothers."

"So, what happens when they're filled? Then what?"

"That's what I need to find out next. I think we know someone who can help us."

"Really, who would that be?"

Curtis was looking rather self-satisfied.

"That would be your old friend, Howie Gardenes. When we get back, I want you to talk to him. Find out if there is anything in his trade journals or on the grapevine amongst his realty buddies about new developments in the bay area. I have a hunch about what's going on with the Lust Brothers, but I still need a few facts to back me up."

"Okay, if you think he'll be helpful, I'll ask him."

I couldn't help feeling Howie wasn't the best source, but then what did I know about real estate. When we returned, I went over to Howie's place and disturbed Jack from his late afternoon nap. Howie was probably napping, too, but was alerted by Jack's barking. I reached down petting Jack on the nose.

"How come you always bark at me when you know who I am?"

Jack just walked a circle around me, like he always does, and led me to Howie.

"Hi, Howie. Did you try some of that Snook yet?"

"Oh, Frank, it was so sweet, so succulent. Such fish, I don't deserve. You are a prince to bring me such a delicacy."

"I should tell you some time how hard they were to catch and *keep*. Anyway, I have a question for you. Have you seen anything in your trade journals or heard anything from associates about a large building project coming to the bay area recently?"

"No, I can't say that I have. Is there something of interest I should be looking for?"

"No, not exactly. My boss is interested in any big developments right here in the bay area. If you see something like that, could you let me know?"

"Of course, Frank, I'd be glad to if it helps you in your work."

"Okay. Thanks, Howie. I'll be in touch."

"Right. Say hello to Sandy for me."

I thought, *that's something I need to do. I haven't spoken to her in over twenty hours. She's probably wondering what happened to me.* I called Curtis right away to let him know what I learned from Howie. Then, I told him I'd be heading home, if he didn't need me anymore that day. Then, I got a surprise.

"I won't be needing you today, but I will tomorrow night. Meet me at the Cove tomorrow after five p.m. I'll brief you then."

"Sure, Curtis. I'll be there."

As I answered, I had a feeling in my gut there was something about to challenge my capabilities. It dawned on me what it might be, but I put it out of my mind intentionally, refocusing on home. I didn't want anything to cloud my mind when I was with Sandy. When I arrived, I could see her out back on our deck watering plants. Coming up the walk, I heard the watering can drop on the deck. She was at the door before I turned the knob. As I entered, she put herself in my arms immediately.

"Where have you been, fly boy?"

Before I could answer, she was smothering me with kisses. I could hardly say hi. Once she stopped, I tried to explain.

"I would have called, but I wasn't near a phone for quite a while."

Once she stood back, she took in my full presence.

"Whew, where *have* you been? You stink?"

"Well, we had to work late on the aircraft and…"

"No, you didn't. You were not anywhere near that hangar. I called and talked to the mechanic there eight hours ago."

"Oh, yeah? Well, ah, I guess you got me there. Why don't you sit down and I'll try to explain why your husband is a liar?"

Sandy crossed her arms over her chest waiting instead for the great explanation.

"Curtis has had me out in the field with him. It was necessary I go with him not only as his bodyguard, but also as a witness. We are working a sensitive case that needs further development. I want to tell you everything, but I don't want to jeopardize you with the facts."

"Just what is that supposed to mean, Frank?"

"It means, the less I tell you about what we're doing right now, the better off you will be. Or, would you have me tell you all about it, and then have you lose sleep and worry about me?"

"Oh, I don't know which is worse, Frank. I just thought when you took this job you would be your ordinary, household, corporate pilot. Now, you do all sorts of things you can't tell me about."

"I know, honey, but Curtis is working a case that is so important to all of us I can't help being a part of it. It is for the good, and we are working against something that must be stopped. Those responsible must be brought to justice. There's a lot at stake. Money is one major issue, but public safety is even larger on my scope. Please do try and understand, Sandy."

She stood there looking at me making my plea and took pity. Wrapping her arms around me, she reassured me with her tight embrace that she would go along with my chosen path. It meant so much to me that I held her there in my embrace until I kissed away her tears. Later, we decided to cook out on the grill. It was a beautiful moonlit night perfect for making up after dinner.

When I entered the Cove the next day, I saw a pair of coveralls hanging over one of the barstools. Curtis was nowhere in sight. So, I walked into the semi-dark room like a lamb to the slaughter. He appeared from the back office with what looked like a small toolbox in hand. I was on time at eight a.m., but Curtis slipped behind the bar and brought down two shot glasses and a bottle of Chivas Regal.

"Sit down, Frank. Let me pour you a drink."

"Now, I knew I was in trouble."

Curtis' eyes lit up with a burning intent in them. I could see he was serious as a heart attack.

"Frank, I've been all through this in my mind. I've planned to the last detail. Now, it's time for you to make my plan happen. I won't insult your intelligence by leading up to this. You know it's about the Lust Brothers' case and we're in the heart of it. I need photographic evidence of what the Brothers are doing at their compound. I can't do it without you. If I were ever found on their property, it would destroy all credibility of my case against them."

One thing Curtis had not told me was his clients had removed him from the case. He justified keeping that secret with the fervent hope he could put together enough evidence to persuade them to put him back on the case.

"What do I have to do, Curtis? What does that little black box have to do with it?"

"Drink up, Frank. I'll tell you."

Curtis clasped his glass in hand and emptied it before I could reach mine. As the remnant of scotch slid down the side of his empty glass, I put mine to my lips and took in the smooth stimulant. Feeling the burn all the way to breakfast, I watched Curtis pour two more. He was clearly trying to get me in a receptive mood.

"Once more, for old times' sake, as they say."

He quickly downed another, beginning the same routine again for a third time. For a moment, I felt I was being challenged to keep up. I rarely turn down a challenge. With a third scotch under my belt, I quickened my pace before he poured again.

"Out with it, Curtis. What's your plan? As if I didn't already have an idea."

He quickly turned and picked up the black plastic box placing it on the bar.

"It's quite basic, you know. Most good plans are, of course."

The last part was meant to stiffen my resolve.

"I need you on top of that stack taking pictures when they dump those containers in the slurry pit. It's what I suspect they are doing, but I need proof. You can get it for us with this."

He stood with his hand atop the black box, opening its clasps revealing its contents. Inside there was a high intensity flashlight, a

Rolex 450 high-speed miniature camera, heavy duty wire cutters, black leather gloves, a small first aid kit and two small towels.

"Just so I get this straight, you want me to cut my way into the Lust Brothers' compound. Then, I climb three hundred feet to the top of one of the gypsum stacks and wait until day break to take pictures of containers being dumped into the pit. Is that it? Is that all?"

"Yes, Frank, basically, that's it."

8

If it weren't for the look of intent in his eyes, I would have thought it was a test of my courage. There was nothing I could do but to agree.

"I'll get started right away. Do me a favor. Check the weather for tomorrow night. I need to go home and prepare, so I'll take your little black box and be getting along."

Curtis sat back on his bar stool as if the weight of the world just came off his shoulders. "I'm grateful, Frank, and encouraged by your dedication."

"Wait 'til you see my bill."

Curtis smiled, giving me a thumb up as I left the Cove for home. When I drove up our winding drive, Sandy's car was in the garage. I thought, *this is going to be a hard sell.* I stepped through the door with a smile on my face ready to tell a lie.

"Hi honey. What have you been up to?"

Sandy gave me a look of surprise that quickly turned into a big smile.

"Well, you certainly are home early. What's up with this?"

She slipped beside me and gave me a big kiss.

"Oh, and we've been drinking, too. What a surprise. Is there a party I didn't hear about?"

"No, I just heard from Curtis that I'll need to fly him out to California to meet with some new clients and I wanted to get some sleep first. You know how hard it is for me to sleep in the day time, so I just thought I'd have a few drinks with Curtis to help me get to sleep."

"So much for a day off with you, then, huh?"

"I'm sorry dear. I'll make it all up to you when I get back."

I took her in my arms and made it seem convincing. Fortunately, she bought it and I prepared for bed knowing I'd need the rest for sure. I awoke around 6 p.m. and went into the kitchen. I found Sandy preparing one of my favorite meals.

"Wow, beef stroganoff. What did I do to deserve this?"

"Oh, I just know you'll probably be away for a while and you would appreciate a hot meal."

"Yes, indeed, I would."

I tried fighting back the feelings of guilt knowing I wasn't going anywhere near California. I finished and cleaned up putting on my usual flight garb. I kissed Sandy goodbye at the door, then hurried off before anymore was said. Several blocks away I stashed my Cobra in Howie's carport. I backed in, then took his old Mercury, as arranged. Back at the Cove, I found the ubiquitous dark mechanics' coveralls lying on a table near the bar with a note pinned to them. It was from Curtis.

"Be very careful tonight. I saw those two men again sitting in the car by the hangar today. Good Luck, Curtis."

I waited and left at 10 p.m. I figured that would give me an hour to reach Riverview, then I could start climbing later that evening around midnight. That would leave me a good seven hours to get through the fence and up that stack with time to spare before dawn. I strapped the black box to my forearm with plastic straps, so I wouldn't be encumbered by it on my climb. When I drove to the area, I got off on a service road the electric company uses. I put the car down along a drainage ditch as low down as I could. The rest of the way would be through head high brush, palmetto bushes, and weeds. My jungle boots made me feel a bit safer around rattle snakes that occupied palmettos. It was slow going, but my little flashlight held down low ahead of my feet helped. When I arrived at the perimeter fence, it was chain link. No problem for my military wire cutters. Soon, I had a panel cut out and crawled in holding it above my body.

At the stacks edge, I found it wasn't as steep at the base. Going up, I made pretty good time at first. Now came the last two thirds of the climb on the stack. Insidiously, the slog upward was becoming increasingly difficult. The mixture of gypsum and sand dredged from the bottom of the slurry pit was porous and light. It stuck to my clothing and everywhere else. There was the vile taste of dust I kicked up trying to surmount that slope of sandy pollution. I was now in full crawl position moving slowly. With each crawl forward, I slid half way back. I hadn't counted on such an arduous climb. The crest of the stack wasn't in sight.

Breathing heavily there in the darkness, for the first time, I thought of abandoning my climb. I quickly dismissed it. The ache in my back muscles told me I wasn't physically prepared for this feat. Yet, I was two-thirds up. *Better up than down,* I thought. Continuing this fight between us and the Lust Brothers had become too personal. So, I climbed on towards the precipice. Slip-sliding along finding my way up the chalk colored sand-like formidable gulfs of slag, I was coated ghost-like in appearance. Then, slowly, I raised my face over the precipice to witness what the brothers were creating. It's one thing to behold a giant stack from across the bay. But, to behold the great slurry lake from its precipice is another.

The sun was just breaking over the horizon. Early light reflected off the surface of the deep white colored lake bigger than two football fields. No workers were present, no trucks. It was too early. Only one lonely looking guard shack stood on the opposite end of the vast slurry pit. I knew it was occupied, so I stayed low. Being covered in white dust was the perfect camouflage lying there blending into the side of the stack. I was exhausted after my arduous climb. Waiting, I drifted off in restless slumber.

Later, I was awakened by a loud banging of metal on metal. I peeked over the edge of the stack and saw my prize. A flatbed truck was parked up on an incline with a shipping container just then sliding off the bed into the slurry pit below. I wondered, *how long do I have to wait for the next delivery?* Thankfully, I didn't have to wait long. As soon as the flatbed pulled out, another was positioning to drive up on the incline to drop its load. I spotted a crane near the edge of the pit. This time some workers approached the container and attached clamps from the crane. Then, the container was lifted off and swung over as far as the crane could reach and dropped into the pit. I could tell the object was to spread out the containers on the bottom, thus forming a type of foundation.

For whatever came later, I didn't know. I stayed long enough to watch this type of offloading of containers repeat itself twice while taking pictures. Propped up on one knee focusing on my photography, I failed to realize what a target I made standing in silhouette with the sun behind me. I really stood out against the rim of the stack. Suddenly, I heard several shots ring out from an automatic weapon. The white sandy gypsum flew up just beside me. Instinctively, I threw myself to the ground and rolled.

In an instant, I found out rolling wasn't a good idea. From the rim of the stack, I continued to roll out of control. Over and over, I couldn't stop myself. In a whirl of sand and dust, I was on my way down the stack. I couldn't have gotten down any faster. Somewhere along the way I saw the black box flying away from me. Fortunately, the camera was still hanging from my neck. When I finally rolled to a stop, I was on the lowest incline of the long slope. I sat up immediately assessing the damage done to me.

I felt a sharp pain in my left ankle when I tried to rise. *Oh God, I hope I haven't broken my ankle!* I forced myself up, convinced I had to run. Soon they would be around the stack looking for me. I hobbled along the fence and gratefully found the cut-out panel I'd made. I stumbled into the brush and fell secluded amongst the palmettos. I wasn't the only one there. To my right, under a palmetto bush, a large rattlesnake lay coiled in response to my sudden intrusion. I forced myself not to move taking heed of its warning rattle to come no closer. This is where I stayed, me and the snake. For at least ten minutes, we stared at each other until it uncoiled and slithered away. Maybe my white chalky appearance bothered it. All I knew for sure was that I was very lucky.

Apparently, those seeking me must have gone beyond the point where I was lying. I staggered on until I found a dead gray oak and broke off one of its branches for a crutch. Slowly, very cautiously, I limped out of the brush to the service road and found my car. Now, I wondered, *did they really search for me after all? Maybe not, I'm here and they're not.* I didn't wonder for long. I just got in the car and drove.

By the time I got back to Safety Harbor, it was afternoon. Howie took me in and helped me clean up. Then he bandaged my ankle. While he was at it, he had a few questions for me.

"Where in the hell have you been to get so filthy? You could have crawled here and looked better."

"I practically did, but I can't tell you much about it. It's all in the line of duty, I can assure you. Listen, Howie, I need you to help me out. First, I need to stay here a couple of days until I can walk better. I'm afraid I sprained it badly."

"Well, sure, you're welcome to stay here awhile. Me and Jack will take care of you. Right, Jack?"

"Hearing his name called, he stepped forward toward me in Howie's recliner."

Jack seemed to sympathize placing his long snout on my leg looking up at me with warm brown, imploring eyes. I thanked him for his solicitation with a gentle pat on the head.

"Howie, I also need an ace wrap for an ankle."

"I'll have to go to the drug store for that. I'll be right back. Jack can keep you company. Just stay off that leg and keep it propped."

I just sat back looking up at the ceiling. Soon, I realized I was very tired and closed my eyes as I slowly stroked Jack's willing head. In moments, I was asleep. Entering a dream world, I was transported back to the spring of 1972. I was in a small forest hiding from the North Vietnamese who were searching for me. I felt trapped in my little place under brush next to a large log covered with green moss. I overcame my fear of being discovered long enough to extend the antenna of my radio above the brush. I was desperate to call in an airstrike to get these goons off my back. My ankle had been sprained in my rough parachute drop from a tree I found myself hanging from. I needed time to formulate a plan, a way out, someplace where I could call in an evac rescue attempt. I just desperately needed a break, a getaway of some sort. Suddenly, my hopes were dashed when a North Vietnam Army soldier spotted my antenna protruding from the brush. Now, I heard his shouts to the others. Then, I felt the muzzle of his AK 47 assault rifle entering the bush poking me hard in the ribs. The jig was up. The wide grin on that soldier's face proved it.

Soon, I was riding down a bumpy road in the back of a truck face down with hands tied behind my back. From the corner of my eyes, I could see soldiers sitting on either side smoking and joking with each other. Apparently, I was the catch of the day and they were clearly jubilant over the matter. We continued for what seemed like hours with my face on the roughhewn boards of the truck bed that came up to meet me like I was riding in a buckboard on my belly. My neck muscles were strained beyond endurance. I could no longer hold my head up. I was just letting go. Watching my head bounce up and down with each bump was a new source of humor for my guards.

I awoke to Howie's jostling the headrest on the recliner to wake me.

"It's time we got this strapped on, but first I'm going to ice your ankle down. He stood above me with the Ace wrap in a box.

"We gotta get this swelling down."

Soon, with Howie's care, I was lying back on Howie's recliner with an ice pack on my left leg. After an hour of that, the swelling had subsided. Howie put the Ace wrap on with care.

"Now, I've got a crutch somewhere in the garage. I'm going to get it, then we're going to get you down the hall to a bed. I can't have you cluttering up my living room in my chair when I want to watch my favorite shows."

I remembered Howie was a devoted fan of *Jeopardy* and *The Price is Right.*

"Okay, Howie, I'll get out of your way. Just wake me for breakfast."

I didn't know what time it was when the pain finally eased up. I was just grateful for uninterrupted sleep. Sometime in the middle of the night, I was jolted out of my sleep by the sound of rapid gunfire! In a second, I rolled out of bed to the floor. At that point, I could still hear the constant sound of automatic weapons. Bullets were riddling Howie's house. Glass flew in from the window with the curtains. The pattern of fire raked the entire house back and forth! I kept my hands over my head face down in my sheet hearing the rip and tear of the bullets shattering glass for at least twenty seconds, which seemed a lifetime on the floor. Finally, it stopped as quickly as it started. I lay still for a moment longer, then my thoughts of Howie made me go into action. Assessing the damage, I realized I wasn't hit, thank God. I started crawling on my belly towards the hall, when I heard Howie moaning. I shouted down the hall.

"Howie, are you all right?"

"No, I've been hit in the arm. I can't move it."

"I'm coming, Howie."

I continued my crawl entering the living room where I found Howie on the floor clutching his left arm. I could see he'd already lost a lot of blood, so I reached up snatching down a tablecloth and got over to him. I could see his upper arm was where the bullet smashed into his body. Fortunately, it missed the vital brachial artery. I began wrapping the cloth around, then, I tied a tourniquet knot. Howie's home had just been strafed in a drive by shooting. I got to the phone and dialed for an ambulance.

Briefly, I wondered, *Why would Howie be the target of an attack like this?*

Then, it came to me in a heartbeat.

Howie's car. They got his license plate. No wonder they didn't mess with the car. They needed it to track me down.

Amidst the heart racing reaction to my brush with death, I began to feel pangs of guilt. I had nearly brought down the curtain on an innocent seventy-three-year-old friend. Because of me, he faced death from unknown assailants. My next call was to Sandy. It was high time she knew the truth.

"Sandy, it's me, I have something important to tell you. I'm at Howie's. I'm okay, but there's been a drive-by shooting here."

"What? A shooting, by whom? Is he all right?"

"Well, he's been hit in the arm, but he'll make it. The ambulance is on the way. Please come over as soon as you can."

"Of course, you're sure you are okay?"

"Yes, I wasn't hit. Just come over here, please."

"I'm on my way!"

When Sandy arrived, she could see Howie being loaded into an ambulance. She tried going to him, but a police officer stopped her abruptly. He held her back with his upraised arm. Jack stood underneath the gurney licking his master's hand.

"Sorry, Ma'am. This is a crime scene. You can't come over here."

"But, my husband is in there!"

Just then, I came through the growing crowd of investigators calling to her.

"I'm right here, Sandy. Officer, I just want to talk to my wife. I'm not leaving the scene."

"All right. Just stay inside. We'll need to get a statement from you."

"Don't worry, officer. I'll be right here."

Sandy then was permitted to join me. I didn't know where to begin, but I knew there was a lot of explaining to do. The distraught look of worry on her face was almost too much for me to bear.

"Honey, this is all my fault. I lied to you about going to California. I did it because I didn't want you to worry. Now everything's gone wrong."

"Where have you been all this time? I don't understand why you thought you would have to lie to me, Frank. I'm upset. What have you been doing?"

"I've been doing my job. Lately, it's been a lot more dangerous. I just want you to know I'm terribly sorry about all this. I've been doing some industrial spying and apparently they followed me here."

"Why here? Why would they follow you here?"

"Because I used Howie's car and they tracked it here."

A man in a suit walked up to us flashing his badge. He identified himself as Detective Jarvis.

"Sir, I need to get a statement from you about what happened here. Would you mind coming over here at the table where we can talk?"

"Yes, sir. I'll be right there."

"Sandy, there's nothing more you can do here. Why don't you go home? After I talk to the detective, I'll be home right away."

"All right, I'll go. After lying to me, I'm not sure what good your promise is though."

She spun around going off in a huff.

I watched her get in my Cobra. I couldn't kick the guilt. Then, I let the detective interview me for the next twenty minutes while trying to understand how a man like Howie and I got into such a mess in the first place.

9

One of the first things I did when the shooting stopped was call Curtis. Detective Jarvis let me loose with the usual proviso. Don't leave town and let us know of any further developments. Of course, I would unless it interfered with a much more important case. My next move was to get photos developed as soon as possible. Curtis found them revealing. He apologized profusely for the drive by, which none of us could really anticipate.

I wondered what's around the corner. After all, Curtis was demanding when he was closing in on a case. Now, I waited silently at the bar in Pilot's Cove.

To my surprise, he entered with a smile on his face.

"Frank, you've really come through this time."

I replied, "Yeah, tell the wife about it."

"No, I mean these photos are remarkable. The lighting is great considering conditions. Really, you've nailed these guys illegally dumping in a slurry pit. The environmental consequences are formidable."

"What does that mean in court, Doc.?"

Curtis assumed a casual tone. What it means, my Mr. Nikon, is you've turned good evidence.

Eight weeks later on the east side of Hillsborough Bay, a foreman from Nuccio Brothers strode into the field office of the "Bay View

Towers" project, slurry mud dripping from his boots. He spoke to the supervisor of the towers project, Joe Bandy.

"Joe, we've got a hell of a problem at the pit."

Terry Riggens, an experienced foreman with fifteen years' experience, knew his business. Strong willed, he could impress his opinion on any man. He had seen a lot go south on ill-conceived projects. This was threatening to be one of them.

"Overflow is what we've got. You have us dumping too many containers full of concrete into that pit. Do you wanna know what happens then? You get displacement. Do you understand what I'm talking about? The more you dump, the higher the slurry level gets. The pumps aren't keeping up. If this keeps on, we're gonna have an overflow from this stack and there'll be hell to pay from the E.P.A. Last week you saw me establish a drainpipe twelve inches in diameter a quarter mile long to the other pit. Well, we've been pumping steady and now the other pit is reaching a dangerous level. We simply can't keep up with the rise in the damn slurry. Something's gotta give."

"I'll be out to look at it right away, Terry. Maybe we can figure out another way to deal with the stuff."

"Well, you'd better kick this one upstairs for some action. Otherwise, we're all gonna be up to our hips in slurry. You and I both know what that stuff is made of and my boys already are griping about it. They know somethin' ain't right with this pinkish, milky white crap. We gotta do somethin' soon."

After Terry left his office, Joe sat down and pulled on his knee-high rubber boots for an inspection. He was sure Terry was right about the situation, but he had to witness it first hand to bring to the men upstairs. This would not be an easy sell with the cost over runs already building. As he approached the stack on foot, he could feel the rumble of the steady line of Nuccio Brothers' trucks delivering containers. A routine was established in the last four weeks of delivery on a carved roadbed all the way up to the top of the 300-foot stack. At first, trucks had difficulty making the grade with their loads. At times, they would get stuck in the sandy soil. White rock had to be poured over the entire delivery road to keep trucks from sinking. This was another unforeseen expense for the Lust Brothers' project.

When Joe reached the crest of the pit, there was an inspection path laid out made of wooden pallets. The only thing that prevented a man from slipping and falling into the pit was a line of heavy rope stretching along the edge of the pit attached to metal fence posts at intervals. At least a man could use the rope as a handhold as he traversed around the treacherous sandy edge of the pit. It didn't take long for Joe to complete his inspection. The slurry level was clearly too high. At one point, thirty feet was all there was left between the slurry and the edge of the pit. Joe could see something must be done and fast. Turning back on the path he hurried to his office. Picking up his phone, he called Peter Lust's office.

He oversaw day-to-day operations at the executive level.

"Let me speak to Peter, please."

"He's on another line. Would you like to hold?"

"Not for long, honey. This is Joe, the supervisor at the pit. I have a serious matter to discuss with him."

"Yes sir, I'll ring his office as soon as he's off the other line. Thank you."

Joe sat down drumming his fingers nervously on his desk. He couldn't help thinking. *If I can't talk to him soon, they'll blame me for all this.*

Meanwhile, the secretary got up and left her desk for the break room. Thirty minutes later she returned after her coffee break and a chat with some of the girls on staff. Joe had called back twice receiving a recording offering to take his message. Not waiting any longer, Joe got into his truck and headed for the executive office in downtown Tampa. When he reached the guards desk down stairs, he flashed his project badge to the guard expecting to be admitted. Instead, the guard insisted on calling ahead to the office. Joe stood in the lobby tapping his foot nervously calculating the time it might take before overflow at the pit would become a reality. Finally, the guard admitted him.

He stepped off the elevator on the thirty-first floor where large windows overlooked the skyline of Tampa. At that level, he could see both pits through the largest window. At a distance, they seemed benign; almost insignificant.

He thought, *I hope I can convince Peter of the urgency involved. From where he sits, it probably looks like just another day.*

When he entered the main office door, he encountered the secretary.

He spoke without introduction, "I called for Peter over an hour ago. Did you forward my message?"

"Well, of course, I did. But, he's been busy and I—"

Joe was in no mood for excuses. He walked into Peter's office and found him practicing his putting on the carpet. No one else was in the office.

Joe announced, "Boss, we've got a problem. A *big* problem."

Peter looked at Joe's face and realized something important was on his mind. Peter rested the putter on a lounge chair and invited Joe to take a seat.

"Please, talk to me. Tell me what it's all about, Joe."

"Well, sir, down at the pit we're filling we have a major problem. The dumping of the containers has got to be stopped. They are displacing the slurry too fast. Something must be done to reduce the volume of slurry or else we'll have an overflow!"

Peter took this message in stride, giving it adequate consideration. "I see, we must reduce the level or face a catastrophic overflow. Is that right?"

Joe hesitated in answering, knowing the expense for an alternative would be great. The weight of Peter's aggressive self-assuredness fell upon Joe as he unleashed a tirade upon him.

"Joe is that not your purview? Are you not the supervisor in charge of this stage of development?

"Yes, sir, and we have taken steps for drainage to the second stack for control, but it isn't enough."

"Joe, if I had the time, I'd dispense with you right now. However, I'll give you a solution."

Peter was known as a man of action. His orders exemplified his character. "First, stop dumping containers. Then, contact shipping headquarters in Port Tampa. Tell them I want ten tankers with barges brought in on the coast next to the stacks. Tell them to make ready to receive shipments of slurry pumped into their holds. I'll give them direct orders after this is done. I want you to make sure you can put on enough pumps with enough pipe lines to handle the volume of this influx of slurry to the tankers. We'll need to off load this cargo carefully in the Gulf somewhere. Tell them I'll be in touch before they sail. Is all that clear?"

"Yes, sir, we will need new pumps and lines to accomplish just what you said. Can that be added to the budget?"

"Dammit, man! Do it. The time is now. Just do it! I'll justify expense with the board. That's my job. Now get out of here and do yours!"

Joe rushed out of Peter's office to take on a major task. As he passed the secretary, parting words came to mind as she finished her nails, but he managed to stifle them. Once in his truck, he grabbed the radio. "Get me procurement at the dock. Then, put me in touch with the Port Master of Port Tampa. Also, put me in touch with the Lust Brothers' Captain on duty."

"Who shall I call first, Joe?"

"Oh, hell man! Get me procurement. I need to talk to them right now!"

Joe left the main office heading back to the project. When he drove up two men covered in slurry ran over.

One large construction worker reached him first. "Boss, it's starting. The west wall of the stack is leaking. We've put up stopgaps along the down slope, but they're starting to erode. What else do you want us to do?

The second man cried, "It's over man. We've got a cave-in and everybody's gonna know it! I want my pay. I'm leavin'."

Joe yelled, "Go ahead. Run to the paymaster and see if I give a damn. You're through here."

On the west side of Tampa Bay, Curtis was briefing Frank on their next photo mission. Since clear weather conditions prevailed at St. Petersburg /Clearwater Airport, he was planning on having Frank do some flyovers to check on the Lust Brothers' progress.

Frank was still feeling guilty about the way his friend, Howie, got shot, but there was little he could do about it for the time being. Curtis finished last minute instructions for Frank. Then, they boarded *Company Business*.

Later, in the air, as they swept over the largest pit under construction, they spied something irregular. Down the west slope, workers were struggling to set up cofferdams to stop an overflow of slurry. When Curtis witnessed this, he made a call from his plane to the Port Authority of Port Tampa.

"This is Curtis Selway. I represent several insurance concerns in the Tampa Bay area. I wondered if you could tell me how many Lust Brothers' ships are at sea now?"

The secretary on the other end seemed a bit baffled.

"Sir, we don't normally get that kind of question about corporate vessel traffic. There are always a good number of Lust ships incoming and outbound, but the volume of the fleet in either place is seldom in question."

"Could you tell me this, are there more Lust Brothers' ships at sea now than not?

"Yes sir, at this point in time, I can verify that. However, there is a constant state of flux. You know, ships come and go."

"Yes, I understand. Thank you for your time. Good bye."

Curtis told me to get *Company Business* prepared for a second flight. When we overflew the stack, he instructed. Fly due west over the Gulf. I want to check something out. As we moved out over the Gulf, just beyond the three-mile limit, a small fleet of ten Lust Brothers' tankers were riding high in the Gulf, towing barges. Obviously, they were preparing to transport cargo. Curtis figured they were there to transport the excess slurry they saw back at the pit.

Curtis turned to me, "I've got to get you on one of those barges."

I thought, *What kind of man does he think I am? I've been shot at, my neighbor wounded, my wife finds me untrue. What more can he expect in this case? Maybe it's time to ask for a raise?"*

Just then Curtis spoke, "This is dangerous and, of course, I can't go with you. Nevertheless, this could make the case against the Lust Brothers. After all, if they're found guilty of dumping slurry in the Gulf, I'll have a lock on this with the E.P.A. to throw away the key. Together we could put an end to this sort of industrial pollution. Do you know what that means to all who live around here?

With that kind of social pressure, what man could resist? Many details must be worked out to mount such a mission, some I didn't expect.

That evening, I went over to Howie's house. Jack greeted me at the back-screen door where I always came for friendly visits.

"Well, hello, Jack. I see you still want to bark no matter who it is. Someday we gotta work on that. Is Howie in?"

Jack gratefully wagged his tail given the opportunity to go and fetch his master. Soon, he displayed his dachshund smile leading Frank to the back door.

"Oh, hello, Frank. What can I do ya for?"

"I just came by to see how you were mending. Are you doing okay? Is there anything I can get for you?"

"Got any brandy on ya? My arm's startin' to hurt again a bit."

"No, I don't, but I could go up to the store and get us a few beers if you wanna sit and talk."

"I suppose that would do. I'll just sit out back here on the deck with Jack and wait for you."

"Do you want anything else?"

"Maybe some pretzels would be nice."

"You got it, Howie. I'll be right back."

I returned with four big 32 oz. cans of Foster's Australian Lager Beer. Howie's face lit up. He took one from my hand, quickly peeling back the tab.

"Aaahh, now that's a sound I like to hear. Here's to you and those that trail ya. May they never find ya outback in Australia."

After downing two of those magnificent dark blue cans, Howie's mood improved. He even went so far as to inquire about the nature of my work. I knew that was forthcoming. So, I didn't resist his questioning. What surprised me was the old man was interested. He followed my explanation of the happening at the stack. I figured he wouldn't give a damn about what I was up to with Curtis, but surprisingly, he did.

"I may be an old man, but I've watched those stacks grow over the years. I always knew there was something evil in them. When I fished the waters of the Alafia River, I watched it dying. It was clear local fishermen like me knew something was terribly wrong with the local environment. Then, when we read articles in *U.S. News and World Report* about the elementary school in Riverview and all the little children being poisoned with radiation from the phosphate mining around them, it made me sick. I want in Frank. What can I do to help? These unknown assailants have wounded me and poisoned my environment. I think it's time for some pay back."

"Well, Howie, maybe there is something you can do. I came over here to borrow your boat for a job I must do. Now, that I think on it, maybe you're just the man I need. I have to warn you though, it could be dangerous."

Howie leaned forward in his recliner with a look of renewed interest whispering, "Tell me more."

10

"Well, Howie, it goes something like this. My boss wants me to go out to the stacks by boat and get on board one of the Lust Brothers' barges outbound for the Gulf. He wants photographs of them dumping slurry in the Gulf. If you could pilot your boat close enough to the barges they're pulling, I might be able to climb aboard and take pictures."

"That does sound a might risky, but you can count on me."

"All right, here's what we'll need. I want to be able to contact you so walkie-talkies are essential. That way, we can rendezvous when I've finished taking shots. You'll need to top off your tanks. I don't know how long we'll be out there before we're finished. I'll have a high-powered flashlight, so if something goes wrong with our communications, I'll send you light messages."

"What if you get caught, then what?"

"Just turn about and leave me there."

Howie's expression was grave.

"What do you expect they'll do with you?"

"I don't know. They shot at me once, and they got you. What do you think?"

"I think what I'm about to do is for a lot of good reasons. I just don't want to see a good friend go to waste."

I laughed out loud, "Me neither, Howie, me neither."

The next few days were spent planning. I spoke with Curtis by phone, but no flying was done. Howie and I spent a lot of time going over what our plan would be. Every morning after breakfast with Sandy, I would go over and talk with him. Sandy knew something was up, especially when I came to her with Jack one night at eight o'clock.

"Can you take care of Jack for a couple of hours? Howie and I want to do some night fishing."

"No, you don't. You and Howie have been cooking something up for the past few days. Has this got something to do with your work for Curtis?"

"If it did, would you try and stop me?"

"No, you know I wouldn't. I know your plans are way too involved for me to try and stop you now. I just want you to try and think this through. Is it all really worth it?"

"Sandy, there was a time not long ago in both our lives when we asked ourselves that question. It was a time when we put our country before our lives. You're still working to heal veterans. I went off to war. You did the right thing. As for me, well, I guess we'll never really know for sure, will we? But now, I have an opportunity to win a real battle for my country and help my fellow man. What do you think my answer to your question will be? Right now, there's an old man out there willing to risk what's left of his life to make this case. I can't just let this go. We both need to get out there and do what's right. So, I'm going. If we're not back by morning, call Curtis."

The actual mission got off to a sloppy start. Sandy got back late from work. She picked up Jack, but wouldn't leave for twenty minutes. Howie marked time nervously moving about tiding up his boat with the lights on. Finally, Sandy said goodbye with a passionate kiss. We shoved off at eight-thirty.

Getting closer to the barges off shore, we doused our running lights. Choosing a night when there was no moon helped a lot. We could hear pumps running constantly drawing slurry through several pump lines that lead back up over the edge of the stack. My plan was getting pictures of those lines pumping slurry into the holds of the barges. Then, I'd get a sample of slurry from under a leaking pump line where it went into the barge. Finally, I would try getting a shot into the hold showing their polluted cargo. I would need a flash for all these shots. The danger was going undetected.

When finished, I would call Howie on my walkie-talkie. Things should go quickly all things considered. Later, Howie got me close enough to a barge being towed into the Gulf. The tossing up and down on the barge prevented me from grabbing a hand hold on the iron maintenance ladder welded to the back of the barge. I slipped twice banging my knees on the ladder. If pain weren't enough, it was slippery on the ladder soaked with salt water and slurry.

Once onboard, I found myself on the cold hard deck pitching more than I'd hoped. My efforts to crawl on the deck left my legs feeling numb. When I reached the first hatch, I struggled tugging on it. Finally, it slid off. My first photo would be directly into the hold. Next, I stood up to take more pictures on top the barge. Lastly, I was going forward to photograph the back of the Lust Brothers' ship revealing its name and owners. Creeping forward, I kept to the right side of the barge. Then, I felt like someone just hit me with a baseball bat between the eyes! A white flash appeared racing through my brain.

The next thing I remembered, Howie was bandaging my bleeding forehead. Back on the boat again, I realized I must have been in the water. There was a blanket on me. My clothes were soaked.

"Oh, my head. What the hell happened?"

"You were knocked overboard, that's what happened. Good thing I had my infrared binoculars. I was watching you walk up the barge. I saw a man come up behind you. Too bad I couldn't warn you. It happened so fast there was no time. Just when you turned toward him, he wacked you on the forehead with a steel rod. I can't believe you didn't drown. Anyway, I came ahead full speed and pulled you out of the drink."

"Howie, my head hurts so bad I can hardly stand it."

"I understand. I'm heading for home as fast as I can, Frank."

I started to ask a question, then blacked out again. Howie got back on the throttle after lying me down near him. The next time I awoke, I was in the hospital. Sandy was looking down at me. I thought I was dreaming.

"Well, you're a very lucky man mister investigator. Sometimes I wish you would stick to your calling as a pilot."

"Oh, Sandy, I'm sorry you had to see me this way."

"Better than not at all! We gave you morphine for pain and we'll be taking you down to x-ray that solid stubborn head of yours next. Just relax and let us do the driving."

The following morning, I woke up still in the hospital. Sandy came in after I had a light breakfast, which came right back up again. Sandy had to show up.

"Sorry, honey, I'm a mess."

"No, for someone who had a severe concussion, it's normal. You'll be back in business in no time. Speaking of business, how did you fall out of the boat?"

"I didn't fall out of the boat. Well, you sure got wet with a huge bump on your head somehow. Talk to me. Howie's clammed up and won't tell me a thing about what happened out there."

Rather sheepishly, I explained I wasn't in the boat. I fell off a barge."

"A barge, now this I gotta hear."

"I was trying to get some photographs of a Lust Brothers' barge being towed to sea. I was going to take a picture of the ship when someone struck me in the head and I fell overboard. Thank God Howie was close by, he saved me from drowning. Is he here now?"

"No, but he said he would be by to see you after lunch."

"Please don't remind me of food."

"Just lay back and take it easy. Howie can talk to you later."

Sure enough, Howie came that afternoon.

"How are you feeling, Frank?"

"Well, I feel okay. I also feel grateful. You saved my life."

"I know but you'd do the same for me. What are friends for?"

"It's good news for me and I want you to know how much I appreciate you're being there for me."

"I don't wish to upset you, Frank, but it's not all good news."

"Why what is it, Howie? Did I talk in my sleep?"

"I'm afraid it's more serious than that."

Howie hesitated for a moment.

"Go on. Don't keep me in suspense here."

"You see, I brought my infra-red binoculars with me that night and I was keeping track of your movements on deck. When you were hit by that crewman with the steel rod…"

"Ouch, I don't remember that."

"I told you when you came to on the boat."

"Well, right now, I don't remember a thing."

"After what you've been through, it's no wonder."

"But, I'm afraid there's more, Frank. That guy who wacked you also took the camera off your neck, then he kicked you overboard."

"Dammit, now we've lost it all."

"That's right, including your walkie-talkie."

"Don't feel too badly, Frank. You came away with your life and that's really something."

"Yeah, I guess you're right. Listen, Howie, please don't tell Sandy we lost the camera. I don't want her to think all this was for nothing."

"Oh, don't you worry. That will be our little secret."

"Howie, I'm really am glad you came by. We'll have to get together soon and go over our experience. Maybe a few beers, huh pal? I'll be buying."

"That's for me, my friend. I won't stay long now. You need your rest."

"That's what they tell me, but I feel I'm about ready to get out of this place."

"We'll see, Frank. So long, and get well soon."

As Howie left the room, he placed a little card on the nightstand where I could see it. It read, "Best wishes for a fast recovery. I'd sail with you anytime. Your friend, Howie."

As soon as he left, I dialed Curtis. He picked up right away.

"This is Curtis Selway, how can I help?"

"It's me Curtis. I'm in the hospital."

"My goodness. What ever happened? Did something go wrong?"

"Yes, terribly wrong. I got knocked out by a crewman who caught me taking pictures on one of the barges in the bay."

"Tell me you're kidding, please."

"Sorry, boss, it's the reality of it all. What's worse, he took my camera."

"How many shots had you taken?"

"I got five photos of various parts of the cargo operation and had a sample of slurry in a tube on me, too. I'm afraid it's all gone."

"Damn, that's too bad. Are you all right, Frank?"

"Yes, though I got a pretty good thump on the head. I'm here at Bay Pines Hospital. You know the one where Sandy works?"

"Yes, I know. I'll come see you as soon as possible."

"Don't bother I think they're going to release me soon. Either way, Sandy's taking good care of me."

Just then, Sandy walked in with a doctor. He was holding an x-ray envelope. I told Curtis I had to talk to my doctor so he hung up.

Sandy said, "Frank, this is Doctor Anderson."

"Hello, Doc, what have you got for me?"

"Well, I've read the x-rays we took last night. You received quite a blow to your forehead. You're a very lucky man. Had you been struck in the temporal area of your cranium, we probably wouldn't be having this conversation right now. How are feeling today?"

"I still have pain, but I think I'm going to survive."

"Good. You have a severe concussion. I'm sending you home today with a prescription for pain. I want you to take it easy at home. No work for at least three days. If you should feel nauseous, dizzy, or have a temperature or headache call immediately. You'll need to take this blunt trauma to the forehead seriously. Your frontal lobe has been bruised by the blow and there is some swelling. That should subside when you take the other medication I'm sending home with you, all right? Do you have any questions for me?"

"No, Doc, except how soon I can leave?"

"I think the nurse can get you out of here later today. Remember take your medications as prescribed and no working."

"Sandy tells me you are a bit of a hard head. I guess that makes you lucky in this case. Do as she says and stay home. Okay, Frank?"

"You got it Doc."

Dr. Anderson left the room. Sandy came closer to Frank's bed.

"*You're* gonna get it, if you don't follow orders. That includes no running over to Howie's for a beer, get it?"

Frank raised his hands in front of his face feigning his fending off Sandy. She relented and smiled, how could she not? Secretly, she shared the stress and fear any good wife would experience when their spouse is seriously injured. It didn't matter she was a nurse; the emotions were the same. Frank grudgingly endured his confinement. Vacillating between reading, watching TV, and calling Howie, he chipped away at the hours. Frank thought to himself, *Sitting around the house is for old folks.* When he finished his time in *stir,* he felt much better. Out of respect, Curtis only called Sandy once to see how he was. Frank was just as anxious to pick up where they left off as Curtis.

On Monday afternoon, Curtis called Frank. Though he was always a quiet, conservative gentleman, he could barely contain his excitement.

"Frank, are you okay? I mean, can you talk?"

"Of course, I can talk, Curtis. It was my forehead they hit. They didn't shoot my mouth off."

On the other end, Curtis was too elated to let his sarcasm faze him. He just learned something that could blow the top right off his private investigation of the Lusts. He dared hope it might even get his clients to reinstate him on the Lust Brothers' case.

Curtis was in high-spirits, holding back and anxious to toss out his leading question.

He forced himself not to rush it, but rather let dramatic pause fill the void between them.

On the other end of the line, Frank was confused. Curtis should have been in the depths of despair following the debacle aboard the barge. Instead, it sounded as if he were head over heels. Frank broke the silence.

"What is it you're trying to say?"

Curtis asked, "Do you remember all the flap in the newspapers after the explosion at the plant about the missing Pinkerton guard. The one who supposedly vaporized in the conflagration?"

"Sure, I remember it made good copy 'cause all they found was his badge and the shield off his hat. They blew it up big claiming he died valiantly at his post. While other newspapers trumped it up saying he was the mystery man; the witness who must be found."

"Well, Frank, that witness has been found."

"What the hell?"

"It's true, Frank. Norman Howard was arrested last week in Las Vegas with a gun and $34,000.00 in cash in his room. It seems he was gambling hard and drinking a lot when surveillance cameras picked up a gun tucked in his waistband. When he returned to his room, police arrested him for carrying an unregistered concealed weapon. Finding the gun and cash didn't make it any easier for him, I'm told."

"My God, this is outstanding news!"

"What do you think will happen to him?"

My contacts at the Hillsborough County Sherriff's Office were contacted by the Sherriff in Vegas, after he learned there was an A.P.B. put out by them for Norman Howard's location after the explosion. Now, Hillsborough County wants to extradite him to face charges in Tampa for felony arson and flight. Isn't that grand?"

Frank's mind was still reeling at the news. He couldn't think of what to say. He pulled himself up in his chair feeling his pulse quickening as he gripped the phone. Instinctively, he glanced at the clock on the wall, then at the door, imagining someone would burst in snatching this revelation from his realm of reality. Then it occurred to him. He thought, *What if the Lust Brothers' attorneys get to him?*

He blurted, "Curtis, what can we do to protect our case?"

"First, we must do everything we can legally to make sure he is charged without infringing upon his rights. Next, it's going to take a while in Vegas for the Sherriff's Office to resolve his case. Norman Howard will get his one phone call. It's a safe bet he'll call the Lust Brothers."

"What can we do in the meantime?"

"Not much, we must let the law take its course. The Governor of Nevada must sign for him to be extradited to Florida, but only after his case is resolved in Nevada, however long that takes. As soon as that takes place, we can contact the District Attorney here in Tampa. We can ask if he would like to see any additional material we have on the Lust Brothers. In the meantime, we need to keep a close eye on developments here at the stacks. That means more flights, Frank. Are you up for it?"

"If they don't try to shoot us down, sure, boss."

Curtis winced, but said nothing.

"Then, I'll look for you at the Cove about 10 o'clock. Okay?"

"I'll be there early to pre-flight *Company Business,* boss."

Curtis winced again putting down his phone.

As promised, Frank was at the hangar early checking out the beautiful blue and white Gulf Stream II, *Company Business.* He didn't find anything out of the ordinary except for the two men alongside the hangar in the same black car he saw in the past. He just shrugged his shoulders as he got in his Cobra and went over to the Cove where Curtis was waiting.

"Good morning, boss. It's a beautiful day, isn't it?"

"Yes, indeed, Frank. Are we ready for takeoff?"

"Yes sir, all pre-flighted and fueled. We're ready to go. By the way, that reminds me. There are two men in a black Mercedes parked between our hangar and the National Aviation Academy hangar."

"Yes, Frank."

"Well, I don't know if it's just me, but they are always there before we take off. Have you noticed?"

"Yes."

"What do you make of that?"

"What I make of that is they're probably spying on us."

"Well, how do they know when we're about to fly?"

"Shame on you, Frank. I thought you would have figured that out by now."

"What do you mean, Curtis?"

"They have someone in our hangar who calls them every time you start to pre-flight the plane."

"You mean, we've got a spy who tips off those guys in our own hangar?"

"We're about to take off and spy on *them*, aren't we? Don't worry, Frank, I've already had them tailed. Every time, they go back to the Lust Brothers lair on Ballast Point."

"So, we have a cat and mouse game going on here."

"Just as long as this cat gets his report from my surveillance camera, I'm not worried. Let the little mice play. They are relatively harmless on airport grounds. They know this area is federally protected by the airport authority. If they cause any mischief, they'll be arrested or thrown off the airport at the very least."

Curtis bent down picking up his briefcase.

"Come now, let's go flying."

"Yes, sir," Frank saluted and climbed the stairs to the cockpit.

Curtis thought, *At least he didn't call me boss.*

As the Gulf Stream soared over the bay, it sparkled in the early morning sunlight. Looking at the surface, no one could tell what pollution was doing to the marine life below. Nevertheless, in the flawless sky, it was indeed a beautiful day. Curtis sat in the right seat of the cockpit looking out thinking to himself of an old Irish saying, "*The better the day, the better the deed.*"

Frank interrupted his thought.

"Do you want me to fly the same heading out over the stacks?"

"Yes, I want to get some shots of their progress on dumping the containers."

"We'll be there in two minutes."

As they began flying over, Curtis noticed the slurry level was down and back to normal. The other stack level was also down. There were no more trucks hauling containers to the stack. That stage of their operation appeared complete.

Curtis said, "Now, take us out over the bay to the Gandy Bridge site."

Frank complied and soon it was apparent no barges were loading containers with concrete.

"That's it, Frank. They're finished with that phase of filling the stack."

Frank said, "I wonder what comes next. They still don't have that pit filled."

"That's why we're going to stay on top of this. My guess is the cheapest and most economical source of fill would come from the other stack. I think their pumping will continue just as their dumping in the Gulf will. I wonder how much luck we would have doing over flights of the barges with infrared photography. Do you think we could detect their dumping in the Gulf that way?"

Frank replied, "I could have our crew fit some infra-red lenses on the cameras. The only way to know if it works is to try it."

"Okay, now let's fly over the other stack."

Frank turned around and was over the stack in a minute.

Curtis observed, "It looks like they are filling barges for tonight's run. So that part of the operation hasn't ended. All right, Frank, let's head back to the Cove. We've seen enough."

"Sure, boss, I'd like to see those goons in the Mercedes waiting for me when I land. I'd like to see them figure that one out."

After landing, Frank taxied up to the fuel pumps near the hangar.

"Damn, those two guys are sitting right there by the hangar. Now, how did they do that?"

Curtis replied, "Easy, Frank, they have a radio in the car. They can listen for all flights reporting inbound to the tower. They already have your call sign and numbers."

"Those goons are really starting to get under my skin."

"Don't worry about it, Frank. By the way, are you sure you're all right. It seems your head injury has affected your logic. Twice now you failed to figure how those guys come and go."

Frank shut down the engines and sighed heavily.

"What are you saying Curtis? Do you think I should have my head checked?"

"Well, it couldn't hurt. It's just you don't seem as sharp as you used to."

"Thanks a lot, boss. I think I'll go home and see a nurse."

Curtis cringed, but waved goodbye.

Frank walked slowly back to the Cove after making sure the aircraft was secure. He wondered, *Does Curtis really think I'm not up to par? I'd like to chase those goons right off the airport. As a matter of fact, I think I will.*

Frank jumped in his Cobra and drove around the back of the hangar and up the other side pulling up right behind the black Mercedes. It was running. Frank figured they were ready to leave. He thought, *This time you're going to get an escort, boys.*

I leaned on my horn twice giving them two loud blasts. Their heads turned immediately. They weren't aware I was behind them because I took my car out of gear coasting up behind. I was laughing the whole time as they sped away. I even followed them all the way to the exit gate. As soon as the Mercedes reached the gate, they sped off. I laughed some more. Come on, boys, who do you think you're foolin' with that

German engineered Cadillac? I can blow your doors in any time. Now the black car raced up the oyster fill road leaving me in a cloud of dust. This only made me more determined to pursue and harass. Onto the highway the men in the black car proceeded to head south towards Largo. When they reached Gandy, they realized they made a mistake and had to make a U-turn in front of me.

Frank thought, *What is the matter, boys? Did you forget the bridge was closed? That's all right, I know where you're headin' and you aren't worth the gas.*

I followed more slowly keeping in the clear so they could see I was still behind them. I wished I could hear the conversation they must have been having. As I neared the Causeway Bridge, I let them go out of sight. Then, I took the little winding road that skirted Safety Harbor Bay heading home. As I reflected on what I'd just done, I thought, *Maybe I should have my head examined, but it sure was fun!*

As I pulled into my garage, Sandy stepped out the kitchen door to greet me.

"Hi, honey, I'm glad you're home. I'm fixing something special for you for dinner."

"It's not my birthday, is it? Lately, I'm beginning to wonder what I know anymore."

"Did you have a hard day?"

She bent down and kissed me while I was still in the car.

"Well, I must say it is getting better. What's for dinner?"

"I'm making you beef stroganoff with those little pearl onions you like, and if you're good, there will be key lime pie for dessert."

"Wow, are you sure it's not my birthday? Seriously, why are you going to all this trouble on a work day? You don't have to work so hard. Wait just a minute. Did Curtis call you today?"

"Why, yes, as a matter of fact he did."

"What did he say?"

"Come in the house, honey. It's too hot out here."

"Just tell me, what did he say?"

"Oh, he just mentioned something about work, that's all."

"Okay, I get it. I know what you're talking about now."

"Curtis thinks I'm slipping after having my head injured, doesn't he?"

"Well, he did mention your performance and asked me a few questions. I called the doctor and—"

Frank interrupted, "Sandy, I'm okay I was just getting used to being back on the job, that's all.

She gave me that same understanding patronizing look nurses use to pretend they're attending to *your* every need while they're thinking what the patient *really* needs is something entirely different than what they're asking for.

"All right, this has gone far enough. I'm calling Curtis. I'll tell him if he wants a flight physical, I'll get one. If he wants me to see a shrink, I'll go."

"Please don't do that, darling. I've already scheduled you for a C.A.T. scan at Dr. Anderson's office."

"You did? My, my, it seems everybody's made up my mind for me, at least what there is left of it."

"Come on, dear, sit down and let's talk it over."

"Never mind, I'll go. I have had some persistent headaches lately."

"Great, dear, I knew you would do the right thing. You always were a conscientious pilot."

"All right, Sandy, you can stop patronizing now. I said I'm going and that's it."

"Fine, dear, whatever you say."

Frank sat down in his chair staring at the ceiling wondering if he'd been bamboozled. It was days before the appointment time came. There was no flying until then. When the results came back there was some evidence of a small clot on the left frontal lobe. When Dr. Anderson explained this to Frank, he took the news in stride.

"Where do we go from here, Doc?"

"I would like to start you off on Coumadin, a blood thinner, and see where we go from there. At your age, I'm cautiously optimistic we can dissolve the clot and that will immediately reduce the pressure on your brain. If that works for you, there will be no need for surgery."

"Thanks again, Doc. Oh, and can I go back to work?"

"On the ground, yes, but no flying until I see you again in two weeks, all right? Do you have any questions?"

"No, I guess I'm good to go."

Sandy stood by Frank during the visit. Now, she stepped forward and grasped his hand and held it tight. It's going to be okay, Frank. "It's not as serious as you thought, is it?"

"I guess I'm a lucky guy." He chuckled, "I always said, I'd rather be lucky than rich."

11

Across the bay in Tampa, the Lust Brothers gathered around the mahogany table in their headquarters. From the twentieth floor of their office building, they could overlook the Bay View Towers construction site. Big Jim was just finishing up.

"Brothers, we are moving to a new phase in our plan without hindrance from local officials. Thanks to brother Martin's work, we have several people in key positions who are on our special payroll. I don't anticipate any interference with our plans."

All present seemed satisfied with Jim's report. He concluded by stepping forward to unveil an artist's conception of the Bay View Towers project in its final state of completion. The brothers were all visibly impressed. Like a work of art, the conception depicted the twin fifty story towers rising above the bay atop the three hundred-foot hill that was formerly the ugliest, most polluted sight on Hillsborough Bay. It would stand as an engineering feat hitherto unequaled considering the soft sub-stratum beneath those towers.

Each tower displayed jewel-like architecture providing a megalithic facade of strength and unassailable grandeur complete with statuary and balconies providing a glorious view of the Bay Shore and Tampa below. The twin structures were to become Tampa's most recognizable edifice overlooking the bay area. The architect left no detail unattended in the aesthetics. The "Bay View Towers" prominence would provide palatial, prestigious, posh accommodations for the most discriminating of investors. These accommodations would consummately rival the best seen in Tampa. Once completed, the Tower's alabaster walls would stand shimmering above "the land of the flowers." Yet all this was, presently, only an artist's conception. Much remained undone.

The meeting adjourned with Sam being selected as the ram rod on the construction site. Assertive and quick on the uptake, Sam was the brother best suited for the job.

At the job site, the final filling of the pit phase was over. Now, the work of placing concrete abutments was underway. It was early spring, and the work was going well for a change. Terry Riggens work was finished now. Todd Fuller was foreman on site. Todd turned from his blueprints to his foundation engineer. Over the din of diesel engines powering heavy cranes, he shouted to him.

"How much longer will it take to get those abutments in place?"

Bill Jackson replied, "It should take a couple of days once the forms are set. The plywood will have to dry after that. This is one hell of a project, isn't it?"

Todd shouted, "You got that right. Just keep it on schedule, Bill."

Bill nodded and turned back to his work. As he did, Todd spotted the limo that constantly haunted his project. It was Sam coming for another conference. Putting on his best smile, Todd approached the limo. Another session of nagging questions would precede a harangue about time and money, as if Todd had no conception of either. To complain to higher ups was tantamount to asking for a window seat on a Roman galley. He *was* the higher up. Anyway, he knew from experience, it was best to ride out the storm letting him vent about his imagined shortcomings in the way the project was being handled. Sometimes Todd fantasized that he greeted him saying what he really thought.

He imagined saying, *Hello, you old bastard. I see you've come on my site to nag and threaten me again. Why don't you make yourself useful? Go stick your head in that cement mixer over there. It might improve that prudish look on your face.* He snapped out of it just as the limo's back window slid down revealing that face.

"Well, I hope you're on schedule here, Todd. I don't see much progress over the last time I came by to inspect. Do you need more men or material? Just what is it you need this time to keep things moving?"

"Why, nothing, sir. We're just now setting up the forms for our next pour. Once they dry out, we can start setting in the abutments."

"How long will that take?"

"A couple of days, sir.."

"Well, put that gang to work doing something else. I don't want any slackers sitting on their asses waiting on forms to dry. You got it? You've got to employ your manpower judiciously. One slacker leads to another, you get my meaning?"

"Yes sir."

"I'll be back in a couple of days to see what progress you've made."

The dark shaded limo window snapped shut. The meeting was over.

Todd watched the large black car bump along the dirt access road disappearing over the edge of the hill top that used to be the top of the gypsum stack. Todd turned to his assistant.

"That man missed his calling. He should have overseen the building of concentration camps."

The problem Sam and his brothers contended with was far worse than Todd's problem. Ever since the inception of the E.P.A. by executive order of President Nixon in 1970, they had been the bane of every industrial polluter. With the game changed, the E.P.A. was in the proverbial cat bird's seat. Fortunately, for the Lust Brothers, bureaucracy begets bureaucracy. In other words, a state E.P.A. was created. It was easier to bribe local officials. So far, the brothers were successful keeping the feds at bay, but it was a race to see who would prevail.

Hence, the pressure was on to complete "Bay View Towers."

Their connection with the Nuccio Brothers provided the concrete needed, but it was a problem for brothers Joe and Martin. They didn't entirely trust the quality of the Nuccio Brothers' concrete. They were both suspicious of them, not only because they were mafia connected, but they remembered why the Gandy Bridge was being replaced so soon.

Whenever cost over runs occurred, they would conveniently use saltwater from the bay to mix their concrete. This led to the early crumbling of the bridge that provided the Lust Brothers with all its rubble. Joe, especially, remained cautious in his dealings with the Nuccio Brothers. He trusted them as far as he could sling a grand piano by its bench. He sent two of his men to the site where the Nuccio Concrete Company did their mixing with sand and water to make sure the trucks were not receiving any saltwater in their loads. As it turned out, his suspicions were largely unfounded. The opportunity to use saltwater wasn't feasible, or even available, in the case of the Lust Brothers' project. Nevertheless, true to his nature, he remained suspicious. Despite both Brothers' misgivings about the Nuccio Brothers, every time they came to Big Jim they were talked down. He would invariably make a case of how much they were saving by working with an outfit whose union worked under the table.

The work proceeded into the summer and foundations were laid and walls began to rise. It was an exciting time for Big Jim as he watched the progress from his penthouse window. The one element that detracted from it was the handling of the ex-Pinkerton guard, Norman Howard, and his case. The Lust Brothers' battery of attorneys was attempting to sway Norman's testimony, but, so far, no enticement equaled the plea bargain deal he'd been offered to testify against the Lust Brothers by the District Attorney.

The head of the Lust Brothers' legal team, Jared Phelps, invested many hours with the accused Mr. Howard to no avail. His last overture at the behest of Big Jim himself left Norman in a quandary. They had already posted his bail, now every time Jared came around he had a new deal better than the one before. Howard, who couldn't be accused of having a backbone by anyone, was beginning to weaken. Jared visited with one last appeal.

"Mr. Howard, I've been instructed to tell you that a very large figure can be deposited in a personal bank account in the Bahamas with your name on it, if you'll only agree to our terms. We don't want any harm to come to you. We just want to help you disappear. When you do, you can be assured of a very comfortable lifestyle in the Bahamas away from any authority seeking to extradite you."

"Are you really sure about that, 'cause the D.A.'s office says they can get me wherever I go?"

"Now, that's not true, Howard. I should know. I'm a Doctor of Jurisprudence. It's my business to know these things. My client only wants you to settle with him and not testify. You know you can't be forced to testify, now can you?"

"Right."

"Also, Mr. Howard, the D.A. isn't offering you any money, is he?"

"No."

"All right, then, let's add both sides up."

"If you go with them and testify against the Lust Brothers, you'll still have to serve some time in jail. After that, who knows what your future will be like? It's a dangerous world out there. On the other hand, you could serve no time and live in luxury just for remaining silent. Which, by the way, is your constitutional right?" "Now I ask you, Mr. Howard, which course of action seems more appealing to you right now?

"Well, of course, I'd be a fool not to take the money and run but they say—"

"Forget about what *they* say, Norman. They're just trying to pressure you into testifying. They're not obligated to do any of those things they say they'll do once you're behind bars. Did you know that?"

"Well, they said it's like a contract that they have to keep."

"Now, I'm not saying they won't, but what if they didn't. So, you spend less time in jail, get out on parole, and get some flunky job because you still have a criminal record. Seriously, Howard, how many reputable companies are going to hire someone on parole with arson on his criminal record? I ask you?"

"I'd like some time to think about it. Okay?"

"Sure, Norman, take your time. Just call me when you decide, all right?"

"I will. Thank you, Mr. Phelps. I'll let you know."

"I'll be waiting to hear from you. Goodbye."

Jared returned to his law office. In two hours, there was a call from Norman.

"I guess I know what I'm going to do next."

Jared said, "Just stay right there. I'm going to call the folks who will drive you to the airport. It will take a couple of hours to arrange for the flight to the Bahamas, so just be patient. You will get a call from our chauffer and he will give you further instructions."

Howard sat down in his apartment and picked up a magazine to read. He had no television. In fact, his apartment was sparsely furnished. He had no time or money to furnish it, since he had been brought back from Vegas. Time passed slowly for him as he worried if he had made the right decision. He also wondered if the police were watching his house. He thought, *What if they stop me and prevent me from leaving.* Then, the phone rang.

"Hello? Yes, this is Howard. Who is this?"

"Howard, I am your chauffer. I'll be taking you to the airport."

"Oh, all right."

"Howard, I advise you to pack lightly as you will be getting new clothes where you are going. I want you to walk to the nearby 7 Eleven just as a precaution. I will meet you there. I will be driving a black Mercedes Benz. Okay?"

"Sure, okay. I'll be there. When should I meet you? Plan on being there in half an hour. Okay?"

"All right, I'll be there."

Howard went to his room to pack. His instructions were easy to follow as he had few clothes with him anyway. Soon he was ready to leave. Feeling paranoid, he opened the door a crack and peered out. Nothing seemed out of the ordinary. Just a few cars he recognized were parked along the curb and kids playing on the sidewalk. He stepped out cautiously and began walking down the sidewalk toward the store. He knew he looked out of place carrying a suitcase, which made him all the warier. He saw nothing that tipped him to police surveillance. It was only a few blocks to the 7 Eleven where he saw the Mercedes. There were two men in it dressed casually. He worried, *"I wonder if they aren't really the cops trying to fool me."*

He shrugged his shoulders putting the thought from his mind saying to himself, *Cops wouldn't come in a black Mercedes Benz, now would they?"*

He walked right up to the car and said, "Hi, I'm Norman."

The driver smiled, "With the suitcase, we figured you were. Come on, get in. We'll take you to the airport."

Howard settled into the plush black leather interior of the new black Mercedes.

"You folks really know how to travel."

The driver replied, "Mr. Lust spares no expense for his guests."

"What about airline tickets and a passport and money. I could use some right now."

"Don't worry," said the driver. "Everything has been arranged."

"Well, if you say so. I just figured I could use a little cash at the airport and where I'm going."

"When you get to your destination, you'll have everything you need. You can count on us."

With that assurance, Norman sat back and began to enjoy the ride. The man in the front passenger seat turned and explained. "We must drive to Sarasota/Bradenton Airport to get a flight straight through to the Bahamas. That way, we don't have to go through Miami customs. They are much more attentive to persons leaving the country."

Norman replied, "Oh, I see. Better that way, I guess."

The drive continued down U.S. Highway 41 toward Manatee County. Not long after they crossed the county line, the Mercedes slowed down and made a right turn on a secondary road. They traveled west for a few miles before Norman asked why they left the main highway. The driver told him he had a sister who lived out that way he wanted to visit a little while. Norman went along as if he had a choice until they made another turn onto a dirt road.

"Your sister lives out here?"

The car came to a stop on the lonely dirt road with nothing but palmetto scrub bushes around them. The front passenger turned to Norman.

"This time, he had a gun in his hand."

"Get out, please, and stand beside the car."

In shock, Norman trembled as he obeyed.

"Take off all your clothes and put them in the car."

Norman's hands fumbled with the buttons on his shirt as he tried to obey.

"Now, get back in the car."

Norman lowered his head as he entered. Now, he was crying and shivering. The man in the front kept the gun trained on his head as the car drove further down the dirt road to an abandoned fish farm. Several twenty by ten pits where arranged in rows where fish were raised commercially. They were filled with rainwater though their surface was murky with moss and stagnation.

"Get out of the car. Stand on the bank facing the pit."

"Oh, please, please. You don't have to do this. I can go away. Whatever you say. Please don't kill me I just want…"

The man with the gun said, "Shut up, put your arms above your head and spread your legs."

The driver stepped forward with a set of diver's weights and buckled them around his midrift.

He ordered, "Walk forward towards the pit."

Howard's entire body shook uncontrollably as urine ran down his leg.

Then came the rapid phutt-phutt-phutt sound from the suppressor of the gun pressed to the back of Norman's head sending him directly to his destination.

A half hour later, Big Jim Lust got the word. Silently putting down the receiver, he smiled with satisfaction.

The news reached Curtis a day later. After a routine check on Norman by the Sherriff's Department, they reported he was missing. Curtis was disheartened and crest fallen. His entire case of arson had gone up in smoke.

Frank caught up with Curtis at Pilot's Cove. Curtis was well into his bottle of Chivas Regal that stood on the bar beside him. Despite the trim, Irish flat cap on his head, he was in a state of dishevelment leaning on the bar. He peered from under his cap as Frank entered. The sudden shaft of daylight thrust through the door upon him made Curtis more aware of his presence.

"How much does it take to keep an eye on one man in one apartment on bail? Did they not think that he would be contacted by the Lust people? This is crazy. All of our work, for what? I spend my own money on this case. I put all I've got into it, and these jokers can't watch a fish in a barrel."

Frank consoled, "It's all right, Curtis. There's still more we can accomplish. We can beat these guys at their own game. You'll see. I've got an idea on how we can build a case on their own turf."

Curtis raised his head long enough to say, "Really?"

Frank sat down by Curtis explaining his plan.

"I can apply for a job in construction on the "Bay View Towers" site as a general laborer. Then, I could get soil samples from the whole area. I'd just collect them in my lunch box, you see. We should be able to get enough samples to prove to the E.P.A. the whole project is contaminated. We could still shut them down, Curtis."

Curtis replied, "Well, it's a long shot, but it's possible."

He raised his head and pushed the bottle away.

"It's worth a try, Frank. Thanks for sticking with me. I know I'm a mess right now, but I'll get straightened out soon as I can. Then, we can make plans."

"That's great. I knew you'd come around to see it my way."

"I'm so impressed by your commitment to this case, Frank. To think a jet pilot would put himself in a general laborer's position."

"What the heck, I'm grounded right now anyway. I might as well get my hands dirty on this case. It's the best I can do for now."

Soon Frank was ready to apply for a job with the Lust Brothers' "Bay View Towers" project. Dressed appropriately with blue jeans, work shirt, and lunch box in hand, he approached the general foreman on site. He had no difficulty in getting an application. They were always looking for general laborers at this stage of construction. No one had seen him or knew him so he used his real name on the application. When he finished, the foreman told him to wait while he turned it in to the office. He went to a trailer marked "Construction Office, Bay View Towers Site, Lust Brothers, Inc." When he returned, he told Frank they would check his references and call him soon.

Two days later, the construction office called.

"This is Todd Fuller, general foreman, on the "Bay View Towers" construction project. Are you still looking for work as a general laborer?"

Frank answered eagerly, "Oh, yes sir, I sure am."

"Well, report to the construction office tomorrow morning and bring some leather gloves with you. We'll supply the rest. Okay?"

"Oh, yes sir. Thank you. Good bye."

He was in. Now, he must find enough of the right samples without being caught.

On Frank's first day, they put him to hauling cement building blocks to the masons. All that morning Frank took blocks off a straight truck's bed and carried them, one in each hand, about a hundred feet to where the masons were laying block on a wall. By noon, his gloves were already showing the wear from friction against the rough cement blocks. Holes were starting to appear. That was a little problem compared to the way Frank's upper arms felt. To him, they felt like rubber. The strain on his muscles was terrific. Clearly, he was unprepared for such labor. When lunch break came, he sat down on a pile of sand grateful for the cool feel of the sand giving way underneath him. He hardly had the strength to finish lunch.

When he did, he looked around himself and saw a pool of water collected on the ground not far from his area. He thought, *That should be as good a place as any to start. I'll scoop up some of the mud from that puddle in my Tupperware container.* He looked around himself careful to make sure no one was looking and pretended to rinse out his container in the puddle. Then, he quickly scooped a sample from the bottom and returned it to his lunch box.

Frank soldiered on for three more grueling weeks with Sandy tending to his blisters and using a heating pad to assuage his discomfort at night. With random sampling, he felt he was able to give Curtis' people a broad view of what the site was like. At one point, he felt discovered when a fellow worker came next to him. He was a Mexican, probably illegal, but that didn't matter to the Lust Brothers. He was busy practicing his English and sat down beside Frank at lunch.

"I see you take bits of earth and put them in your lunch pail. Why is this, amigo?"

Frank replied, "I just want something to remember from such an important project as this. You know, like a souvenir."

"Oh, yes, I see, a souvenir."

Frank replied, "Si".

When it became clear Frank could no longer go on with the charade as a laborer, he left the job without notice. That wouldn't be enough to arouse suspicion if it weren't for the keen eyes of Sam aided by his binoculars. He often watched the workers from the construction office trailer and he noticed something peculiar in Frank's behavior on the job site. He was just getting ready to close in on him when he quit. Using the address from his application, he decided to do some investigating.

In the meantime, Curtis was happy to pass on the samples collected by Frank to his lab. It was no surprise, they all read high on the radioactivity chart. The entire area was contaminated with radioactive gypsum slurry. The list of substances read like the top forty E.P.A. list of hazardous substances that posed significant threat to human health, as well as reading high on the chart for radon contamination.

All indicators were pointing to one inevitable conclusion. In phosphate producing regions, telltale environmental damage is the legacy of the industry. Reclaimed land emits high levels of radon. People who build on this land stand a greater chance of developing lung cancer and leukemia. Phosphogypsum stacks are piled up to 300 feet and leach toxic chemicals into the aquifer and toxic dust into the atmosphere, not to mention their deleterious effect on phosphate workers and nearby residents.

12

It was crazy, but who could know how clearly the "Bay View Towers" was taking on exceptional character as the most imposing edifice on the bay. Elsewhere nefarious plans were underway. The consequences of the endeavor could not be measured. Nevertheless, dark bitter waters continued to rise.

Brother Michael Lust, trusting, quiet, withdrawn Michael, was talking to the Nuccio Brothers. He had overseen the slurry dumping operation. Now that it was finished, he had a scheme to re-employ the ships that were idle. The Nuccio Brothers were nearly ready to foreclose on a bad debt. Jack's Cookies of Tampa Florida had outlived its usefulness for the mafia. After having sold *through* it as a business front and stole *from* it enough, the business was teetering on the brink of bankruptcy. The Nuccio Brothers informed Michael he could purchase the business for a song and use it as a front for any activity he might think of. Michael had his mind on a venture for some time. This was the opportunity he'd been looking for. Always the younger brother, always under Big Jim's thumb, so to speak, he longed for the chance to use his own business prowess to build a nest egg of his own.

Michael foresaw using the Lust Brothers ships to distribute raw materials for cookies from Miami to the company in Tampa. In addition, the cargo they would include cocaine purchased wholesale in

Miami to be re-distributed in Tampa retail. The fleet of trucks that came with the distribution contract of Jack's Cookies would be perfect. All he needed was to convince Big Jim he could make a go of it, that is, without his knowledge of the additional cargo. Michael figured Jim was so involved with "Bay View Towers" he wouldn't mind his younger brother operating a small business on the side.

The Nuccio Brothers would complete the connection in Miami that came from South America. Now, Michael must present his business venture plan to Jim. He chose his time wisely knowing timing was everything. On a Friday afternoon after Jim had finished overseeing the development of his dream project, "Bay View Towers", Michael entered his office.

"Jim, I want to tell you about an opportunity presented to me by the Nuccio Brothers." Jim leaned forward listening with interest. Anything that had to do with those brothers caught his attention. He knew they were a contriving lot. Doing business with them was one thing, but he learned from experience, they were to be kept at arm's length. In other words, they weren't entirely acquainted with the word *trust. Beyond that,* he could abide their saving the Brothers' substantial amounts in their construction costs.

"I've spoken to them about acquiring Jack's Cookies. I think you're familiar with the product."

"Yes, I am. They've built up quite a territory over the years. Their brand is well known as a quality product. However, lately, I've heard some talk about it being on the ropes."

"That's what I wanted to talk with you about. They need a financial shot in the arm to keep them going. The Nuccio Brothers have made some loans with them, but they're not able to pay off. Now, they want to sell. I thought with our backing, we could save the good name and go forward with their distributorship and still allow them the manufacturing rights."

"You thought of this?"

"Well, yes. It could keep some of our ships employed delivering their supplies wholesale from Miami."

"I see. Would the Nuccio Brothers, by any chance, be related to the wholesaler in Miami?"

"Yes, they are related. I think Jack's Cookies could benefit from the savings they'd make on their supplies. I propose we would just lease our shipping and use their distribution fleet to keep the business going and see if we can grow it."

Jim remained silent for what seemed like an eternity to Michael.

"You know, Michael, I think you might just have something here. We should diversify. I've been thinking about that ever since we got out of the fertilizer industry. We might be able to use a legitimate business with a good name like Jack's Cookies to front some of our, let's say, less tasteful ends of our business. Let me run it by all the brothers at our next meeting. In the meantime, you can tell the Nuccio's we're interested. Just watch those fellows. Don't make any commitments yet. You never want to get in too deep with them. Okay?"

"Sure, I got it Jim. Thanks for hearing me out."

"Oh, no problem, any time, little brother, any time."

Michael left the meeting feeling he had cinched the deal. Jim's interest was virtually his approval. Getting it past the rest of the brothers was like a rubber stamp on the outcome to Michael. He did as Jim suggested and forwarded his thoughts to George Nuccio, the titular leader of the brothers, with a meeting set up at Carmine's Restaurant in Tampa. Michael sat outside waiting to greet him before he entered. George arrived in a Chevy Impala to maintain a low profile, as usual. He was dressed casually smoking a cigar that he was seldom seen without. George was a middle aged, balding man with a paunch around his middle. He walked with a noticeable limp from a stray bullet he received once in the foot. The one who shot him never walked again. He always wore glasses with shaded lenses to hide his baggy eyes. He stepped out of the passenger side and greeted Michael.

"So, we meet again my friend. I must congratulate you on your "Bay View Towers" project. It's really taking on the shape of an elegant place to live. Maybe I should move in soon, huh?"

"You know we'd always save room for you, George. Come on, I've got us a table in back the way you like, huh?"

"Sure, let's go. I'm hungry."

The two of them entered the Italian restaurant where many a deal had gone down between Tampa's movers and shakers. Today would only be a preliminary meeting to make some assurances and receive some, as well. The plans had to be drawn more finely with proposed details in mind. Michael was going forward as planned. This meeting would determine the outlines of the whole plan with one main ingredient left out — the funding. That would be the part that would cement their business relationship.

When they were seated, George summoned the waiter and ordered a glass of burgundy. Michael never drank and ordered water with lemon.

George began, "You know much can be gained from our partnership. We can use this relationship to further our commitment to your other project. So far, your older brother only sees us as a supplier of raw materials. But, we can do so much more for you with this new partnership. Forgive me if I speak out of turn, but I trust you have your brother's ear or you would not be here today. Am I right?"

"That is correct. It is with my brother's consent that we can finance our undertaking. I drink to its success. Salute!"

"It is with complete understanding that I accept your toast."

Michael drank his water and studied George's face over the rim. George never missed a glance. When the meal was finished, Michael left George with assurances the deal could be made. A week later, Michael met with Big Jim.

"Do we have the necessary finances lined up for the investment with George Nuccio?"

"Yes, after our meeting with the other brothers it will be set. You can go ahead and make a commitment to the Nuccios. Remember always, though, the one who takes advantage first assumes last in our business. Do you get my meaning?"

"Yes, brother, I do."

A week later after the mechanics of the deal took place, the current management of Jack's Cookies was shown the door. Then, the hard work began. Michael had to rely on the Nuccio Brothers' connections in Tampa to set up a network of buyers. Some were already in place on the streets of Tampa, since the Nuccios already did business with a few. Michael's plans would call for more, many more. The Nuccios made it clear they wanted to work the wholesale end of the business.

Michael would need some key introductions to those who could help make the necessary connections with those on the streets holding pre-paid dummy accounts directly with Michael. No money would change hands between delivery drivers and street dealers. To receive shipments on account, they must be paid up in full with Michael vis a vie Jack's Cookies. Then, the prospective dealer could sign for the merchandise. Michael had to make some rounds about Tampa getting necessary buyers in line. However, he soon found he was in over his head. He needed a trusted person to handle the buyer/seller connection end of the business on the street level.

It wouldn't be easy, but he made a calculated decision. He would approach brother Martin. Michael considered, *Since my brother is already engaged in the underworld dealings of bribing local officials, perhaps he could be persuaded to see the advantages of being in my business.* In this situation, he absolutely needed someone he could trust completely. He thought, *Who would be better than my own brother?*

In two weeks, the entire operation took on a new look with brighter signs and more colorful street billboards offering free delivery for all Jack's products no matter how large or small the order. Soon, local restaurants in Tampa were placing extra orders. Distribution tripled in less than two months.

Now, the shipments of raw materials started to arrive in Port Tampa. At first there were only a few kilos. Once these were safely distributed in

Tampa, shipments began to increase. Delivery drivers for Jack's Cookies were instructed. If an "X" appeared in the bottom right hand corner of a bill of lading, the driver could be credited with a twenty-dollar bonus for making sure it got into the hands of the waiting customer (drug dealer). No one else would do. If that person wasn't available, they would return their cargo to the shipping dock. From there, Martin would contact the street dealer to straighten out the problem.

The transfer of product would occur in the Jack's Cookies storage facility where all incoming shipments from Port Tampa came in by unmarked straight truck. If any authorities questioned a driver, he was to tell them it was company orders because marked trucks were having loads hi-jacked. Usually, it was the Nuccio Brothers' guys who were doing the high jacking. It didn't work, though if they gave the cops that story. They had a number to call Martin, and problems would magically disappear.

In a few months, the distribution network was set up and underway. The money received from sales by street dealers went to local bosses who did the final count and determined their percentage. Everybody got a decent cut right on down the line. It was rare when street dealers tried to scam the system. They rarely got away with it either. Martin saw to that. Michael made sure his bosses were paid well enough to ride herd on the rest of the dope dealers. Soon, the money was coming in and it was more than enough to order another shipment from Miami. Where to put it; how to account for it? That was Michael's job. He was doing it well. He never had a problem with income.

In fact, he was considering another type of business when the Nuccios stepped back in with a new proposition. First, they wanted a cut off the top for their risk involved. Then, they wanted more for their shipments of cocaine, too. At first, Michael refused. When he saw himself in over his head, he went to Martin. He knew he would not tolerate what the Nuccios were trying to do.

Martin confided, "If they want to muscle in, you have two prospects with the Nuccios. They play hardball. I thought we would have a better experience with these guys, but I see it's starting to get out of hand. You can make your move by cutting back on buying shipments or you can get tougher by offering to take over their distributorship at the head in Miami. That should shake them up.

Michael considered both propositions. Before he did anything rash, he did some research. He found out through some links on the dock in Miami that the connection was willing to meet with Michael. After all, he felt he wasn't getting his share of the action either and was looking for a new buyer. That prospect seemed fortuitous to Michael. So, the initial breach with the Nuccios came over a new and separate issue. Michael set up a clandestine meeting with the supplier from Miami, who incidentally turned out to be Colombian.

They determined to meet at a restaurant in Orlando, the Fourth Fighter Squadron (a WWII themed restaurant) on the periphery of the airport. It was a small airport shared with the U.S. Air Force. It was named McCoy Airport, after a hot shot B-47 pilot Major McCoy drilled in during an airshow. It made no consequence to Michael, it was just an out of the way dark place open by noon, just the way he liked it. In keeping with its WWII aviation motif, the walls were covered with black and white photos of the Fourth Fighter Squadron in action with the famous Eighth Air Force in Debenshire, England.

When his contact entered, he was alone, which made Michael slightly more comfortable. He hesitated, as all did when entering, allowing his eyes to adjust to the dark interior. As planned, it gave Michael a chance to look him over in case there were any last-minute misgivings. So far, he passed muster. He caught sight of Michael at a candle-lit table. Innocently, he moved toward him. Michael always kept a nine-millimeter berretta with him, which made him feel a bit more comfortable in these types of exchanges. He knew by now he was way out of bounds by Big Jim's standards, but he had the guts to carry on.

When the portly man reached the table, he introduced himself.

"I am Mister Barcelona. Have I the pleasure of meeting Michael?'

Out of politeness, Michael rose and put his hand forth.

"It is a pleasure to meet you, Mr. Barcelona. Since you know my first name, may I ask yours?"

"Por Supresto, how clumsy of me. It is Garcelaco. Garecelaco Barcelona. It is a mouth full, no? My mother must have been in a talkative mood when she named me. He smiled revealing two gold teeth prominently displayed in his mid-upper jaw.

"Make no apologies. Your English is excellent, by the way."

"I've been looking forward to our meeting today. I hope you are enjoying your stay with us."

"Oh, yes, very much so. This is only my third time in your country. It is so busy compared to mine. There is so much new construction since I was here last. I have yet to see your much talked about project on the bay. I hope to see it before I leave."

"Oh, I promise you will. It would be my pleasure to show it to you. If you will permit me, I would like to discuss future arrangements with your shipping company, Garcelaco."

"Yes, indeed. I trust we will be dining together. I have had nothing but disgusting peanuts since I left the airplane."

The conversation went on amicably until lunch was served. Garcelaco ordered Chilean Sea Bass, which left one of the chef's running to the nearest seafood restaurant to procure the necessary delicacy. Fortunately, Garcelaco had a taste for wine, which kept him occupied during his absence. Garcelaco was a quiet man like Michael. He was careful not to tip his hand. Michael noticed he doted on his every word not wishing to speak, but listen. An older man than himself, Michael recognized the revelation of knowledge being transformed into wisdom in his action.

Michael broached the subject of transport and delivery saying he wished the shipments to be delivered to Port Tampa. Garcelaco smiled as he toyed with his wine stem. He was waiting, listening to hear something else, but he did not know how to express it.

Finally, Michael asked politely, "Are you comfortable with the idea of transporting your goods on your own ships?"

Garcelaco patiently replied, "Actually, no." I was in hopes of making a deal to lease your ships since they are well known in ports like Buena Ventura and Port Tampa. It seems to me it could make them less suspect for search and seizure."

Michael was taken aback, at first, by his suggestion. Though with proper consideration, he believed there may be some merit to his idea.

"How many would you need?"

Now, it was Garcelaco's turn to be surprised.

"How many can you offer?"

Now, it was Michael's turn to display the markings of a true Lust brother. He couldn't resist bragging. "I have twelve ships at my disposal for this operation, though I doubt you will need that many to keep us supplied. Of course, we must arrange for other cargo to disguise the product."

Garcelaco seemed favorably impressed smiling at his tentative offer. In truth, his men had done their homework. He knew how many Lust Brothers' ships and their tonnage were committed to Michael's last enterprise, hauling slurry barrages into the Gulf of Mexico. He was thinking, *I could have enough ships to expand my operation all over Florida.*

Garcelaco asked, "Would you consider leasing me transport of my goods along with other profitable cargo, in return for a good price on the drogues?"

Michael shook his head from side to side only slightly.

"Be careful, Garcelaco, even in this place someone might hear you and get the wrong idea, *comprende?*"

Garcelaco noted the sharpest hue of blue in Michael's eyes, contemplating, *He must be of Irish decent.* He took no offense at his remark. In his youth, he might have resented a future partner's warning. But now, his youth had vanished like a morning mist. Ever since taking up his chosen wayward path, he was never easily frightened. He was positioned to profit greatly from a new operation. That was all that concerned him presently.

13

Where it began for the Nuccios was their interference. Known in the business as muscling in, it was starting to happen to Michael and Martin. In the beginning, it was tolerated. Now, Michael felt pressured. If he was to save all they had worked for, he must find a better way. After all, it was business.

"Martin, I just finished talking to George Nuccio. He's saying his supplier is giving him the bump on his prices and the risk is too high unless he gets a bigger part of the action. He wants a percentage off the top from Jack's Cookies profits."

"Did you tell him to go straight to hell?"

Michael just shook his head in dismay. He understood the paranoid side of his brother.

Martin complained bitterly, "Michael, if you give them what they want now, where does it end, huh? You know the ropes. Once they're into us, there'll be no end, until they break us. Then they'll sell us and start all over again for themselves, right? It must stop here, Michael, I'm tellin' ya', you can't back up no more. There's no sense pushin' a worm. This is it."

Michael weighed his brother's words patiently. He placed his hands together interlocking his fingers, tapping his hands on his chin as if he were a Buddhist monk chanting a prayer for wisdom before speaking.

"Martin, I think it's time we make a change in suppliers."

"That could take time. What about the interruption in deliveries? That could cost us business. The people on the streets don't like interruptions. They're gonna go someplace else."

"Don't worry. I already got something else in the works. I'm more concerned with what the Nuccios will do when they find out we're changing suppliers."

"Well, I don't think they'll be sending you a fruit cake. Let me know when you get something solid."

"Sure, don't worry, Martin. I'll let you know."

Martin left the office to talk to his men on the loading dock. Michael picked-up the phone to call Garcelaco.

"Hello, may I speak to Mr. Barcelona please?"

"May I say who's calling, please?"

"Yes, tell him it's Michael Lust."

A full minute passed before he heard Garcelaco's voice on the phone. In the meantime, Michael sat nervously tapping his fingernails on his desk.

Then, came a familiar voice.

"Michael, I'm sorry I couldn't get to you sooner. I had to straighten out some things."

"No worries, Garcelaco. How are things going?"

"Do you mean that thing we talked about at the restaurant?"

"Yes, I was wondering about your connections."

"Oh, yes, Michael. Everything is fine with that. We are ready when you are. Would you like to come over to my store front and check it out?"

Michael didn't want to seem over anxious, so he hesitated a moment.

Then he said, "Let me check my calendar for an available date. How about next Monday? Do you have some time in the morning"?"

Garcelaco patiently raised his eyebrows at his ploy, but answered affirmatively.

"Sure, we could make it at ten o'clock Monday morning. How does that fit into your schedule?"

"Ah, let me see. Yes, I think I can get over there for a little while. Is it the Salvation Navy Store on Franklin Street?"

"That's the one right in downtown Tampa?"

"All right. Then I'll plan on seeing you there on Monday morning. Thank you, Garcelaco."

"No, thank *you*, Michael. I'll see you there, goodbye."

On Monday morning, Michael's long black limo arrived in the parking area in the alley behind Garcelaco's newly acquired front business, The Salvation Navy Store. It was a shabby looking, two story, second-hand merchandise store that operated under the guise of a non-profit charity. This provided Garcelaco a base of operations in downtown Tampa where he could keep his finger on the pulse of happenings in Tampa. Ironically, one could view through the grimy 1920's building windows construction continuing on the rising edifices of the "Bay View Towers" near the eastern shore of Hillsborough Bay. It was a brisk day in early January. Michael stepped out of his limo wearing a scarf wrapped around his neck and a black bowler hat. He was dressed for success and to impress, even his black hand-made Italian shoes shown like mirrors. No one could doubt he was a man in charge who knew his way about town. Today, he hoped to make a deal that would change how his business would operate in the future. He came with two men escorting him. As a show of faith, each was unarmed like Michael. They were greeted at the back door by a man dressed in a shabby wool coat and sock cap who was wearing tennis shoes. He could have easily passed for any homeless bum on the street. The only difference was he had a .45-caliber model 1911 Savage automatic pistol tucked in his pants.

"Good morning. Welcome to The Salvation Navy."

He winked as he spoke the name, as if everyone was in on it. Michael did not appear amused.

"I am here to see Garcelaco."

The greeter's smile slid slowly from his face. "This way, please," was all he said as he led the men up an old wooden staircase that would cause anyone trepidation just to step on. When they arrived on the second floor, Michael was not impressed seeing a large dimly lit warehouse room full of old clothes on racks that captured the odor of mildew. Just then, two of the large racks on wheels parted and Garcelaco appeared smiling.

"Welcome to my headquarters in Florida. How do you like it?" he said laughing.

Michael returned a trim smile and stepped forward grasping Garcelaco's hand.

"I thought we might talk in your office."

Returning Michael's grip firmly, he said, "Of course, right this way gentlemen."

He turned and approached two other large racks of old clothes. Parting them, he revealed a modern glass, enclosed, office suite. They found it air-conditioned and well-appointed with stylish office furniture. There were all the amenities e.g. refrigerator, coffee maker, and small kitchenette. Another room led to what appeared to be a private bedroom.

"Welcome to my home away from home."

Michael replied, "I see you take ample precautions. That is commendable in our line of work."

The walls of the room were paneled in Brazilian pecan and complemented with leather furniture and a large black walnut table in the center of the room.

"Please sit down and make yourselves comfortable. Is there anything you would like — a drink, cigar, or something to eat? I can have my assistant make some sandwiches, if you like."

Just then a woman appeared from the bedroom. She appeared to be in her thirties with an exquisite body and long black hair flowing over her shoulders. Her eyes appeared as emeralds set in a classic Castilian countenance. Her skin was flawless and smooth as alabaster. She was at least six feet tall with longs legs complementing her athletic appearance.

When the normally reserved Michael saw her, his heart leapt. He had to concentrate to keep his mind on present business.

Michael spoke for himself and his men.

"Thanks, Garcelaco, we are fine."

He nodded politely toward the woman acknowledging her presence.

Noticing, Garcelaco said, "Forgive me, I did not introduce my assistant, Lamari."

Lamari turned her eyes on Michael, as she parted her lips slightly allowing a curt smile revealing her sparkling white teeth. Tilting her head coquettishly, she looked directly at Michael.

"Are you sure you won't have something?"

Michael did not speak; he just stared, smitten. A connection between their eyes formed. He barely heard his host speaking as he invited them to sit down.

Lamari went back to her room allowing the men to discuss business.

Michael sat on the leather couch trying to clear his head of the vision of Lamari.

Garcelaco spoke, "The last time we met, we reached an agreement to form an alliance. I would supply your company with cocaine in my coffee shipments. In return, you would lease ships to me at a discount in exchange for what we referred to as the product. Is that correct so far, Michael?"

Michael's face looked stony as he returned completely to his business mode.

"Yes, that was the tentative agreement."

"Good, since we spoke I have made my connection aware of our plans. They are prepared to deliver as much product as you need. I sense, at this point, we should set up a contract and let you see and test the product, if you desire. If you wish to complete the deal, we can do all that this morning. I am ready to do business."

Michael took his time in replying, letting it all sink in before he committed himself. Then, he stood up and shook hands with Garcelaco and smiled.

"I think it is time you and I make a contract. Let me begin by saying, I will commit three ships to the deal as well as qualified crews and captains. This should allow us to keep a steady flow of product into Port Tampa."

Garcelaco seemed very pleased with the offering and was also ready to enter into a contract. The two men sat at a table working out the details for the next hour. When they were both satisfied with the written agreement, they each signed.

Then, it was time to test the product. Garcelaco called out to Lamari. When she entered the room, Michael's pulse quickened. Garcelaco beckoned her. She went to him and bent down listening as he whispered in her ear. She then departed for the bedroom returning with a small silver spoon and a small bejeweled box. She placed them both on the coffee table in front of the two men and returned to the bedroom.

Garcelaco smiled, "I think you will find this product the finest Colombia has to offer."

He opened the small, jeweled box revealing a pure white powder. Michael was having an awkward moment. He may have considered himself a drug king pin, yet he never tried cocaine in his life. As he sat staring at the solid white powder, his mind was racing. Garcelaco handed him the spoon with an expectant look on his smiling face. Michael suddenly turned on the couch and called to one of his assistants.

"Jamie, you will be dealing with this product directly soon. Since you have experienced other grades of cocaine, I want you to test this for me. Give me your honest opinion of its quality."

Jamie came forward while his boss held up the tiny silver spoon half full.

"Go ahead and sniff this, tell me what you think."

Jamie stood next to his boss and bent over sniffing the entire amount into his nostril while holding the other shut. He rose up quickly. His eyes went wide as a grin slowly appeared. Clearing his throat, he looked at Garcelaco smiling then turned to his boss again.

"Mr. Lust, this is the best quality I have ever experienced."

Michael and all in the room were pleased. Michael felt he had sealed a good deal and kept his little secret intact. With that, he turned to his new partner and put out his hand to congratulate him. Garcelaco was satisfied he had made a good deal.

"According to our contract, I will begin shipping as soon as your first boat arrives in the Port of Cartagena. Do you need anything else from me now while you are here?

Michael thought, *perhaps you would care to give me a few hours with your lovely assistant.* Then, he straightened up and rose from the couch. He was businesslike again thanking Garcelaco for his time and the convincing demonstration. He couldn't know that Lamari was, in fact, his new partner's wife. Michael and his two assistants prepared to leave. One assistant went ahead to get the car while Michael said his goodbyes, after walking through the room of stinking clothes. Once seated in the back of his car, he shrugged thinking *what an unpleasant cover, although I must admit it would probably be quite convincing for overly curious authorities.*

On the way back to his office, he picked up the phone in his car and called Big Jim. His secretary put him through right away.

"Well, little brother, how is the Jack's Cookies business shaping up?"

"I called you in part about that, Jim. I want to send some ships on a regular basis to Cartagena. I'll need three to be exact. Our business is expanding and we want to add a line of Colombian coffee to our selection. I was thinking I would take three ships off the Miami run and use them for Columbian trade. The shipments from Miami are more expensive and I've found a better deal on flour and coffee."

"As long as it's profitable, I don't see a problem with it. It seems you're getting some good experience out of this new venture. I hope you aren't wearing out those Nuccio Brothers. Sometimes, they're lazy, like the time they used saltwater in their concrete on the Gandy Bridge project. Of course, that turned out for the best for us when I needed that concrete for fill, didn't it?"

Once again, Michael found himself listening to big brother brag. It always disgusted him and he decided to get off the phone.

"Jim, I've got some other matters to attend to, so I'll have to let you go for now. I'll keep in touch and let you know of any new developments."

"Fine, fine, keep up the good work."

"Right, Big Jim." *Bullshit,* he thought, as he hung up.

Now, the way was clear for Michael to make his other move. Dropping the Nuccio connection would not be as easy. He knew there would be consequences. He picked up the phone again and called George Nuccio. Like Big Jim, he was the eldest of his three brothers. He made all the big decisions. He picked up on the first ring.

"George, it's Michael. How are you doing?"

"Oh, Michael, everything's fine here. What can I do for you?"

"I need to talk some business with you. Can you meet me at Carmines' tonight?"

"Ah, that's kinda short notice. Could we make it tomorrow evening say around eight?"

George always wanted to call the shots. He felt it gave him the upper hand in negotiations if he made the arrangements as to where and when. He suspected, in his own egotistical mind, that Michael would accept the recent offer the Nuccios made. He never suspected Michael would have the guts to strike out on his own making a deal with someone else so soon. Michael hesitated on George's postponed arrangement, then he reluctantly agreed.

"I'll meet you at Carmines' then tomorrow at eight. Good-bye, George."

George hung up wondering why Michael was so curt. It didn't bother him for long, though. George was convinced he had Michael in his back pocket.

Eight o'clock on a Wednesday found Michael and his two assistants waiting at Carmines' in the back of the restaurant. It was always crowded on a Wednesday, which was in Michael's favor, should George become unruly. Michael took the precaution of having his two men sit at a table across the room. This time, they were both armed.

George showed up late and slightly inebriated. Michael smelled brandy on him. He hoped his mood would not cause trouble. His men were instructed to watch George's hands while he ate. There was no sign of his bringing anyone with him. It underscored his feeling of confidence in his control over the situation. He was not expecting trouble. He appeared in a three-quarter length over coat. It made him appear small, as he was only five feet five.

When the maître d' removed it, he revealed a man with more than a middle-aged paunch. George had dined on fine foods for many a year and it showed. He had a round face and a receding hairline. His face was smooth as a baby's behind. It disguised the man's volatile nature. He smiled and looked around the room before seating himself. He thought he noticed some men in the back room who looked familiar, but he decided to make no mention of it.

"So, Michael, how are you? It has been a little while since we've had the opportunity to chat. I'm glad we could have this time together. What sort of business did you wish to discuss?"

Michael was a bit nervous. He hoped it didn't show as he subconsciously rubbed his hand across his chin. He caught himself, then stopped. He suggested wine. Wanting to get further into the meal, he decided to make small talk. George went along and they discussed some of his construction plans in town. Ultimately, the discussion led to the "Bay View Towers" project. Soon, the waiter arrived and George took Michael's wine suggestion. They each ordered and returned to the previous discussion.

"So, my foreman tells me, your people are ready to move on to a new section of pouring the perimeter walls. You must be excited that the project is moving along so well."

"Yes, although, my other business concerns keep me busy. My brothers assure me we are right on schedule, thanks to your concrete fill from Gandy Bridge."

"We're always glad to help if it furthers both our business concerns."

Michael continued with small talk until their main courses were nearly consumed. Finally, George abruptly left the polite tact and asked the important question of the evening. So, Michael level with me, why are we out at Carmines' on such a cold night?"

Michael glanced across the room quickly making sure his men were paying attention. They were, so he cleared his throat and leaned forward to speak to George.

"George, we are making some changes in our operation to economize. My accountant informs me we cannot enter into your most recent offer and remain solvent. He recommended several approaches we could try to tighten our budget and stay competitive. Michael cleared his throat again, looked at his men, then said it.

"One major step we are going to make immediately is to change suppliers of our product out of Miami. Now, he had George's full attention. His dark brown eyes seemed to light up.

"What exactly are you trying to say, Michael?"

"Well, me and Martin and the accountant talked it over, and we feel a move to a new supplier is necessary. To tell you the truth, we find your new proposal for a greater percentage of the gross profit unacceptable."

George put his hands on the tablecloth pulling it tight towards him.

"Are you sure that's a wise decision, Michael?"

"It is, in fact, what we are going with, George."

George maintained his composure, looking around the room for anyone else listening. Then, he called for the waiter.

"I believe you better think that over again, Michael. I will contact my brothers, in the meantime, and let them know how you feel. It seems you have some business dealings with someone else. You should not have done that without giving me and my brothers an opportunity to make a counter offer. Did you do that, Michael? I think not, and that disappoints me. I know my brothers will be disappointed, too. Your family and mine go way back. I think you should think twice about disappointing my family."

Michael bristled at his partner's threats and pushed his chair back to leave.

George said, "Have you counseled with Big Jim on your decision?"

"He is not included in decisions made by me for Jack's Cookies."

George returned, "Maybe he should be."

Michael stood up gazing down at the flustered little gangster and said, "Those who don't when they may, will find themselves lacking another day."

"Yes, well, I strongly advise you then to prepare for a day that may surprise you."

Michael said coldly, "Good evening, Mr. Nuccio."

He left the bill with George, adding insult to injury, as his men hurriedly followed him out of the room.

14

The only thing left for Michael was to prepare for receipt of shipments from a different direction. In other words, Michael was in the cat bird's seat, and he knew it. An inner voice told him, *Enjoy it while it lasts, Mister Drug Kingpin*. He was emptied after the exchange with George. Hoping for a better future, he felt drained. He was shaken by the thought of the Nuccios possible revenge. They were the same cats under the skin. That's what bothered him.

He remembered all too well the incidents and accidents that occurred across Ybor City in the late fifties… local officials attempted throwing off Santo Trafficante's control of the city. Then came retribution. Every cop on beat in Ybor City had his knees blown out by two thugs in a car that stopped to ask directions. In those days, no one could alert the other unless they could reach the call box at their post. None could survive the Italian '00' shotgun blast to make that call. That was enough to make even the toughest cop shiver.

For the time being, Michael put it out of his mind. He must prepare for the shift in delivery of shipments. Often, he would go to the shipping dock and talk with the men working there. He enjoyed bantering with the men. He remembered the days of his youth working for his father's shipping line. On the wharf, his body was sculpted by the heavy lifting of a stevedore's life.

Michael had nicknames for drivers he enjoyed chatting with. One driver he called Country Joe came from Riverview. He lost his job when the plant blew up. Michael saw to it that he got another job driving trucks for the shipping line in Port Tampa. When Michael took over Jack's, he asked him to come drive for him. Country Joe always had a joke to tell or some homespun homilies that would make Michael laugh or at least forget his troubles for the moment.

"How's it going, Joe?"

"Oh, just finer than frog fuzz, boss. Though I was just thinkin', that forklift driver inside sure is independent. I told him I was ready to leave on my route if he could load me out next. You know what he said to me? He had a loading chart and I wasn't next on it. He said he had a certain order when he loaded and nobody was gonna change that. Why that fellar is as independent as a hog on ice."

Michael chuckled, "I'll see what we can do about that. It wouldn't do to have my drivers sitting around idle. Keep an eye on your count now. I'll talk to you later."

Michael strolled down the loading dock dodging an occasional forklift and talking with the other drivers. Soon, it was time for lunch and another boring meeting with the brothers in Big Jim's office suite. Every meeting started the same with Big Jim giving a blow-by-blow account of the recent progress made at the "Bay View Towers." Then, the accountant would give them a full report ending with his usual admonition to stick to the budget and watch for over expenditures. Every brother would then report on his assigned area of construction. That is, except for him, since he had Jack's Cookies to report on. The only consolation was the meetings were only held monthly.

The new supplier's deliveries went through seamlessly and soon better quality coke was hitting the streets of Tampa. Then, things took a nosedive. Country Joe's truck was late coming back to the loading dock. Martin asked the other drivers if they had seen him or his truck. None reported they had seen him since he left the factory. That night, Martin started a search of his route stop by stop but found nothing. He called every delivery point the next day and received no word of him being seen. Then, he received a phone call from Joe about mid-morning.

"Hey boss, I've been hijacked. I'm out here at Hooker's Point. I've been tied up and blind folded for hours, seems like all night and then some."

Martin nearly dropped the phone in his office.

"Are you hurt?"

"Nope, just my hands a bit. I've been workin' that rope right along. I guess they didn't do too good a job or I'd still be at it. Some fellars here at a warehouse let me use their phone."

"Are you sure you're not injured, Joe?"

"No, I ain't poked nor punctured, just a might dusty. I've been rollin' around in a ditch all night trying to get shed of that rope."

"Tell me where you are exactly and I'll send someone out to get you."

"Well, do you know that spot at the end of Hooker's Point Road where they off load the new foreign cars from the ships?"

"Yes, I know the place, Joe."

"I'm at the last warehouse on the right."

"Okay, Joe, just stay where you are. We'll come get you."

Michael sent out another driver to pick up Joe. When he returned, Michael called him into his office.

"Are you sure you're all right, Joe? Do you feel okay to drive?"

"Like I said boss, I'm all right."

"Just the same, I'd feel better if you took a couple of days off (with pay of course); I'd feel better if you did, Joe."

"Well, all right, since you put it that way. I'm sure my wife can find plenty for me to do at home."

Michael laughed, "Yes, Joe, I'm sure she probably can. Come back Thursday bright and early. Okay?"

"That's just fine with me, boss, so long."

After Joe left, the smile dropped from Michael's face. He thought, *So the battle begins. I've got to get Martin's take on this.* Just then, Joe popped his head back in the door. I almost forgot to tell you those guys who pulled me off the truck had a message for you. They said they didn't want to see me on another one of your trucks again."

Michael heaved a sigh, "I see, does that bother you, Joe?"

"Oh, heck no, if they didn't have guns it would have been a whole different story, I'm tellin' ya."

"Thanks for your loyalty, Joe. I appreciate that. Now, go on home and take it easy. We'll take it from here."

As he left, Michael reached for the phone and called Martin for a meeting in his office. While he waited for him, Michael's mind drifted back to a time when the Lust Brothers were embroiled in one of their many lawsuits. It seemed ironic at the time. The Lust Brothers Corporation provided the county a low-cost lease on land near their plant in Riverview, so an elementary school could be built.

Years later, they were being sued for leasing radioactive, contaminated land to the school system. They ended up winning the suit at the time, but Michael remembered a larger than normal number of children attending the school contracted leukemia. Two of Joe's children were affected and one eventually died. He remembered Joe never complained to the office or protested, he just allowed the courts to settle it. More sensitive than his other brothers, he felt remorse over the tragedy. He wished he had done more for Joe's family in the past. Martin interrupted his thoughts barging into the office.

"I told you they played hard ball. This is only the beginning, just you wait and see."

"I don't want to just wait and see. That's why I called you, so we can discuss this."

"Well, if you're asking me, I say we should put an armed guard in the back of every truck."

"With fifty, correction, 49, trucks in our fleet that could get expensive. Besides, it could lead to gunplay in the streets. That's something we don't need, considering what we're delivering all over town. Martin, I'm not exactly sure what the answer should be. I'll have to sleep on it."

Martin said, "Don't sleep too long brother or we won't have much of a fleet left to worry about."

The following afternoon the police notified Michael there were two trucks from his fleet found completely burned out on the roadside. The drivers of each truck were listed as missing.

A few days passed and no other incidents occurred. Michael thought, *Maybe they're just testing our resolve and waiting to see what we'll do next. After all, what would they do with 50 twenty-five-foot trucks?* His second thought was, *with their connections in the auto industry…plenty!* It was five thirty p.m. Most trucks just finished their routes and were returning through the gates to the loading dock. Suddenly, one truck entered the gates with its horn blaring. It was out of control. Several drivers jumped out of their trucks surrounding the truck that rolled to a stop on its own. Its driver sat bolt upright belted into his seat with the horn wired to the wheel. There was such a commotion Martin ran out to the crowd around the truck.

He yelled to the drivers, "Don't touch anything. This truck could be wired with a bomb!"

The drivers suddenly jumped back allowing him to see the gruesome sight immediately. It was Country Joe, with an ice pick embedded up to the handle in each ear! Like others, he gasped at the grisly sight, then felt like puking. Some drivers already were. Martin yelled to the crowd.

"Don't touch anything. I'm calling the police. Get an empty truck over here and unload this truck NOW!"

One of the men saw a note pinned to Joe's chest that read:

EVERY TIME A TRUCK LEAVES HERE, SOMETHIN' BAD HAPPENS!

A lot of drivers' voices grew louder and more agitated around the truck. Soon the police arrived and a crime lab truck entered with a crew prepared to investigate.

Michael was distraught and blamed himself for waiting to see what the Nuccios would do next. Now, he picked up the phone and called his insurance agent. By the time they arrived, there was not much to look at. The crime lab left with all the evidence they could find and the ambulance took Joe to the morgue.

Obviously, they would have to rely on the results of the police autopsy and subsequent investigation. They told him life insurance was available and they could notify next of kin unless Michael wanted to. At that point, he refused, saying he would be taking care of funeral arrangements. He felt that was enough. He did not want any connection or knowledge of his association with the murderers to surface. He knew Martin and himself must remain outside of the circle of people that could implicate their dealings with organized crime. They must lay low. The insurance agent who arrived on the scene later made a good recommendation when he spoke with Michael.

"You know I have seen similar cases. As unfortunate as they seem, they do occur. Also, a case like this might have extenuating circumstances, if you know what I mean."

At that, he considered Michael's eyes, speaking sincerely. "I think you and your company would be better served through a private insurance investigation agency, that is, if you so desire. Now, I know of an excellent one if they have the time and inclination to accept your case. Here is their card. Think about it anyway." The agent went out the door leaving the card he mentioned on Michael's desk.

Michael picked up the card, it simply read:

SPECIAL INSURANCE INVESTIGATIONS, ALL FIELDS

Chief Investigator
P.O. Box 662
St. Petersburg, Fl. 33613

Michael heard back from Martin that there were drivers on the dock overheard grumbling about having to go out the next day. Michael quickly decided to address the drivers immediately.

"Martin, I want you to call a meeting of the drivers right away before they leave on their routes. I need to speak to them."

Martin got on the p.a. system and announced.

"There will be a meeting held on the loading dock in twenty minutes for all drivers, only drivers. No other employees need attend. Thank you."

Most drivers came together in a large knot, some grumbling, some bewildered, nevertheless, almost all were there.

Michael soon appeared and stepped up on a desk with the use of a chair. He was dressed in his suit because it was a bit chilly. He did not wish to try impressing the men; he only wanted to assure them.

"Thank you, men, thank you all for coming. I know you have routes to run and I will compensate you if you run late tonight."

Martin stood beside the desk Michael was standing on in a show of solidarity.

"Martin, see to it every driver gets a bonus for late driving this evening."

Some men shuffled around; others looked down. Then, one voice raised out of the crowd.

"How much?"

Michael answered, "Martin, make it fifty dollars for everyman who is here."

Now that Michael had the men's attention, he addressed them.

"Men, I know what some of you had to witness was difficult for you. First, I want you to know I will be personally paying for all Joe's funeral expenses. Also, I will set up a retirement fund for his wife and child. Many of you knew Joe and those who did, liked him. In his own way, he was a trusted, friendly, loyal guy. Personally, I liked his little jokes. He really did brighten our day. I want you all to know I have taken measures to prevent this from happening again. I have applied to our insurance company to allow guards to ride on every load that leaves this lot.

"Also, I'm having radios installed in all your trucks so that you can radio a dispatcher here if you think you see any trouble. In addition, I am authorizing a raise of 20% for all drivers effective at the end of this pay period. I know money is not the whole answer, but your loyalty means a lot to me especially in the upcoming days. So please stick with it and trust me. We will come out all right."

Michael looked around at the men's faces trying to glean something from their expressions in their eyes that would assure him he got through to them. Most just turned away walking off in small groups; some in clots of twos and threes. His only take on their disposition was at least he wasn't booed down. Martin was soon by his side reassuring.

"You did a good job encouraging the men, Michael. I just hope you can come through with all you promised."

"Well, with any luck, maybe I won't have to."

"Whadda ya mean?"

"I plan on setting up a meeting with George Nuccio. Maybe with all his brothers, I don't know yet. Whatever it takes, Martin. I've got to get this violence to stop. I've looked at it from both sides. Far as I can see, it's a no-win situation. If I give in entirely to the Nuccios, then they will just keep pushing us like you said. They'll squeeze us like an orange, eat the fruit, and throw away the peel. Yet, if I keep on going this way, we'll lose drivers and trucks. In addition, we will call down attention by the authorities on our entire operation. That's no way to run a drug ring. Am I right, Martin?"

"No, of course, not. But, we can't show weakness either."

"Right, so do you see the dilemma I'm in as President? So far, I've lost three trucks and a driver. God only knows where the other two will end up. Some drivers want to quit. Wasn't it you, Martin, that told me I must not back up! You said if we didn't stand up to them they would take it all. Remember? Well, what now Martin? Should we have all-out gang war in the streets of Tampa? How about this, Martin? Maybe I could have all our trucks armored? How would that ring as a jingle,

'You can trust Jack's Cookies.' 'They arrive sealed in armor for guaranteed freshness.'

"Michael, I never told you this would be easy, did I?"

Michael put his arm around Martin as they walked together toward the office. Michael spoke closely to his ear so he wouldn't miss a word.

"No, Martin, you did not say it would be easy."

At the end of their walk to the office, Michael went to his desk picking up the phone without dialing. He just held it in the air.

"So, Martin, since it's not going to be easy, I think I'm going to have to ask you to go along and strong arm someone or bribe an official. Do whatever it takes to keep us afloat. I'll make some calls and try to straighten out this whole mess without your sage advice."

He gave Martin a look of good-bye in his eyes.

"Please do shut the door on your way out, thank you."

As it proved between the two brothers, it was nobody's fault unless over ambition be considered. The point at hand remained Michael must untangle the mess before it became deadly for them both. He sat still for a long moment, then he put the phone back in its cradle doing some more thinking. With nowhere else to turn, he decided to write to the special insurance investigator. Two days passed before he received a phone call from them.

"President Lust, this is special insurance investigator, Curtis Selway. Your secretary was good enough to put me through. What can I do for you?"

Michael was surprised he had returned the call so quickly.

"Yes, this is President Lust. I'm so glad you called. My insurance agent recommended you and gave me your card. I must say, you don't advertise much. Is there a reason for that?"

"Yes, there is. We only take on special cases by recommendation only, so we don't feel the necessity for a high profile."

"I see. From what I described in my letter, I must be a special case then."

"I would say it's worth considering further. I must remind you, however, my associate and I would be in the employ of your insurance company, should we accept the case. Since your letter was sent by special delivery, I assume you must want to get started soon."

"Yes, as soon as possible, if you please."

"In that case, I promise you I will be in touch by tomorrow one way or the other. Thank you, President Lust."

"Thank you, Mr.—" the connection was gone.

Curtis let up the receiver button and called Frank.

"Frank, I'm glad you're home."

"I'm not. I could use some work, preferably flying work."

"Well, I think I've got something for you."

Frank sat up on the couch simultaneously turning down the volume on his TV, giving his full attention to the call.

"What is it?"

"Well, you won't believe who I was just talking to. It was President Michael Lust and, get this, of Jack's Cookies. Can you believe it?"

"Jack's Cookies sounds familiar. Did you see on the news where one of their drivers was murdered in front of their company? He was still in the truck with ice picks in his ears."

"No, I missed that ghouls' parade, but my client informed me of the details. They want to know if we will work the insurance claim for President Michael Lust."

"Whoa, how did he get so far from the barn?"

"I'm not sure, Frank, but I have a suspicion this case could lead us somewhere."

"I think you're right. It would be good to get out of the hangar and work a real case again and maybe even do some flying, boss."

Curtis winced, "Well, yes, maybe. Right now, this looks pedestrian. Unless I missed my guess, we'll be in Tampa mostly. Nevertheless, I'm intrigued as to what our younger brother Lust is up to, aren't you?"

"Oh, yeah, I'm with you there."

"Good, I just wanted to make sure you were ready to be on a case, especially this one."

"I'm ready to go. Just let me know where and when we begin."

"Okay, Frank. I'll deal us in tomorrow and call you later. So, get your walking shoes on."

"Fine, Curtis. I'll be ready."

"Sandy, I just heard from Curtis. We've got some work right here in the bay area."

Sandy replied, "That sounds promising. Can you tell me anything about it?"

Frank acting coyly said, "Only that it's a pretty sweet deal."

"Oh, really. How so?"

"The company we will be working for is called Jack's Cookies that's how."

"Oh, wait a minute, is that the cookie company that had one of its drivers murdered in their truck lot?"

Frank tried playing that down. "Yeah, that's the one."

"Frank, I don't want you going into some sort of gang war or labor dispute. That one sounds pretty gruesome."

She walked out of the living room confronting him as he was dressing in their bedroom.

"I know how that man died, Frank. I watch the news, too. I don't want you getting mixed up in some gang land war."

Frank defended, "It's not all that. This is about insurance coverage on their fleet of trucks. Besides, it's work again. I need to get out of this house. It's tying me down."

"Well, I could stand living in a clean house again."

"What did you say, honey? I didn't hear that?"

"Oh, I just thought it will be nice for you to be back at work again."

"Yeah, sure, I agree."

Frank finished pulling on his Jodhpur boots, hoping this job would turn into one that required a pilot. He leapt to his feet looking himself over in the mirror. Dressed in a long sleeve dark blue swede shirt and charcoal grey dress slacks, his black boots provided just the right amount of accent. After pulling on his brown short-waisted A-2 goat's skin leather flying jacket, he checked the mirror again.

"That's right, this pilot is available."

"Honey, I'm ready to leave."

"Okay. Here, I've got something here for your lunch."

Frank protested, "Honey, I can't go off to work carrying a brown paper bag. I'm a pilot, for gosh sakes."

"Oh, it's just some crab cakes Howie made up special for you."

"Just let them stay here in the kitchen. I'll eat them when I get home."

"Come now, take them. Howie would be devastated if he found you wouldn't take them. He said they would bring you luck and to just put them on the dash board of your plane and they would warm up plenty.

"Oh, all right. If it's for Howie, I'll do it."

Frank made it out the door to his red Cobra waiting in the curving drive. Sandy must have pulled it out of the garage for him. He tossed the bag of crab cakes into the front bucket seat. Cranking her up, he loved to hear the throaty roar of his twin Holley duo flow carburetors metering out the power to that 427cid Ford engine. He drove away slowly, so as not to disturb the neighbors waving good-bye to Sandy. On his way to the airport, he could see a storm brewing in the east. It was only ten a.m., yet it was getting very dark. Frank said to himself, *I'll have to keep an eye on that baby.* As he wheeled up to Pirate's Cove, only Curtis' Bentley was there. He looked over towards the hangar for the black Mercedes with two men, but it was gone. Frank thought, *Good riddance, we can sure do without your kind around here.* Frank entered to find Curtis leaning over the bar with the lights turned up. He was staring at a large map of the Tampa Bay area. When he heard the door, he looked up seeing Frank.

"Good, you're here. Just in time to give me your opinion."

Frank quipped, "It's always free, you know."

"Yes, at least, this time it's welcome. Look at this map of the Tampa Bay area. Do you see any possible pattern between the Jack's Cookies factory and areas of Lust Brothers' activity?" Frank perused the map, then rose facing Curtis under the bar lights.

"No, I don't see any connection. Most of the Lust Brothers' activity is around the docks of Tampa and Port Tampa and, of course, that monster condominium in Riverview. That's just what I see. Michael Lust has his operation separate from the others for the most part. I wonder if he is completely on his own or is he using his connection to stay afloat? I know damn well he's got something more than just cookies going on."

"Frank, I'd like to work out something from the air. Why don't you go out and give *Company Business* a preflight?"

"Roger that, but I must warn you, there is a pretty bad winter storm building in the east. It looks like its heading towards Tampa."

"Just the same Frank, get her ready."

I was almost finished with my pre-flight when the hangar phone rang. It was my line.

"Frank here, what's up?'

"Yes, Frank, it's Curtis. I just talked to the Flight Service Station on the field and they say the weather will not be good for the next four hours. So, I want you to do a bit of ground surveillance for me. Get the binoculars out of the plane and borrow one of our mechanic's cars. Then drive to Jacks Cookies. I have a hunch I want to play out. The delivery trucks are out on their routes now. I want you to let me know when the larger truck arrives that supplies them. Then, trace it to its home base."

"Is that it?"

"Yes, that's it."

"All right, I'm on it, boss."

Frank thought, *I hate stakeouts. I wonder how many hours this one's gonna cost me.*

He took his black bag out of the Cobra and put the top up. Then, he walked into the hangar. He walked out the back door to the employees' parking lot. Before he left, he wanted to find the best car available. The little lot behind the hangar would have to suffice. He strolled amongst the cars as if he were in a used car lot.

"Ah, yes, this should do. His eyes settled on a lemon yellow 69', 396cid Chevy Malibu SS. Returning to the hangar, he spoke out. Who belongs to that Chevy Malibu out back?"

Ricky, one of the senior A & P mechanics, stepped forward.

"Anything the matter, Frank?"

"No, I just wanted to borrow your car for a while."

Ricky hesitated, "Ah, boss, that's my pride and joy. I've only had her one year and I was planning…"

"Don't get nervous Ricky. Do you see these? They're the keys to a 1972 racing equipped Cobra. I'll trade you for a day, no questions asked. What do you say?"

Ricky had that look on his face as if he'd died and gone to heaven. He raised his hand up in the air as if to keep his customer on line. Hold up there, just a second, while I go get my keys. Frank stood motionless in the hangar having second thoughts.

I can't believe I'm doing this. My beautiful Red Cobra with the black speed stripes…

Ricky returned in a flash. "Mine only has a quarter tank of gas."

"That's all right. You'll use that much just getting off the airport in mine."

Then, he motioned Ricky outside and took him over beside the Cobra. Ricky bent down and ran his fingers just above the front-end lines as if in a state of worship. He could only hum.

Frank stood back from his car looking Ricky in the eye. Then, he put his hand around the back of his neck and spoke closely to him.

"You see this car?"

Ricky said, "Yeah, I see it, Frank."

"When I get back and we trade cars again. If I see so much as a bug's ass on my bumper, I'll have you waxing this beauty until your clothes are out of style, you get me?"

"Oh, yeah, I get you, Frank. No problem."

I wished him good luck and walked out to the Malibu. It fired right up giving me a big smile. I took hold of the four-speed shifter and put it in gear and drove out of the grass parking lot slowly. Before I could get out of the parking lot, it started to rain. It was a typical Florida downpour. I waited to pull out into traffic on Highway 686. Soon traffic slowed to a crawl under the pelting rainstorm. So, I decided to go back home for dinner and set up my stakeout later that night.

I was home early. Sandy seemed pleasantly surprised.

"Hello dear, what brings you home so early?"

"This storm is partly why. Now, Curtis wants me on the night shift."

"What do you mean?"

"Oh, he just wants me to watch over a client of ours and take notes."

"That doesn't sound dangerous. Did you enjoy your crab cakes for lunch?"

"I'll be damned, I forgot all about them. They're still in my bag."

"Well, I hope you get to them before they get stale. Do you want me to go out and get them?"

"No, it's raining. Don't worry about it. Come over here with some wine, though, and I'll set a fire."

Sandy shivered, "I was hoping you'd say something romantic like that. I'll be on my way soon with a plate of crackers and cheese, too."

I laid myself back on the couch. "Sometimes I wonder why I go to work at all. How can I leave you alone? I must be clear out of my mind."

15

I sat in the Chevy Malibu outside the gates of Jack's Cookies. It was one thirty a.m. The monotony of a stakeout was already forming creases on my butt. Traffic was slow. All the daytime deliveries were made and trucks parked in the main parking lot. I was looking for something else, though.

I was looking for a large delivery, something that came by tractor-trailer. I was after the main supplier, the one that kept the factory alive churning out those delicious cookies. It's rare when people get murdered over cookie deliveries, especially in such a brutal gangland way. Curtis and I agreed the only way to find out why was to get to the source that delivered to the manufacturer.

Another pair of headlights pierced the night lighting up the entrance road to Jack's Cookies. This time, they caught my attention. It was a semi tractor trailer entering the gates. I watched him back up to the loading dock as I reached in my bag for my binoculars. As I scanned the front of the truck, it didn't take long. There it was; an entry permit sticker on the windshield. It was for Port Tampa. Now, I knew the source of their supplies. I stayed a while longer watching them off-loading the truck. There was little I could learn from it though.

Everything was palletized making it difficult to see any labels telling me what was being off-loaded. I could guess the main ingredients were flour, sugar, chocolate, etc. but that wasn't what I was looking for. I needed to get out to Port Tampa if I was to learn anything about this shipment. Even then, I might come up with nothing, but I had to follow the lead where it led.

The drive across Tampa was almost wonderful. I missed the ride of a high-powered Chevy. This one was tuned perfectly. *Of course, why wouldn't it be? It was my head airplane and power plant mechanic's personal car.* I crossed four-lane Dale Mabry Highway with a thump, thump at sixty. I was on Interbay Street. *Better slow down,* I thought. *It wouldn't do to be pulled over in this part of town at this time of night.* Mainly a blue-collar neighborhood, Interbay was an angling street opposed to the others. It led directly to the Port Tampa dock entrance.

As I rolled up to the gates, I pulled out one of many insurance inspector identity badges that Curtis provided. The guard waved me in without a care. When I was on the dock drive cluttered with abandoned forklifts and cranes, I wasn't sure which way to turn. I knew what I was looking for, but which way? A sailor walking down the dock towards the car gave me an idea.

"Hey, sailor, I'm looking for the Lust Brothers' ships. I'm here to pick up some friends."

He raised his arm over his head with thumb extended without looking back saying, "They're all down there. Watch 'em at poker, they're a cheatin' lot."

"Thanks, I'll remember that."

I rolled along the dock cautiously, looking up to see the shipping line name on the bow of each ship I passed. Soon, I was there down and in front of a Lust Brothers' ship. It flew a Columbian flag next to the American flag. I thought for a moment, *Chocolate, yes; flour, no; milk must be fresh, so that's a no. Could this be my ship?* I thought, *I'll wait awhile and see. The ship looks abandoned.* I settled in for a long wait and that's what I got. Near dawn, I decided to pull the plug on the stakeout.

Before I left, I thought I'd take pictures to show Curtis I wasn't out here dreaming. I spied a stack of lumber, so I decided to take my pictures from behind it in case anyone else was watching. When I got out, I was glad I had my parka on. The wind was coming straight down the dock. It was bone chilling stiff. After a few photos to identify her as the Lust Brothers' *Seven Seas,* I got back in the car.

Then, I remembered the crab cakes from Howie that I stuffed in my bag the day before. I wondered, *Are they still good? Well,* I thought, *only one way to find out.* I leaned over reaching for my lunch bag on the top of the dash on the passenger side. Just as I did so, I heard the crack of a rifle shot and heard a thud inside the car! Then, another hit the wheel. Then, a third shot hit just above me, entering the door next to me. I lay still not having another place to go. I stayed there lying over the seat for a good twenty minutes. Nothing more occurred, so I reached up slowly and turned over the key. Then, I jumped behind the wheel with my head way down, looking through the steering wheel. My foot floored the accelerator. The tires let out an awful screech, but I didn't care. I was only hoping another round wasn't coming through my rear windshield!

The gate guard was startled as I whizzed past his little shack. In a hurry to save my neck, I had no time to spare. By the time I reached Dale Mabry three miles up the road, my heart was still trying to pound its way out of my chest! Then, I had the oddest thought, *Those crab cakes saved my life.* Right then, I had a strong urge to be home safe in Safety Harbor. I would return Ricky's car later since no one was up at this time of morning. When I snuck in the house trying not to wake Sandy, I failed. Sometimes I think she has the ears of a bat. When she found me in the kitchen, she offered me breakfast. I was delighted to be with the one I love and allow her to wait on me. Bacon and eggs would be great with me, just hold the crab cakes.

After a sumptuous breakfast, I kissed her sweetly, not saying a word about the shooting incident. I went down the hall mumbling about long stakeouts and being ready for sleep. I made up my mind she'd never hear about my harrowing escape. The next day, I didn't get out of bed until eleven o'clock. It was too early for lunch, so I decided to meet up with Ricky and settle for the damages. This was going to be some meeting. I felt like I'd rather chew tin foil after razzing him about caring for my car.

When I arrived at the hangar, I had to go looking for him. Nobody else had seen him lately. I finally located him inside a twin-engine Bonanza pulling out some wires with a needle nose pair of pliers.

"Hey, Ricky, how's it going, *muchacho?*"

"Oh, you're back. That's good. Now, I can take my car to lunch. After what you said, I got the sweats just sittin' in that beast of yours. It sure is one fine set of wheels."

"Ah, Ricky, I need to talk to you. Can you come out of there for a minute?"

"Sure, Frank I'll be right there. Where did you park my car?"

"Oh, it's just outside the hangar doors."

"I'm sorry if I was kind of rough on you about using my Cobra. You did the company a big favor and I want you to know I appreciate it."

"Oh, that's okay, but I want you to know I took good care of her. I even washed her off after the rainstorm. Have you got my keys?"

"What"?

He said, "Have you got my keys, man?"

"Oh yeah, here you go."

"What did you want to talk to me about, Frank?"

Just as he asked the question, we rounded the corner of the hangar door. There in the sunlight was a beautifully restored Chevy Malibu SS with no driver's window. Ricky was shocked. He ran up to the car looking it all over. Then, he opened the door. Small shattered pieces of glass fell out. He saw the mangled headrest. Then, he saw another bullet hole on the passenger side.

He started repeating, "Oh, my God, oh, my God, what have you done to my car?"

I tried consoling him.

"Now, all this can be fixed in a day, Ricky. Don't worry. I'll get it in the shop today and you'll have it back soon good as new."

"Oh, no, it won't. It'll take days just to match the paint. It's custom you know."

Ricky turned to me with his hands on his hips looking at me with a scowl.

"Just what is it you do exactly, besides fly jets?"

"Well, Ricky, I'm prepared to remunerate any damages this unfortunate incident has incurred."

Ricky got in his car and started it.

"Well, at least it still runs. I'm going to lunch, but believe you me, I'm not happy and Curtis is going to hear about this."

"That's fine, Ricky. Go get some lunch. I'll let *you* tell me where you want the body and paint work done. Then, I'll get right on it."

I decided to get over to Pilot's Cove and have a chat with Curtis myself. When I entered, he was checking paperwork he requested from Michael.

"Well, he returns. How did the stakeout go?"

"Boss," Curtis winced, "there's both good and bad. The good part is I found the source of their supplier."

Was it the Lust Brothers' Shipping Line?"

I was a bit flabbergasted.

"How did you know?"

"Well, with a bit of deduction, that and some of these shipping records Michael has handed over to me with little protest. Obviously, he's anxious to demonstrate his business is legitimate. Also, the fact that he's a Lust brother seems a likely guess. He uses family ships to do business. I also learned the only port of call they do business with is Cartagena. That also leads me to believe, somewhere along the line, he is shipping drugs. I further submit the only operation in town that could satisfy his demand would have to be the Nuccio Brothers because they have all the connections he would need."

I sat down on the corner of his desk and waved my hand in the air.

"Well, la de da. Don't you ever get tired of being right? What was my stakeout all about? If you knew so much, why didn't you just put that in your little folder and complete the investigation, Sherlock?"

Curtis looked surprised, "Are you angry about something, Frank?"

"You're damn right, I'm angry. You sent me out on a fool's errand already knowing what I was supposed to learn. Which, by the way, took several hours of keen observation leaving me with callouses on me callouses from just sitting around waiting."

"There was something else I needed from you."

"Oh, really? What could I possibly do for you?"

"Pictures, of course. I need pictures as evidence to corroborate my case."

"I got pictures all right and when Ricky gets back, I'm gonna take some more. You might just find they're valuable as evidence in a big way. Of course, I guess it wouldn't surprise you I was shot at and narrowly missed three times last night."

"That's outrageous! Tell me about it."

"Oh, I will, all right. Then, maybe I'll get a raise, since this has been the second time I've been shot at in the line of duty. Last night, I was on stakeout at the Port Tampa docks near a Lust Brothers' ship, *Seven Seas.* I took some photos discreetly outside my car of the ship. When I got back in, I leaned over in my seat to reach a lunch package and the first shot narrowly missed my head and entered my headrest. Another shot hit the steering wheel. Finally, the third hit the inside of the passenger door above my head. Of course, my window was blown out by the first round. After that, I stayed down low waiting for a break in the shooting. When I felt I'd waited long enough, I reached over, started the car, and sped away."

"Oh, my gosh! You *were* fortunate."

"I must say it really got my heart thumping like a snare drum."

"I'm sure it would be nothing less than akin to what Winston Churchill once wrote about his experiences in the Boer War."

He said, "The most exhilarating experience ever is being shot at and missed."

"Indeed, Curtis, now what about that raise?"

"All right, we'll see if we can do something about that, too."

"Tell me, now, did you see the one firing at you?"

"No, I had my head turned in the opposite direction. After that, I was busy keeping down. I could tell it was a high-powered rifle though, judging from the sound of the shots and the damage done to Ricky's car."

"Yes, well, I'm sorry about that. I must get it made right for him. How's he taking it?"

"Not well. He says he's going to complain to you about it."

"Did he ask any questions about how the bullet holes got there?"

"Not exactly, he just wanted to know what else I do for a living."

Curtis laughed, "I see, I must talk to him soon and take care of that. Nevertheless, you probably got good photos, which I'll get developed immediately in the dark room."

Curtis stood up from his desk to congratulate Frank on the job he did.

"Great job, Frank. You've proved what I thought all along. Those photos should be solid evidence."

Frank replied, "I'd wait and see how they come out, but what we still don't know is what the real cargo is, do we?"

"No, we don't, but I'm sure if you put your mind to it you'd come up with something like I'm thinking of, and it wouldn't be chocolate."

"I'd say cocaine comes to my mind."

"Exactly, and what comes to my mind is a check in with the Lust Brothers' project tomorrow. I want an overview to see if there is any connection between Michael's operation and theirs. I'd say you need to rest up a bit, Frank, before we go flying tomorrow. Take the rest of the day off. I'll see you back here tomorrow morning, say eight o'clock?"

"Sounds just great to me, boss."

Curtis winced, and then smiled congenially.

I was so pleased when I returned home. I had pizza in the car for Sandy, a late lunch surprise. The sky was clear. I thought, *Maybe red snapper might be biting later if Howie wanted to take his boat out.* When I drove up, another car, a black sedan with government plates, was in my drive. I knew they were F.B.I. and, of course, I knew why.

When I entered both suited gentleman were questioning my wife at the coffee table, that is, until they caught sight of their real prize. Both turned from my wife on the couch.

Each stood up like marionettes to greet me.

"Mr. Barrett, I'm Officer Pruitt, Federal Bureau of Investigations. This is my partner, Officer Benez. May we ask a few questions? "

I replied, "It looks like you've been doing that already with my wife. Should I refuse now?"

Sandy looked helpless. Her eyes pleading as if to say, "Don't screw this one up, Frank."

Officer Pruitt maintained a stony professional profile.

"It would not be wise. I can assure you. However, if you would like to accompany us to headquarters, I'm sure we can work this out."

"Never mind, Officer Pruitt, what have you got on your mind?"

"Like I said, Officer Benez, and I would like to ask you a few questions. Particularly, on the night of January 26th where were you and who were you with?"

"Well, let me see. I think I remember staying out all night with a friend of mine, whom I was consoling about his lack of being promoted. It seems as hard as he worked within the Agency, he couldn't get ahead because he interrogated suspects in the field without a court ordered writ of interrogation of the suspect."

"You needn't say anymore. Officer Benez and I were merely following up on a lead. If you don't wish to talk now, if you feel we are disturbing you, we can come back another time."

"Presently, I think that would be best, Officer Pruitt, my pizza's getting cold."

Frank closed the front door peacefully behind the erstwhile agents. Events following in the Barrett home would be in question.

Sandy started in the usual way, "So, Frank."

All the bells and whistles were sounding in my ears! Clearly this was *not* the position I wanted to be in.

"Sandy, I—"

"Wrong answer, buddy boy. Do you wanna try buying another vowel? I got several just waitin' for ya. I think your mouth should start forming some different vowels like i-o-u. or i.e. which, by the way, form most of your message. You lie. Where am I supposed to plug that into my life? Tell me, Frank, where? I'm torn by what *you* want and where *I* fit in. You see, Frank it's hard for me.

"At work in the hospital, when I know you are working long hours alone, it stresses me out. My supervisor has caught me asleep at my nursing station more than once. It can't happen any longer. If I don't know what's going on when you're gone, if I continue to see you come home bedraggled and beat up, what am I to do? Can you possibly think the filthy coveralls, the blood-stained boots and underwear are all about a hard day's work at the airport?

"For God's sakes, Frank, your life insurance card lists you as a jet aircraft pilot. For most guys, that's excitement enough. What is it? Do you want something more? Do I not fill the bill? Is your need for action that great? You're in deep, whatever it is. I know it. Most pilots don't have the frickin' F.B.I. coming by to ask questions.

"I'm not a child, Frank. Either you put me in the loop, or I'll just go pack one of *my* little bags and stay out 'til all hours and not have something to tell about it. Maybe *I* could live the life of danger. I'm warning you, Frank. This is the last time I look away. *Let me in!* Please, dear God, I implore you."

All the while, I absorbed her words looking down at the floor. Nothing but truth would suffice now, and I knew it.

"All right, please sit down before you burst a vessel. It's true, my line of work has brought me in line with some unsavory individuals. Along with Curtis, our job is to investigate, to learn the truth. Sometimes, these other individuals don't like the truth being known about what they do, or who they do it to. There's big money involved in insurance fraud, not just for me, but for those who engage in it. Look, I'll give you an example. Do you know how much money was at stake when the Lust Brothers had U.S. Phosphoric set on fire? The loss claim was 150 million dollars.

"But, I thought it exploded."

"Yes, Sandy, it did, but not before it was deliberately set on fire. That's *arson* and after several months the guy who did it was found. He confessed to being put up to the job by the Lust Brothers. The F.B.I. was willing to put him in the witness protection program, but the Lust Brothers bought him off so he wouldn't testify. Now, nobody knows where he is. Suddenly, he just vaporized with the Lust Brothers' help, I'm sure.

"You see, Sandy, we investigate some real tough customers to recover great amounts of money in insurance claims for our clients. We're not out there playing badminton. Sometimes, that means danger goes along with the job I chose.

"My only defense here is I felt it was better to try and shield you from events that could perhaps put you under a great deal of duress. That was my thinking. My judgment was impaired by the circumstances that would make you afraid. I meant no harm in trying to shield you from the underside of my work. Maybe I should have let you in on these things, but I was afraid it would be too much stress, in addition to your job, that is all. I swear it."

Sitting still on the couch, Sandy was quietly evaluating Frank's defense. In her initial reaction before he spoke, she felt was justified. Yet, with further consideration, she was allowing her love for the man to sway her to see his side. After all, he was only trying to protect her in the way he thought best. She further reasoned he couldn't be faulted for trying. She looked up at him with a little smile, then, patted the couch next to her.

"Come here, Frank."

I did and she softly placed her arms around me whispering in my ear.

"I'm sorry if I was unreasonable. We'll try it your way for a while longer."

Then, she gently kissed me on the forehead and held my hand. I drew nearer sensing her warmness. I kissed her hard on the lips as she kissed back. We were drifting together, once more. I was enthralled becoming her man, even her love slave. We swirled like two butterflies trapped in an eternal whirlwind. The sun's rays stretched around us guiding warmth over us where we remained until dawn scantily clad on the couch. The morning reigned glorious because the sun was shining. We were together again without any misgivings. That was most important. Despite that little detail, my heart swelled with anticipation of flying again.

16

With the Gulfstream II pointed down runway 18, we lifted off south bound at 150 knots. On my right sat Curtis Selway owner of Company Business. Back in his office, the phone rang. His secretary picked up.

"Special Insurance Investigations, may I help you?"

"Yes, this is Michael Lust. May I speak to Curtis Selway? I'm a client of his."

"Oh, sorry sir, he's out on *Company Business* right now."

"When do you expect him back?"

"I'm not exactly sure. He said it would be a while."

"Well, if he calls, please let him know I tried to reach him and would he please return the call."

"Does he have your number?"

"Yes, he does."

"Thank you, sir, goodbye."

"Oh, Frank, you don't know how good it is to be up flying again."

"On the contrary, it has no comparison, Curtis."

I was wearing my broadest grin when he looked over making it obvious I too was glad to be back in the saddle again.

"That's right, you *were* grounded for a while. I know you'll make up for lost time."

Just then, I spoke into my headset microphone.

"Roger, St. Pete ground control, switching to departure control on 118.9 MHz. Have a nice day. Switching now, departure control, this is Gulfstream 1331 Whiskey Bravo off runway heading 18. I'm over the outer marker, request further instructions."

I heard a tiny crackle over my headphones as transfer took place from ground control to departure control.

"Gulfstream 1331, this is flight control. Continue your climb to 5,000 ft. on current heading and await further instructions."

I turned to Curtis, "These Feds in the tower are tightening up everywhere."

Curtis spoke, "Yes, my friend, the President's War on Drugs is in full swing now. I hope we net a few."

I held my finger to my lips as departure control issued further instructions.

"Gulfstream1331, maintain 5,000' on 180 degrees until you are clear of the control zone, acknowledge?"

"Roger that St. Pete departure control, 1331 Whisky Bravo out."

"Curtis, we've got some open sky ahead now, if you want to stretch your legs."

No thanks, Frank. It's a beautiful day. I'd just as soon enjoy from this vantage point."

"Yes, it's a beauty out there, all right. Visibility is 10 miles plus and no clouds in sight. Look at the way the Gulf sparkles in the morning. It kinda makes you wanna go down and jump in. I only wish we could say the same for Hillsborough Bay. Now, there's a place where you can smell the 'bay roses.'"

Curtis queried, "What do you mean 'bay roses'?"

"Oh, it's just a saying my Dad used to have about the stench in the bay caused by all its industrial pollution."

"Whatever brought you to Florida in the first place, Frank?"

"Well, you could say my Dad did. After the war, he was assigned a flight of B-29's to take a training flight to MacDill Army Air Force

Base. He used to tell us when he landed and looked around himself he said, 'This is the place for me." So, when he returned to the farm in Illinois, he took a thirty-day leave, and moved the family down here. That was in 1945. I came along later in 1950.

"So, I guess I arrived by default, but I haven't regretted a day of it since. My dad was a Colonel by then and I didn't have to move from base to base like my siblings. So, I enjoyed uninterrupted schooling in grade school. When in high school, I, too, learned I wanted to fly, so I joined the Air Force R.O.T.C. In the sixties, I took a little ribbing about it, but it gave me a good foundation for what I wanted to do. In my first year of college, I learned to fly at Sarasota/Bradenton Airport in the Aviation Technology Program."

"Now, that's sort of a coincidence. My father founded an aviation business on that airport. That was back in the sixties."

"Really, what was it called?"

Curtis had sort of a twinkle in his eye when he chose to reminisce for a moment.

"He named it Cavalier Aviation."

"You've got to be kidding me! I knew that business. It was on the other side of the field from where I worked at International Aviation as a lineman. We fueled Eastern and National Airlines and everything else that flew. We always wanted to go over to Cavalier to see what was going on with the P-51 Mustangs they had over there."

"Yes, you could say that business was the cornerstone of my father's wealth. He used to fly for a couple of airlines in South America over the Andes Mountain routes, that is, until he grew tired of it. He said he was always looking out for an opportunity to break into his own business. With his pay as a pilot and being a family man, I guess you know that wasn't easy.

"Yet, one day he got a break. He'd heard about the Ecuadorian Air Force re-vamping their aging fighter planes, which happened to be P-51's. He talked another pilot into partnering with him and they bought the entire lot for ten cents on the dollar at the Army Surplus auction. It turns out, just in time, too. Another bidder was supposed to show at the auction, but they were delayed by weather.

"Later, he learned those bidders were representatives of Pan Am Airways and were prepared to offer top dollar. However, the Ecuadorian General in charge was impatient and took Dad's bid. Later, he almost lost the entire deal because the impatient General wanted the old P-51's off the field so he could start training his men in the new jets, which were soon to arrive.

"Now, it became a race against time for Dad and his partner to round up enough of their old WWII buddies, and any other airline pilots, to get the planes ferried out of South America. It was a frenetic time, he later confided, but with a flurry of phone calls they managed to put together thirty pilots willing to fly from Ecuador to Florida.

"Dad and his partner managed to lease an old hangar at Sarasota/Bradenton Airport. That was the destination of the pilots they hired. Some had never even flown a P-51. They held a crash course and checked out all the pilots under the watchful eye of the Ecuadorian Air Force General. Eventually, all the planes made it to the U.S. save one that went down in Brazil and was determined irrecoverable."

"That's so interesting. I never knew your Dad was the owner of Cavalier Aviation. Me and some of the other linemen would get over there for any reason just to see them working on those great old fighter planes."

"Yes, Dad had a vision, all right, and it paid off. Not so much for him, but me. I worked there daily in that drafty old hangar as a mechanic until I went off to college. I was probably gone before you got there.

"Anyway, Dad and his buddies' dream was to completely restore the venerable P-51 Mustangs. They installed new air navigation radios, and painted them in spinach and sand camouflage scheme. They even restored the gun ports to look authentic. They even converted a couple into twin-seaters so they could train their pilot/owner customers.

"Things went very well for a couple of years, then Dad's partner died. Dad took on the load of owner/manager. However, not long after that, he suffered a heart attack and died.

"I came back from college to run the business for a few more years. By then, it developed a sort of cult culture amongst aviation circles. Most every pilot who could afford it, wanted to own one. They became a rich man's toy. By then, I developed interests of my own and sold the business for a handsome profit."

"That's some story, Curtis. Imagine, you and me at the same airport a few years apart with similar dreams. I always wanted to fly one of those planes. Sometimes they would let us warm them up for the check pilot so they would be ready to demonstrate. Wow, that was a thrill, I tell ya."

"Well, maybe, we can arrange that for you again one of these days. I know a few pilots that are still flying the Mustang."

"Wow, that sure would be a trip. I understand some of them are worth a lot now."

"Imagine, I saw Astronaut Gordon Cooper from the Mercury Program. You remember the one who orbited the Earth 22 times back in the sixties? I watched him purchase one of those Mustangs for $65,000."

"A very astute investment, I must say. Considering a fully restored one goes for $250,000 now. Oh, well, all this talk about aviation has left me thirsty. Would you like me to bring up a drink for you?"

"Yes, thank you, Curtis. I'll have a Coke."

Curtis went to the galley in the plane. He thought, *It's fortunate the judge didn't ask him to reveal his identity testifying at the arson trial of the Lust Brothers. Instead, the lawyers of my clients kept my identity a secret. Otherwise, Michael would be aware of me on the previous arson investigation.*

"Here's your Coke, Frank. I'll grab those binoculars and get a closer look now that we are over the building site. That first pass wasn't bad, let's come around again. I believe I see some activity with some cement trucks. Take her out over the bay and hold her steady. I want to get some pictures."

Curtis adjusted his camera and began taking shots outside the front passenger window. What he saw next surprised him. The trucks coming back from the construction site were lining up at the settling pit of the second gypsum stack. Since it was a shortcut, construction should accelerate. None would be happier than the old bastard who supervised the construction. For Curtis, inevitably, all these actions led back to Jack's Cookies. Curtis completed taking a full set of photos. Once he had done so, he instructed Frank to turn around and fly over the same point. He, then, took another full set and was satisfied with what he had seen so far.

"Let's take it back to the barn, Frank. I think I got all I need here."

"You got it, boss. We're on our way to the barn."

Curtis winced amicably.

"Curtis, why do you suppose the Nuccio Brothers are using that slurry to mix with their concrete? That's a cost-saving measure, for sure, or is something else a foot?"

"That's a good question, Frank. It makes me wonder, too. I wouldn't put it past the Nuccios to try every corner cutting measure. However, I can't help wondering — are they using the slurry to damage the construction?"

"It would seem they have something against the Lust Brothers beyond maintaining their partnership. I can't help thinking it might have something to do with Michael's operations. He can thank the Nuccio Brothers for getting him into this business. So, I can't help wondering why are they working against the rest of the family? They certainly must know the slurry is radioactive. You and I proved that conclusively with samples we took from their barges."

Ten minutes later, *Company Business* banked onto the base leg of runway nine. After taxiing into the hangar, Curtis quickly left the plane headed for the dark room. I stayed with the aircraft securing all the control surfaces. As a wiser pilot once said, "The flight is not over until the plane is secure in the hangar."

Two years passed since I secured *Company Business*. The Bay View Towers were complete in 1975. It was now the spring of '76. In all their resplendent glory, the towers had little trouble filling vacant condominiums with the rich and influential of Tampa. Yet, within their walls, they hid something insidious like a time bomb ticking. Not only were the walls weakened by polluted concrete slurry from the second gypsum stack, they contained the permeation radioactive material in the walls like a tomb that surrounded every resident of the towers.

By now, the operation of Michael Lust revealed itself when one of his drivers got involved in a fender bender. Because the driver was discovered driving drunk, the vehicle was impounded. As a matter of routine, the vehicle was searched. Street ready cocaine was discovered in the delivery van. All things return to their source, as was the case with Michael. His operation was shut down.

Now, it remained with the courts to determine his fate. In the meantime, he turned to the solace of drink numbing his pain. His brother, Martin, was later caught up in a street battle over turf amongst dealers. It ended with a shotgun blast to his chest. Soon, Michael's entire operation was coming apart at the seams. Desperate and lonely, he sought out someone to share his pain. His thoughts turned to Lamari when he received a call from Garcelaco.

He told Michael he was leaving for Cartagena to settle some business with his partners. Seizing the opportunity, Michael decided to pay a visit to the Salvation Navy and Lamari. When he arrived unannounced in the garden, tennis shoes guy greeted him. Michael quickly dispatched him with $50 and a wish for a good lunch. Once he was out of the way, Michael made his approach to the upstairs office. He found Lamari in her room. She welcomed him in and offered him a drink. Michael was ready for both. The ensuing afternoon was spent in pleasurable pursuits. Michael experienced what he was hoping for, almost living for. His dreams spent on her he realized. They could be closer still, if she resided with him. The time that Garcelaco was away was filled with future encounters. So much so that the guard entrusted with the entrance quickly gave over his intelligence to Garcelaco when he returned. This would only contribute to the fall of Michael's business with Jack's Cookies.

While all this was underway, two ten-year-old boys in Bradenton, Florida went fishing. Sam and Bill hoped an abandoned fish farm might provide the catch of the day. When they began fishing from the banks of the old farm pits, they had no luck. Now, Sam lowered his hook trolling the bottom hoping to snag a catfish. Instead, he hooked into something unusual. He hooked the rotting weight belt attached to the skeleton of Norman Howard. He thought he had something big on the line.

Turning to his friend, Sam cried, "I think I got a big one here! It's really giving me a tug-of-war. Watch me bring this baby in, Bill." When he reached the end of the reel he found he was pulling something heavy. Suddenly, the long-submerged weight belt that had been rotting on the bottom of the pit came apart. Sam's line went slack and a muck covered skeleton arose from the depths of the pits with Sam's hook in its rib cage. At the site of the slimy skeleton looking up at him, Sam fell backwards on the bank of the pit. Bill ran over to see what happened. He slid down slowly on the side of the bank next to Sam staring in disbelief. The boys, then, quickly left their poles on the bank and scampered out of the abandoned fish farm. Both went to Sam's garage, where his dad was working that day. They told him all that happened. Sam's dad was soon on the phone to the sheriff.

When the sheriff's deputies arrived, they retrieved the skeleton and laid it carefully on a tarp, hoping not to lose any potential evidence. The forensic pathologist was called out and the investigation began. Eventually, the investigators were able to match dental records from the skeleton with Norman Howard, the missing Pinkerton guard. It didn't take long before authorities were able to find criminal records connecting Norman with the burning of the U.S. Phosphoric Plant in Riverview, Florida. The District Attorney in Hillsborough County decided to reopen the case of arson in the plant. When Curtis got the news, he was elated. Right away, he contacted Frank.

"Frank, they've reopened the case of the U.S. Phosphoric Plant."

"That's really great news, Curtis. What do you think we should do next?"

"Well, Frank, I think it's important that we somehow connect the Lust Brothers with the payoff they gave Norman for the arson job. I believe we need to talk to that F.B.I. agent who questioned him shortly before he disappeared. I think the way to start this investigation is to bring in our evidence connecting the Lust Brothers with all the pollution, too. That way, we can approach our former clients to convince them of what the Lust Brothers were really trying to accomplish by having their own plant blown up. I believe with a copy of the F.B.I. agent's interview with Norman and all our other evidence, we can convince them to re-enter their charge of insurance fraud."

"Yes, Curtis, I agree. That's a good place to start. How soon do you need me to come over?"

"Well, I believe, we should get started on this right away. Some of our evidence will be useful to the D. A."

"Okay, Curtis, I do have a few things to clear up here at home, but I think I can meet you tomorrow around ten, if that's okay?"

"That should be fine, Frank. I'll get my files in order and meet you at Pilot's Cove. We just got a real break on this case and we need to be careful when we follow through. I don't want these sleazy brothers to slip the noose once more."

Frank replied, "As they say, once more into the breach."

The job remained convincing the DA. There must be more evidence put before the judge when they reopen the case. With the exhumation of Norman's remains, there should be no problem. The hurdle would be overcoming the battery of lawyers working for the Brothers. If they presented evidence to the contrary, like the former defense, they could discredit the prosecution. That ploy saved them in the first place. More like a cat and mouse game; it would entail legal chicanery. The defense would obtain continuances of deliberation through the courts keeping the fight in litigation ad infinitum.

Curtis said, "I only hope we can find a place for these guys before it takes too long."

While I was encouraged by recent information, I wasn't too sure. Mostly, what I hoped, was Curtis and I could build a case that would stick. Some of the deck was already stacked against us. I faced a case as tough as they can be. I had always believed it was the big guy who won. After all, I was raised in a culture that taught me in America you get all the justice money can buy. Of course, I thought we were on the right side with all the evidence we compiled. I felt there had to be a case. These guys just couldn't get away with this kind of pollution on such a grand scale.

A new day dawned. I walked from the hanger to Pilot's Cove with information from the Flight Service Station. It was discouraging. The tropical depression named Carlos was forming into a category two hurricane. It would only gain strength out in the Gulf of Mexico directly west of Tampa. If it continued to build, I knew we could be in for a real walloping. Warmer sea temperatures in the Gulf were feeding the storm system. The waters in the Gulf were like glass in front of the hurricane. It was as if the hurricane was being invited to slide right into Tampa Bay with little effort.

The emergency preparedness teams were active ever since the storm threatened to become a category two. Now, most of the preparations were made. All the residents could wait for was a pure disaster on its way. I finished my preparations at the hangar early. Now, I was ready to ride it out at home unless I was ordered to evacuate.

Earlier in the day, I had gone over to Howie's place to help him secure his boat and work on some of his large windows in the back of his home. With everything lashed down and the windows taped, I felt reasonably sure we could ride it out in Safety Harbor. The little town earned its name as a relatively safe harbor tucked away from the main body of Tampa Bay.

As for the "Bay View Towers" their height over Hillsborough Bay was not a safety factor. All the normal precautions have been taken and most of the residents evacuated voluntarily. The Sheriff's Department gave the remaining occupants stern warnings. The next 24 hours proved to be a relentless onslaught by Mother Nature. The storm worked its way up to a category five by 3 a.m. Carlos made landfall directly at the mouth of Hillsborough Bay. By now, winds reached 160 mph driving solid sheets of water into walls of buildings surrounding the bay.

The towers were taking a terrific beating. In some cases, the higher balconies enclosed with steel railing began to weaken. The slurry infused concrete was revealing its weakness. Some railings lost their footings and came completely off. In the high winds, they spun like steel missiles. Whenever they encountered sliding glass doors, they completely shattered them, sending the thick glass of the doors flying into the condos. Anyone standing near would be cut down by a fusillade of flying glass. Beaten for hours by relentless pounding rain, the façade of the buildings cracked in places, then crumbled, leaving huge patches of underlying cement block. The block permeated with water leaked into the residences of hundreds of occupants causing massive flood damage to expensive furnishings within.

Carlos reached its peak intensity early on the morning of September 4, 1976 with maximum sustained winds of 160 miles per hour. Hurricane winds raged for 13 hours. Thereafter, it began to weaken leaving the Bay Area and headed northward through the state of Florida. In its wake, coastal flooding had destroyed nearly 50% of buildings. 5,200 residents were made homeless. The previous evening the storm surge reached 12 feet rushing up to 10 miles inland.

However, the most devastating destruction with long-lasting effects was the second gypsum stack in Riverview, which had its embankments broken resulting in millions of gallons of radioactive slurry flooding into Hillsborough Bay. Over 1 million fish were killed and other marine life with some species never to be returned. The collapse of the wall on the second gypsum stack created catastrophic pollution in the Bay Area. Losses would be estimated in the billions. Sadly, the recovery of the bay would be a very slow ecological process.

I remember the time when Hurricane Donna struck the bay area. I was only 12 years old. That was in 1962. Winds and gusts were similar and sustained over 150 mph. My parents lived about 2 miles west of the bay. After Donna passed, we were astonished to see all our roofing material on the lawn. A blanket of gray shingles, roofing nails, and wood were everywhere. Also, tall palms that were planted along the streets, originally in our development, were crisscrossed down the road. Every one of them struck down taking power lines with them blocking all transportation. There was flooding in all streets and most backyards in our neighborhood. Continuing its path northwest through Florida, it reached the coast and continued to strike every state on the eastern seaboard, something that has never occurred since.

Compared with Donna though, Carlos was even more destructive causing damage from the Lesser Antilles to New England killing at least 365 people. Property damage was 3.5 billion dollars.

In Tampa, inundated subdivisions were also extensively damaged by the tidal surge. Additionally, 352 boats were destroyed or severely damaged. A total of 50% of the grapefruit crop was lost, 10% of the orange and tangerine crops were ruined, and the avocado crop was almost destroyed. With at least 3.5 billion dollars in damage to Florida alone, Carlos was the worst hurricane ever to strike Florida in its history. The cleanup would entail all the resources the Bay Area community had and more. Not surprisingly, the Bay Area was declared to be in a state of emergency by the Governor.

In the aftermath of the deadly hurricane, reality soon set in. Insurance companies would be hard pressed to cover all the claims for damage. This was a time when Curtis' clients would need his services more than ever. They were inclined to persuade the judge to allow more evidence to be placed before him to reopen the case. This would allow Curtis to present all the samples Frank collected before.

It seemed it would only be a matter of time before the judge saw things their way and the Lust Brothers would be calling their attorneys to court once more. The evidence of Norman Howard's dental records was most damning for the Brothers. Bones don't lie. The discovery of his ID badge and number in the remains of the fire at U.S. Phosphoric only connected Norman to the Brothers as an employee. The rest would remain for the courts and the battery of lawyers to determine. Surely, they would remain in litigation for months.

17

Michael Lust was in a hurry to leave his office. He pushed through his work on Friday hoping to get to Lamari as soon as he could. His plan was settled, simple and straightforward. He was ready to marry Lamari. He intended to get out of his office before the Friday afternoon traffic began. This time, he was driving himself. He certainly didn't need any bodyguards for what he was about to do. With Garcelaco still in Cartagena, all he needed to do is keep the guard at the door silent. He can always be bribed, he thought.

Rushing up the stairs, for a man in his fifties, his heart was really pounding. He could not wait to share his thoughts with Lamari. He knew they made good lovers. He just wasn't sure if she would ever commit to leaving all Garcelaco's money. Although, to come with him would mean she had to leave the old man alone with his money. He thought, *Then she could look forward to leaving those hands cold as ice. She could begin a new life with someone like me closer to her age. After all, we're only 20 years apart.*

Michael pushed his way through the two rows of used clothing. He always hated this part walking through those musty clothes. Yet, he would walk over coals to get to Lamari. As he approached the glass-enclosed office, he looked for her as she sometimes waited close to the door to allow him in. He was happy to see her there already waiting.

She let him in quickly and greeted him with a kiss. More followed then they retreated to her room.

Lamari said, "I was hoping you'd make it soon. I know how hard it is for you to get away from your office."

"Would you like to go out to dinner tonight with me? I'd like to take you to the Columbia restaurant. I have something special to talk to you about."

"I think that would be lovely, Michael. Just let me get my coat."

They both left by the stairs at the bottom landing where the guard in tennis shoes gave Michael a curious smile. It wasn't lost on him. It only peaked *his* curiosity. He wondered if he'd been talking to Garcelaco. If so, he would have to talk to the guard himself. Perhaps he could learn what he had been telling him before it was too late. But now, his mind was on Lamari and the special question he would ask her. As they both stepped into his Mercedes-Benz, he tapped the right side of his coat pocket assuring himself that the 10-carat diamond was there.

They engaged in small talk as they navigated the downtown streets of Tampa until they reached Kennedy Avenue. Michael pulled his car into the valet parking and Lamari stepped out. She had been expecting Michael that evening and was dressed elegantly in a full-length silver sequined evening gown. Soon, they were together walking toward the maître d. Michael's pulse quickened as the excitement of sharing the evening with her was beginning to influence him. When they were seated by the maître d', Michael ordered a vintage year of champagne.

"Are we celebrating something special tonight, Michael?"

"Yes, I am hoping it will be something special. First, I would like you to enjoy your meal."

Lamari took some time studying the menu that evening. When the waiter arrived, she told him her selection. It would be Sea Bass on a Bed of Rice Pilaf with accompanying vegetables. Michael ordered Palomia Steak with Yellow Rice and a side of Black Bean Soup. The meal was sumptuous especially the onion rolls that accompanied the entrées. When the meal was finished, they shared a dish of Spanish Flan for dessert. Soon the time had come for Michael to make his announcement. He reached into his right coat pocket and pulled out the ring case. As he did so, he spoke these words, "Lamari, I am lost without you. Marry me, please. Lamari hesitated looking into Michael's eyes."

"You don't know how much this means to me, Michael. It has been so long since I can think of living with another man, and you are that man. She lowered her head as if in shame and then began to speak again. I fear the vengeance of Garcelaco, should he ever find out about us. How can we live together when he knows you and where your business associates are? He knows all about you and how to find us. I fear what he would do if we did, after all, join in marriage together. You see, Garcelaco and I are not really married. He took me away from the slums in Cartagena where he found me. I had no family then and was living in the streets. He took me away from all that and showed me a world I never dreamt of. As time went by, he began to want more from me. He saw me not as a child, but as his lover. Yet, he could not give me the things a young lover would. Instead, he did his best, I know, but with his attempts and his abilities he was, as they say, ahh 'inadequate.'"

"I understand Lamari. Yet, I believe I can convince him that it is best for both of us. I also feel he will understand because of the business ties we have together. We all have a stake in this, Lamari. I would not want business to fail for either Garcelaco or myself. There are things a man must have, and, in this case, for me, it is you. I am willing to take the risk and talk to Garcelaco when he returns from Cartagena. If you are willing to be with me, I will do that."

"Oh, Michael, I hope it would work out. You know I want to be with you, I'm in love with you."

She reached her hand across the table grasping his. When she did, she looked in his eyes, hers were shining wet with tears. Michael took a napkin brushing away her tears. Reaching into his pocket, he produced the ring box opening it before her. When she saw the precious gem, her hand instantly went to her mouth. It was, indeed, an impressive, breathtaking jewel. Naturally, she was in awe of it. Michael tried placing the ring upon her finger, but Lamari stopped him gently.

"Michael you must promise me something first. If he will not let me go, I do not want bloodshed to take place between you. You should let me go my way and I will not interfere. That is my promise to you."

Michael paused giving due consideration to her wishes. Remaining cautiously optimistic, Michael decided to accept and make that promise.

"All right then, Lamari, I promise I will approach him as a gentleman and make my case for you and me."

"Oh, thank you, Michael. You are such a gentleman. I know we both can be very happy one day. I hope that day will be very soon."

They returned together to Lamari's room, again passing the guard in tennis shoes. He had little to say as Michael reached out pushing a $100 bill in his top pocket. Yet, as they both ascended the stairs together, the guard's eyes narrowed with a hateful glare. As they ascended the stairs, Michael turned around and spoke to the guard.

"Will you be here this evening around midnight?"

"Yes, of course. Those are my orders."

"I would like to have a few words with you before I leave this evening. I'll look for you then."

Michael stood at the top of the stairs. He waited for a moment listening carefully. His mind was on the guard downstairs. Michael cocked his Walther PPK pistol and replaced it in his shoulder holster. He walked down the stairs slowly and quietly hoping to surprise the guard with his presence. Instead, he found him on duty as usual.

Michael said, "I was hoping to find you here. What is your name, by the way? After these past couple of weeks, I thought perhaps we should become acquainted. As you know, my name is Michael and I am your boss' partner. I would like to know if you have been in contact with him lately."

The guard only blankly shook his head as if to say no. Michael was suspicious of him.

"I wish to know, because if you are inclined to tell him I have been here often, I have an offer for you. I can make it well worth your while to keep my business to yourself. Do you understand me?"

The guard only shook his head affirmatively.

"Good, then, we will discuss this again when I come here. Is that understood, also?"

Again, the guard shook his head. Michael climbed into his black Mercedes SSL 330. He thought *he is either ignorant or most intelligent.* As Michael drove home, the guard went to the back of the building. Picking up the phone receiver, he dialed the number for Garcelaco in Cartagena. After reporting all he knew, including what he saw on the hidden camera in Lamari's room, Garcelaco became livid. Then, he began to give a list of instructions to his trusted guard. He was a man he had also brought up from the barrios of Cartagena and in whom he had complete faith.

"I want you to listen carefully, Danios. Follow my instructions to the letter. Find the man in his home. Take him outside and place him in his own car. Then, I want you to take him to a very secure place. Strangle him to death with your garrote. Dismember him and place his parts in a trash bag. Then, deliver the bag to the front door of the Lust Brothers' enclave. Leave a note on the bag that says, 'Dispose of your own trash.' Do you understand me completely, Danios?"

For the first time, Danios spoke. "Yes, Mr. Barcelona, I understand completely."

"I will return home soon. Wait there for me."

Later that evening, Michael received an unexpected visit. Danios slipped silently through the sliding glass doors of Michael's condominium at Bay View Towers. The curtains waved gently as he passed through the opening. His entry was as quiet as a cloud's passing. Soon he was standing beside Michael's bed, tennis shoes and all. Michael heard the click of his large .45 caliber automatic. The rest was rather routine, though he was not asked to dress.

They left in Michael's car to that secure place. Michael made his plea offering all, but the loyalty of the man in tennis shoes had been bought many years ago. The rest ended quickly with three shots to the back of his head. Then, his dismemberment began. Danios was not interfered with in the dark recesses of Ballast Point Park. With the difficult job completed as ordered, Danios entered the gates of the Lust Brothers' enclave.

Security cameras picked up his entry immediately, though the guards were slow to respond because they were tired and it was late. They had not been staying close to the monitors as they were ordered. Fat and lazy, the security guards became rather secure themselves.

By the time they reached the door, Danios was closing his trunk after depositing what remained of Michael in a heavy-duty plastic trash bag. Shots rang out as he sped away. What he had not expected was at the end of the loop that exited the brothers' compound was a rapidly closing steel gate. To gain exit, he would have to back up and ram the gate with some speed. This gave the other guards in the 62' gunmetal gray Avanti time to reach him.

No questions were asked of this interloper, instead he was met with a spray of machine fire from two Uzis the guards fired. It was not exactly according to plan. Garcelaco had wanted that Mercedes for himself.

When the guards returned to find the wicked mess in the garbage bag, they slowly determined it was Michael. Once the brothers were informed, there began an all-out manhunt with all the resources they could combine to find his killer. A thorough search of the shot-up Mercedes yielded nothing. The killing was never reported to the local authorities. Instead, the Lust Brothers arranged for a cover story to explain Michael's disappearance. They concocted the story of Michael's taking an ocean cruise and, somehow, never being heard from again. The authorities had nothing to go on, not a body or a suspect or even a murder weapon. The case was entered in the cold case file.

That is, except for the Lust Brothers who would never really cease their manhunt for the killer. Months went by without a lead. Meantime, Curtis continued to pursue his investigation. He did have some success. The judge that had originally sat on the arson case of the Lust Brothers and U.S. Phosphoric agreed to accept the evidence found at the scene of the missing Pinkerton guard, Norman Howard. Also, he permitted the pollution findings that were compiled by Curtis and myself. Using the EPA ruling of 1970, the judge felt justified in using the wording of the federal government. It stated the original owner of the entity that created the pollution was ultimately responsible for the cleanup of same. This could go a long way towards the conviction of the Lust Brothers as accessories in collusion with the arson, plus insurance fraud, as well as industrial environmental pollution.

Amidst these troubles for the Lust Brothers, a revenant reared its ugly head.

This specter would remain so long as the brothers controlled "Bay View Towers". It came on slowly almost like a whisper of an evil portends to come. Patients were being seen at Tampa General Hospital. Their chief complaint was weakness and vague, cold-like symptoms. When the pathologist received lab work on these patients, he determined each one was experiencing classic symptoms of leukemia. Oddly enough, they were all residents of "Bay View Towers". This information was slow to get out, at first, given doctor-patient confidentiality laws.

However, amongst families and those close to them, eventually the word got out. When it did, the results were catastrophic. Now, everyone associated with "Bay View Towers" were deeply concerned. Family attorneys were retained, interviews completed, and interrogation led to sworn depositions. The entire community living at the towers was involved in one fashion or another. Some suffered out right from the effects of radiation poisoning manifested in the form of leukemia. Others joined in a class action suit against the Lust Brothers to protect their property values and their health.

The upshot of it all was the Lust Brothers had concocted a stew everyone was choking on. For Curtis and Frank, this was justice. They had waited a long time for this and now intended to be in court when that day arrived. There remained problems that the courts would decide about assaults made upon Frank and his friend, but these were ancillary compared to the main charges that would be resolved. The outcome of the trial would be interesting, to say the least. But first, all parties representing the Lust Brothers would have their say. Since every aspect of their defense had put in for an extension for various reasons, fifteen separate attorneys were gathered together before Judge Griffin in a sidebar fashion. There, he admonished them for the extensive use of motions for extensions of time. There were motions from every side.

There were attorneys for the protection of assets, attorneys for protection against lawsuits, attorneys presiding over business relationships, attorneys for medical representation, even attorneys for medical records and their representation etc. The judge now lectured the defense attorneys for their seemingly endless use of extensions. He reminded them, these actions in court did not bode well for them with the media and, especially, the prosecution. Amidst all this litigation, there were also the civil cases that would be brought to bear after the legal ones. There were many gathered together in court with a prepared class action suit against the Lust Brothers for the cause of their physical diseases. Their main charge, of course, would be negligence in the use of contaminated building materials that eventually led to multiple cases of leukemia. The civil cases would have to wait. Criminal charges would be dispensed with first. The Brothers would face charges of collusion, racketeering, accessories to arson, bribery, and federal crimes of pollution of a community water source and vessel pollution.

Once the evidence was weighed and the judgment squarely placed before Judge Griffin, some of the minor cases of pollution were dropped due to the fact they were obtained by myself while I was, unfortunately, trespassing. But, all the rest of the charges stuck and the Lust Brothers were found guilty as charged.

"I find you guilty and sentence you all to 50 years in federal penitentiary without parole. All charges shall run concurrently due to the defendants' current ages.

Each brother appeared sullen, as if some unseen weight had been placed between his shoulders. Each man was ushered from the court with his guards. As big Jim passed Curtis, his eyes burned like two coals. Misery and pitiless hate melded into his countenance. The other four brothers followed Jim out of the courtroom, where they would soon be ensconced in a place where one size fits hell.

Curtis looked at me from behind his steel rimmed glasses. He merely winked. Yet, with all the years we worked this case, I could feel it. I knew exactly what he had on his mind.

Then he spoke, "Frank, my sentiment is heartfelt, when I say there is true joy in knowing these men won't walk amongst our society."

I could only think, *"Amen"*

We chose to stay behind while the defendants were escorted out of the courtroom. Now, they would be taken across the street to another annex of the county courthouse. There, they would have their final photographs and fingerprints taken before incarceration took place. Later, they would be transported to a federal prison.

As we sat talking quietly, there was a sudden commotion and a burst of people literally clawing over each other trying to get back in the building. I jumped up to see what the matter was, but couldn't get to the door for the humanity pressing its way inward. Then, I heard a few shots ring out. To me, they sounded like service revolvers. I finally found a way to slip through the crowd by jumping over a few of the last rows.

From the point of view of the bailiffs, who already descended the steps of the courthouse crossing Franklin St. to the annex, it was mayhem. What they witnessed were two sheriff's vans shooting at them, screeching into their midst forming with the front of their vans nearly touching. Filled with the four sons of the Lust Brothers and two physically daunting guards, they parked in this V-shaped fashion. The guards and three of the cousins leapt out the doors, and were immediately accosted by the tight group of their fathers and bailiffs. Everything was well choreographed. Men heavily armed with Uzis slung over their shoulders had suppressors on their barrels. Other than the screeching tires of the two vans, there was no sound. The five men had their duty forming behind the bailiffs and prisoners. In this way, they could shield the Lust Brothers from being attacked from behind. Everything was going like clockwork as they knelt with two bolt cutters freeing the men of their shackles.

Then, the two large guards commenced throwing the Lust Brothers into the empty vans. Just as they were about to jump in themselves, two sheriff's deputies suddenly appeared in the gap between the two vans. Seeing what just occurred, they started firing upon the Lust guards. They replied with a rippling torrent of bullets. As the two drivers squealed away down the one-way street, two Lust Brothers' guards lay in the back of the vans, each mortally wounded. The windows of the two vans were bulletproof. Only one other was hit in the upper chest. This was Jim Junior, Big Jim's son. The two vans hurtled down the street together to the next turn. Turning left, they sprayed the area behind with fusillades of bullets Uzis are famous for.

When I reached the scene in the street, blood was everywhere, and confusion was paramount. Confusion increased as two heavily armed Sheriff's vans sped through stoplights, dodging around corners, heading for the hiding place prearranged for all five of the remaining brothers.

As I looked down, I knew it was useless to check for a pulse. The Sheriff's deputies were literally ripped in half. As I looked to my left down Franklin Street, there were bodies down. Innocent bystanders were helplessly caught up in deadly pandemonium. I ran to a woman who was still moving. Then, I ran further up the road to another. Now, I realized I must stop and identify myself. If I did not, the cluster of Sheriff's deputies forming on the scene could easily have mistaken me. I immediately stopped, raising my hands above my head holding my wallet with my driver's license. I could see Curtis a block away looking down the street toward me. He remained on the courthouse steps looking helpless, like the rest of us, who were still in shock.

Of course, no one knew where the two sheriff's vans went. Naturally, all-points bulletins were put out only adding to the confusion of who was pursuing whom. The Sheriff's switchboard was immediately flooded with sightings. Of course, that was the Brothers' intention. The whole town was caught up in the frenzy of fear and misidentification. The Lust Brothers were counting on this kind of reaction to further shield them in their attempt to escape. Their plan went off without a hitch.

18

There would be no appeals. With seemingly endless, exhaustive procedures the legal defense went through, it nearly seemed a shame. However, with the brazen breakout of the Lust Brothers, all deals were off the table. While authorities searched the Tampa Bay Area, the Brothers would remain hidden in their pre-planned hideaway.

As they left the courthouse that day, they sped through the back streets on a planned route to a cul-de-sac they could reach quickly. It was a secluded spot where two other cars awaited them. They ditched the two-authentic looking, bloodied Sheriff's vans and sped away in two-toned Ford Galaxies. They sped past the gate guard at the main port in Tampa. He was a replacement the Lust Brothers' guard installed days earlier. The two Galaxies proceeded with the next stage of their plan. They had the two Galaxies stored in shipping containers near the *Seven Seas,* a Lust Brothers cargo vessel bound for Cartagena.

Many connected with the case conjectured that Port Tampa, home base of the Lust Brothers' shipping concern, would be the last place they would try to hide. While others maintained it would be the first.

At Pilot's Cove, a group of executive pilots gathered on Curtis' call. He addressed them,

"Justice has not been fulfilled. There are some things citizens can do. While I am not a man in favor of vigilantism, these men have gone too far for too long. I have backing from clients to search for these violators of federal law. I want you pilots to join me in tracking down these fugitives. We have the capabilities at this airport to keep more eyes in the sky than law enforcement can currently provide. I'll pay you time and a half more than you're receiving per day. I cannot tell you how long that will last. It depends on when we capture these fugitives.

"I cannot tell you how long it will take for me to prepare a grid pattern. What I am asking is, 'Will you fly a search pattern seeking these fugitives of justice?' I will get back to you all. Thank you for your coming. If you chose to meet again, I will have charts and times prepared for search patterns. Again, I thank you for your attendance."

I approached Curtis, "This is dangerous, Curtis. How would you coordinate this with the local officials? Are you proposing to just ride out like Billy the Kid and roundup a group of outlaws? This is the 20th century. We're trying to find some serious felons and killers."

"Yes, I know and this is the only way I have to do it with the means at my disposal. I hope you'll join my posse, because, well, you know the rest! I've got to do *something*, even if it's wrong."

"I appreciate your zeal, Curtis. But, we must approach carefully. They are armed and unafraid. They, *too*, have resources. I know you have considered the angles. Yet, just now try and relieve yourself of emotion. This is the time for caution."

"I never thought I'd hear this kind of talk from you, Frank. In the beginning, I chose you for your outward boldness and your seeming ability to take on projects with firm resolve. In my heart of hearts, I still feel I am correct in my judgment of you. We are nearly at the end of this Lust Brothers' spree. I feel like I have never needed your help more than now. Please, Frank, put your heart in it now. The time is now. Do it!"

"Curtis, again I appreciate your fervor, but the way I see it they are desperate and dangerous. Besides our aircraft equipment will be too fast. Our cameras are good, but I doubt they'll help us in our search on the ground like this. Some of these other pilots you have contacted may be of use. I feel we can be more instrumental on the ground search. We have backers, yes. However, the authorities don't recognize us any more than *Ozzie and Harriet.*

Curtis laughed out right, "Hey, I swear I never thought of it that way. Thanks for bringing me down to Earth, Frank. I'm just so damn frustrated about the outcome of all of this and our work and what it has come down to. I feel strongly we must do something about this or I would call off the pilots' meeting. Now, what is your inclination on how this investigation should proceed?"

"Well, Curtis, I would say let the slower planes fly. Every asset we put into the search can help. If they stay out of the way up there, we don't want any trouble with the authorities especially now."

"All right, then. I'll hold the meeting and set up the pilots with photographic equipment. Then, I want to sit down with you and plan a surgical search. With all we know about these Brothers, I feel we can use that knowledge to pin them down. Many think searching the Port Tampa area would be ineffectual. I tend to agree, but there is another area where they might try to hide out. They could be in the main port in Tampa. They birth their ships there, also. It might just be the place they would try to break out."

On the main dock, only blocks from the courthouse, the Lust Brothers entered two fully furnished shipping containers on the opposite end of the dock from the *Seven Seas.* They were safely tucked away on the docks in the maw of a cavernous potash warehouse behind a huge pile of potash in the center of the building. Their plan provided they could stay in that spot for at least five days. By then, they felt the heat would have gone down enough for them to board the *Seven Seas.* After that, the plan grew deadlier. While things stayed cool in Tampa, they would be hunting Garcelaco Barcelona in Columbia. Just before he died, with a little help from one of the Lust Brothers' sons, they learned where Garcelaco would be headed. The plan was once Garcelaco was removed from his operation in Cartagena, they would muscle in on the cocaine smuggling ring he had formed.

By way of their son, Martin, the Brothers learned of Michael's smuggling ring in Tampa. They never intended to inform him, instead they chose to stand aside and watch his operation. Big Jim figured if there was success for him in this business, then perhaps all the Brothers could combine their resources to enjoy even more profits than Michael's operation. Naturally, upon his death, their plans changed. Taking the operation back from the Nuccio brothers would be especially sweet. However, their legal battle took a turn for the worse. If things went as planned in Columbia, they would covertly return to Tampa. They had business to settle with the Nuccio Brothers, who had ultimately turned out to be the bane of their very existence. When they returned they would be outlaws? Also, they would need even more guards to protect their new operation in Tampa. Unfortunately, they would have to do without their palatial estates, although they were impounded anyway, pending the outcome of the legal suits. Since they were now fugitives from justice, the prospects for any settlement were nil. On the other side of the ledger, they would benefit handsomely with control of both sides of the operation by removing the middleman.

On the dock in Tampa, Big Jim was getting restless. It was the third day of hiding in their side-by-side containers.

"I gotta get out of here. I can't stand living in this iron coffin anymore!"

Joe cautioned, "You shouldn't talk that way. You're gonna get us all going claustrophobic. It's only two days more. Why don't you sleep awhile? It'll take your mind off things."

"Nothing could relieve my mind of this stinking can. Whose idea was this, anyway?"

Joe said, "We all voted on it. Don't you remember?"

Jim laughed, "Oh yeah, what was I drinking that day?"

The other Brothers laughed nervously. They would do anything to get out themselves. Instead, they had to placate Jim. On the fourth day,

Big Jim slumped into a great state of depression. One evening after supper with his brothers, he stood up and bid them farewell. They made nothing much of his statement until they heard a shot ring out from the shower. They found him lying in the shower, pistol still in hand. He left a note explaining he had been dying of terminal brain cancer. Later that night, he was wrapped and weighted down and slipped into the bay he helped pollute for so many years.

In the wake of his suicide, Charlie, the second oldest of the Brothers, sat at the head of their diminutive meeting table. Charlie spoke, "Brothers, this is indeed a time of grief for us all. We grieve the sudden change of fortune thrust upon us by the cataclysmic events that put us in this position fending off the wolf at our door. The only thing that can strengthen us enough to lift us out of this pit of despair is ourselves. It is that same force, when we act as one, that will pull us through this great trial".

Most Brothers looked downward looking dejected until the mention of their collective strength produced a glimmer of a silver lining beginning to emerge. Charlie had always been a great speaker. His words acted as a tonic amongst them.

"We have never faced any crises as crippling as this is in our history. Yet, here we remain as one. This, I propose, will be our saving grace. The lawyers have advised us of our economic prospects as companies, which are dismal at best. Nevertheless, we have combined the resources of our experience and brainpower and persistence. As we fall forward into the unknown never under estimate the power of collective will."

The atmosphere in the room was changing as Charles's well-spoken words brought about a boldness showing in their faces. These broken captains of industry had the temerity and grit to come back. Charles set his jaw in determination before launching into his dramatic proposal. He had been waiting too long for such an opportunity.

"Gentlemen I propose completing the dissolution of our association with the Mafia. The so-called, Nuccio Mafia, who has stood at every crossroad blocking us, ever present, never welcome. I propose a complete break, including any previous personal associations of any kind them, whatsoever. Further, I say the Lust Brothers declare war on the Nuccio Brothers."

There was some shuffling of feet, clearing of throats, but it was a foregone conclusion, as the oldest, Charles, was now in charge. He would represent them not unlike the free-floating apex of a pyramid. Since he was nonetheless established as their leader, for better or worse, the hallmark of his calling them together came from his position, thus emphasizing a solitary future life in the hands of Charlie.

Meanwhile, five general aviation aircraft, two Cessna 180's, and three Piper Cherokee D's flew above the Brothers' heads in a grid pattern photographing the city below. Each was assigned a section of the city that they closely adhered to as the co-pilot kept the pilot online, he also maintained the camera position. As some flew close to the former defunct Bay View Towers, there were no signs of leisure activity below. Only government workers from the Environmental Protection Agency were busily cordoning off the entire premises and cleaning up the towers project that was now declared uninhabitable by the agency.

The movers and shakers in the bay area were rapidly moving through other litigations concerning civil suits against the missing Lust Brothers. In the meantime, the E.P.A. found a new designation for the towers property. The high level of deadly radon gas was determined to be directly linked to the exposure of layers of radioactive phosphate over the past six decades. In other words, land turned upside down can never be made right.

In fact, the entire area was reduced to a category composed of uranium poisonous phosphate. Its moniker consisted of the acronym, N.O.R.M.. So dubbed by the government. N.O.R.M. meant naturally occurring radioactive material according to E.P.A. regulations.

Every acre became the government's responsibility. Subsequently, it was surrounded with a 15-foot-high chain link fence with barbed wire stretched on top. Every 50 yards the fence was placarded with highly visible signs which read,

No trespassing, this area is highly radioactive and extremely dangerous, violators will be prosecuted and fined to the limit of the law. This warning is issued by the authority of the E.P.A.

The only thing left to do was regularly monitor the compounds' radiation levels for valuable information on adverse effects of phosphate strip mining gained through longitudinal study. The former project was rendered totally useless. The failure of the towers concerned the local mafia greatly. The Nuccio Brothers were all hunched over their meals in the dark back room of Licata's Steak House (their favorite eatery), where most of their plans were hatched. George was the eldest, then came Richard, Nick, and Danny. Richard was four years younger than George and Nick and Danny were twins.

The Nuccio Brothers grew up together in the same house on the west side of Tampa, along with other Latino sons and daughters. They were the products of turn-of-the-century cigar makers, which gave the city of Tampa its name. They came as immigrants from Cuba bringing their trade with them. Now, the second-generation of Nuccios evolved under the umbrella of protection offered by the Don, developing a passion for organized crime. They existed in the dark shadows of the rising slumlord Santo Bonaconte. He was the Don of the territory. If any of his wayward sons were in need, they knew where to come.

Now the aged criminal boss was reaching the point where he was searching. Searching for the most loyal of his subjects to pass the scepter along to, the most deserving in his eyes. Years of loyalty gained the Nuccio Brothers that spot. They would never relinquish it without storms of violence. Now, a new storm was brewing between the Lust Brothers and the Nuccio Brothers. After all the misgivings and changed fortunes on both sides with vengeance to spare, the storm was forming.

Because he remained the titular leader of the brothers, George took his rightful place in speaking to the others first.

"Many things have passed between us since we have chosen to deal with the treacherous Lust Brothers. We have been generous in our dealings with their youngest, Michael. Yet, when we find an opportunity to receive repayment, how does he repay? He leaves our office in the dirt with disrespect. Instead, he chooses another supplier when it was we who so generously brought them into the fold. When we had full confidence in the rest of his family as we helped them labor to build, what becomes of us? Again, we are disrespected. Our reputation is ruined just as the towers themselves are ruined. It is time now for us to repay, to leave a message of our repayment, we must act."

Richard reacted emphatically to George's obvious goading of the other brothers.

"We said we listen, of course. We all understand what they have done to us and what they will do to us with their horrendous reputation. Now, that they have gone, it's worse than ever. Everywhere, all my associates are being questioned in the streets. The level of damage done by their brazen escape has caused all of us to suffer. If we are to go on with what we have established, we must seek them out better than the cops."

Danny spoke out, "Richard is right. Listen to him. We have to take them out before they try to bring us down."

Nick nodded in approval at what his brother, Danny, was saying. Although he was a bit more brash than the other brothers, Nick decided he had an answer.

"We need to put our people on the docks wherever their ships are. Because wherever their ships are, that is where their interests lie. We must catch them before the cops corner them, and we'll have to act fast. I suggest, with all respect George, we place at least five guys on each dock to patrol. Let them go out at night and see where these rats are infesting the docks. I say we give them radios and let them tell us if they find anything of these scum Lust Brothers."

George wiped the marinara sauce from his face with a smile. He paused for effect, then encountered every brother with his steely eyes. He peered around the table intently.

"This is not a bad plan. If we are quick enough, we can spring the trap and catch them before they come for us."

Richard reasoned, "What if there is no trap to be sprung? What if they have already gone?"

George returned, "Time, brother, that is what I think they will not have left. They had many loose ends to tie up and, with us, I'm sure they feel the way we do. There are scores to settle. Of that we must be wary, and on guard, before they spring the trap on us. I say we put Danny's plan into action and see how many fish we catch on the docks. At least, we may gain some leads and find someone who wants to rat on the rats. At least, it is a start and better than sitting here planning revenge without substance. Remember, if we find them, their whole empire could be ours."

19

I was sitting in a darkened room with a dozen other pilots. We were reviewing film clips of the search patterns recently flown. So far, I was tired and bored. Soon, I was daydreaming. I found myself back in the past, at the age of 12. My brother, John, and I were taking a shortcut walking through a liquor distributor's warehouse parking lot not far from our home. We were living off base then, in a nice neighborhood near Bayshore Blvd., although, on that day, we were literally walking on the wrong side of tracks. Crossing the parking lot, we walked between some liquor delivery trucks parked close together. One truck had been involved in an accident. Passing between it and another truck, we discovered its side was ripped open in a long gash. We could see right into the cargo bed through the gaping hole ripped in its aluminum side. John froze in his tracks.

"Holy shit, there's bottles of booze just lying there!" Sure, enough I confirmed there were pint bottles of old Granddad Bourbon just lying right there on the wooden floor of the truck. John and I were concealed from view standing between the two trucks. He looked both ways reaching through the trucks open side pulling forth a full pint bottle. With a sneaky smirk on his face, he put it right down the front of his pants.

John said to me, "Let's go."

"Hold it," I said. "I want one, too." At this point, I guess anyone might have accused my older brother of being a bad influence. Yet, let me be the first to say, I had an influence all my own at the ripe old age of 12. I just wouldn't be out done by my older brother. Besides, I had never tasted bourbon, and here was my chance. Opportunity presented itself, and I took it. Now, we each had a pint down our pants and a mile and a half to get home. Too easy, we thought, *no sweat.* All we had to do was walk out of the parking lot, cross the railroad tracks, and walk home.

Once home, John and I hid the liquor in our metal upright military footlockers Dad bought us from the Army Surplus Store. My bottle was secure, as was his, and our caper complete. All that remained was consumption of the evil spirits, the fruits of our labor. Never mind that we stole, or that we were under age, and trespassing at the time. The matter never entered our minds. The two of us were young boys on the cusp of a momentous foray into adult worldliness. In fact, nothing but our prize seemed to matter.

We each agreed we would consume our just desserts together that very Friday night with Coca-Colas spirited away from the kitchen, along with some Planters Peanuts. We were no fools, we'd seen grown-ups in action. However, we were soon about to learn there is justice in this world and payback is a bitch! That's a natural fact. Yes, even the best laid plans… I got mine through direct experimentation and a lamentable introduction to the onerous John Barleycorn.

That same night, under cover of darkness, or should I say under my covers in the darkness. I held the Coke, which John and I opened using the metal side of my bunk bed frame. This trick I learned from John. He already had a head start with his bottle and kept watch from his upper bunk, passing me the peanut can occasionally. The party proceeded. We figured, who needs ice when the booze is free, so we partied hearty under the covers.

I had no idea what those little numbers meant on the bottle. Mine said 100 with the word proof behind it. Later, I learned John's bottle had an 86 on it. If I had only known the difference. At first, I seriously considered opening the window and dumping the entire contents out. Oh, if only I had only done so. Instead, I stubbornly stuck it out until the Coke and the booze were nearly gone. The remainder in the bottle took on a hazy appearance. Then, the age-old question arose. Was the bottle half-full or half-empty? At this stage of inebriation, it really didn't seem to matter much. I was feeling warm all over. My forehead began beading sweat. My brother finished his bottle. I could tell by the way he was acting above. He talked so much I wished he would've slowed down. My brain could not process all that he was saying. Then, I discovered an even more serious situation developing. I had a problem of bed control. I was rapidly losing the battle. The bed continued spinning out of control beneath me. I dared not close my eyes for fear I would lose the contents of my stomach. Yet, the sight of the spinning room was making me increasingly dizzy and even more nauseous.

That was only the beginning of my travail. When vomiting would start, I erroneously believed it couldn't last. How wrong was I? No one ever informed me of the dry heaves. I was trapped in my own bedroom, no water, very little peanuts, air supply suppressed, sweat now draining from my hapless little body down the nape of my neck to nether regions of my body. I had no one to turn to. Brother John had mercifully passed out. My last conscious thought before sliding into a stultified stupor was, "How can this get any worse?"

The following morning, I found out. On that Saturday morning, I distinctly remember Dad was the first image I processed in my blurry field of vision. Just outside my window, he was marching to and fro in the backyard mowing the lawn. I never experienced a hangover before. My whole brain was tightly confined within my little skull. With my skulls shrinking, my head pounded from the inside out to the relentless roaring of the heartless lawnmower. Dad moved right up to my window, so he could yell to John from outside.

"John, it's past noon, already. Get your butt up and get dressed. I need your help mowing the lawn right NOW!" Dad always used this little dad-ism to be emphatic. He always spelled out in capitals whatever it was he wished to stress.

"When I say now, I mean *NOW!* We both heard him again over the din of the mower.

I experienced this familiar rousting and the roaring mower coinciding with one of the worst moments in my life. I seriously thought it would be easier if I just died and went to heaven. Although considering my most recent transgression, that merciful departure was highly unlikely. There was nothing for my condition but time. Sadly, I realized time heals all wounds, and, brother, I was learning it from the head on down.

Later, I managed to peer out of the window through one slit in my eye spotting my brother pushing the lawnmower. From the expression on his face, I felt it exquisite how I escaped this punishment. I can attribute that only to my youth. I speculate Dad could never conceive of my lips touching drink at such a tender age. John, on the other hand, was 16. He was receiving the brunt of Dad's anger at finding him in such condition. It was obvious he had been drinking and Dad was making him pay for his sin dearly. I can still remember him telling me what it was like mowing the lawn in the hot Florida sun in his hung-over condition.

"Frankie, I swear I could hear every blade of grass screaming at me."

I never forgave myself for getting off so easily that day. I felt I'd somehow let my brother down. It just wasn't right. The whole episode marked my first last experience drinking liquor, at least, until I reached the legal age of consumption in the state of Florida.

My daydreams went on. I had just turned 14 and had landed my first job. Of course, I was still in school so it was part-time. I had to fib to get a work permit. Dad looked the other way, knowing, I would gain from the experience. Besides, I had promised to defray the costs of payments on my new Honda 65cc motorbike with my earnings. Good grief, he was an indulgent man. Only six months later, he co-signed again, allowing me to buy a beautiful jet-black trap set of Pearl drums complete with high — hat and Zildjian cymbals. It was a quality drum set for its day, costing over $600. Fortunately, I could play them having played drums in school since fourth grade. I had, at least, mastered the rudiments.

Soon, I formed my first Garage-Band. My employment at the Boys Club Gym as an assistant coach soon fell by the wayside as I dedicated myself to afterschool practice sessions with my three would-be rock star friends. Diligently, our band cranked out incessant Beatles, Rolling Stones, and other renditions rattling half the neighborhood with our amateur outpourings. Dad soon found it necessary to stuff the rafters of the garage with newspaper, attempting to muffle our attempts at mastering pop music. Thankfully, our neighbors also had kids. They possessed a high level of tolerance. Once again, Dad took the prize for being patient. What a guy.

I was jolted out of my daydream with a question directed at me by Curtis.

"Well, Frank, what do you make of all this?"

Slow to respond, I felt the eyes of every pilot there upon me.

"I think we're wasting gas. Nobody who doesn't want to be seen is going to expose themselves to a low, slow-fixed wing aircraft. We need to rely on human intelligence on the ground. I suggest we go back to the docks and nose around with money in hand, in case we find any snitches."

Curtis replied, "Thank you very much for your input on our combined aviation search, Frank. We'll have to consider your original thought on finding our fugitives. For now, gentlemen, I suggest we halt the flights until we give some other ideas further consideration. Thank you for your time and your effort. You have been most responsive. Again, I appreciate your input into this very important investigation. Good afternoon."

I knew Curtis had nothing further to go on, so I suggested we go over some of the finer points of my idea. Curtis was receptive to my ideas, though I could tell he was very disappointed in the results of the air search. I pointed out that we may get further on the docks than any-where else, since we had seen for ourselves how proactive some of the crew were on the Lust Brothers' freighter *Seven Seas.*

"Curtis, I think, myself and two others could come to the docks at night. I think we could find someone who might tell us more about what's going on there."

"What exactly do you expect to find?"

"I don't have it all put together in my mind, Curtis, but it goes something like this. Right now, they're running together with a good number of people. I figure there's Big Jim, Joe, Charles, Peter, and then, there are the four sons. Then, there must be bodyguards. They must have a very large place to stay. I think they're going to try to make it out by cargo ship. After all, that would be a hard place to search and they have a lot of them. I just need to find out which one. If you asked for volunteers from our search team, I'm sure I can get a couple to come along with me."

"When do you want to go, Frank?"

"Tomorrow night should be good. There's no moon. I would like to meet with the pilots who volunteer an hour before. That way, I can explain the mission and what we are looking for. I suggest we start at the Adamo Street Bar. I'll instruct the men to meet me there and bring their firearms for their own protection."

"All right, Frank. I hope this pans out. I'll talk to the men."

That night about 11 p.m., my two volunteers and I met in front of the Adamo Street Bar. I took the time to explain to them a way we could avoid the guard. The docks were open to the street paralleling a train track that ran 6 feet deep right along the docks. This facilitated the stevedores when they unloaded boxcars. The guard at this end of the dock stayed inside warehouse number six. He would walk his rounds hourly. So, we could slip by him to the actual dock without much difficulty.

Once we were down on the tracks, we could easily walk along them and look up to see which ship was birthed there. Cautiously walking along this way, checking all the ships, we could see most had dimmed lights and little activity aboard. I didn't tell the others, but near the end of the dock, I found what I was looking for. It was the *Seven Seas.* There was no activity there either, so I told the men we might as well go back to the bar. Perhaps we'll find someone willing to talk about her. I knew from experience, most sailors were reluctant to talk about their ship or its cargo. I figured it was worth a try, nevertheless, too much liquor can loosen lips.

As we stepped into the bar, all eyes shifted to us, but not for long. I instructed the men to dress in old work clothes so we would not attract attention. We found ourselves a vacant table along the wall. It was late enough by now, if anyone was drunk, we would soon know it. We observed for a while and saw a couple of gentlemen talking. Each of them was tottering back and forth on their barstools. I approached and ordered a beer and stood near them while they were chatting. I told my two volunteers to follow my lead, when the opportunity presented itself. That way, we could learn as fast as we could. My sailors were feeling rather gregarious, since it was Friday and payday at the end of the month. They were buying each other drinks.

I asked, "Are you fellows sailing together?"

One said, "It just so happens we are, young fellow. Now, why would you be asking?"

"Oh, I just got in myself and I thought I'd find out if there was any action around here."

"What kind of action would you be talking about, sailor?"

"Oh, I don't know, a good game, perhaps."

The sailor scratched his head as if he were in deep thought, and then looked at his partner and asked him if he knew of any good games around.

His partner replied, "I thought we quit gambling?"

The first sailor answered, "Why, so we did. I believe we agreed to quit gambling so we could continue drinking. Wasn't that the agreement?"

Turning to me with his glass upraised, he affirmed in my face with a light spray of rum.

"That's it, we agreed to quit gambling, so we could drink more, you see."

Quickly, I realized there wasn't much to be learned here. I returned to my table finishing my beer and sharing what little the others had learned. Apparently, the same was so with the rest of their inquiries. They were either too drunk or not enough. So, I decided to try another tactic. I stood up raising my beer in the air shouting above the din.

"Here's to the *Seven Seas!*"

One single sailor sitting stuffed in a corner raised his glass. I thought, *now I have someone to talk to.* I walked across the bar room addressing the older sailor there.

"Evening sailor, can I buy you a drink?"

"Why would you be doing that?"

"Well, me and my buddies were just talking about the *Seven Seas* and we just wanted to talk to one of the sailors on her."

"Hell, no, I'm not on the *Seven Seas.* Though I was on her a while ago, and I sure pulled in quite a haul. I took the whole pot. Boy, those souls were mad, too. Good thing we're sailing out tonight, or I might not sleep so sound."

"Did they say when they were shoving off?"

"I believe some of them said they was leaving at dawn day after tomorrow on the *Brimstone* with a load of phosphate for Cartagena."

"Were they shipping any other cargo?"

"No, but they said they had some big shots on board. They had to be careful where they gambled. They were talking about the owner of the whole shipping line. The Lust Brothers they said. Some of them were on board and they had to mind their P's and Q's."

"I see. Well, thanks. I appreciate that. I was going to meet up with a buddy of mine on that ship. I guess I'll have time, after all. You still want that drink? I'm buying."

I stayed with him until his drink was finished. Then, I got back with my friends. I was anxious to call in my information to Curtis, so we left immediately. Later, that old sailor in the corner made his way down the docks where he met up with another dark figure. It was a bodyguard for the Lust Brothers. The old man told him what he had said to me and he added I seemed interested in his information. The bodyguard stuffed three $100 bills in the old man's top pocket and thanked him.

When I got to a phone, I gave my new information to Curtis. Although, I woke him out of sleep, he was delighted with what I had learned at the bar. He asked me to meet him back at Pilot's Cove so we could plan our next day.

At Pilot's Cove, Curtis addressed our group of pilots. There was no time for training now. These men had become paid workers of Curtis on this case. They were all ex-military pilots and most had flown forward air control in Vietnam. At least, they had that kind of experience before going into harm's way. Every one of these pilots had served in close arms combat. Their aircraft were spotters for our artillery and rescue efforts. This meant, they had to be down and dirty, so close to the enemy you could see their faces in the muzzle flashes of their weapons. They all knew what it was like to taste fear and look death in the face.

"Men, I've explained to you what this mission is about. You know it can be dangerous and I want you to understand right now. No one fires their weapons unless I give the order. Our intelligence tells us that the ship we're looking for is named the *Brimstone*. Further, it will not leave port until tomorrow evening at sundown. Of course, that is an approximate time, so I will need you men at the dock before sundown by one hour.

"I don't expect too much trouble if we can get the drop on the Lust Brothers and their men. However, if we are detected first, there may be a fight. Since you work for Curtis, I best say you don't have to take on this risk. If you show at the dock on time, I know you'll feel that justice is being done and justice has its rewards, right men?"

The men seemed encouraged. Maybe some thought it was kidnapping with a bonus. Others saw it for what it was, a takedown necessity where gunfire might ensue.

Curtis made it clear that they just needed to stay in the shadows alongside the dock.

When they saw the party, they would close in without a sound keeping them covered.

At dockside the following morning it was evident a few family men found this too much. What none of them knew, including Curtis, was 12 hours earlier a freight container was loaded aboard the *Brimstone* under cover of darkness. The Lust Brothers' scheme was working so far. They had Curtis' men waiting 12 hours after they departed. In the early dawn hours, Curtis realized he and his men had been duped. He resignedly told his men to return to headquarters to revise their plan. He realized the Brothers had, at least, a day at sea upon them. His only resources were planes and men. It was decided they would fly in a fan shaped pattern over the Gulf of Mexico. They would fly out to a safe point of return searching all the while hoping to find that golden needle in the proverbial haystack.

Early that morning, 12 aircraft including Curtis and Frank in a B- 50 twin Bonanza took off from St. Petersburg/Clearwater Airport. From the meeting they had earlier, they reasoned the freighter they were searching for would not possibly sail westward nor would they try for any port in America. They reckoned it was a safe bet to fly southwest over the Gulf. Each aircraft picked a compass radial that would take them out over the Gulf in that fanlike pattern they had discussed. From left to right, they each took a number that would identify them and help them maintain separation. With the sun behind them, fortunately, it would be easier to search the seas. Frank came on the radio speaking on their pre-established frequency.

"Gentlemen I'm checking in to see that you can all receive. Please count down."

The number one aircraft replied, "Number one, loud and clear. Over and out."

Number two replied, "Hearing you loud and clear."

Number three came on confirming in this fashion until all 12 finished.

Frank confirmed, "Roger, affirmative. I understand you read me loud and clear, over."

He received a countdown, "Roger one, Roger two," and so forth."

After obtaining their confirmation, Frank spoke, "I chose not to give you one part of this puzzle that I'm sure will be of great help. I hope you realize I had to be careful making sure everyone here is sure to make the trip. Now that I know you're with us, if you don't mind, I'll refer to us as Curtis' Convoy.

I'm sure some of you are wondering why you weren't told the name of the ship you're searching for. Well, here it is partners. It's *Brimstone*. For some of you guys who aren't sailors, that name is plastered on the fantail, that is, the blunt end of the ship, guys."

His last remark received a plethora of responses. Nevertheless, they continued their search on various headings in a fan shape keeping their eyes on their fuel gages. This formation was necessary. Frank knew they had half the range of the twin Bonanza. Their function was only to tell them where the ship wasn't. The twin Bonanza could fly twice as far. The reports of the others narrowed down their search.

As they crossed the shimmering Gulf, Curtis and Frank discussed their strategy.

Frank conjectured, "If we can narrow their course, we should be able to land nearby. We can refuel and stay aloft again enough to track them down and report to the authorities."

On the bridge of the *Brimstone,* another situation played out. One of the bodyguards captured by the Nuccio Brothers on the docks in Tampa was paid to work for them. He made himself familiar with the radio operator and, eventually, learned to work the radio station while giving him breaks.

At first, the radio operator was suspicious, but soon came around when the ex-guard showed a genuine interest in operating the radio.

The operator confessed, "There's really not much to do when your orders are to maintain radio silence. All you do is stare at this radio scope and log anyone who calls in. It was just the job for the would-be radio operator. He would give the real operator breaks now and then, so that he could get coffee and relax. The rest of the time the other operator, who worked for the Nuccios, could settle in and get used to the operation. When the time came, he'd identify their position by latitude and longitude to his new bosses. Then, they would close in on the ship with their Scarab Cigarette fast boats situated in Cancun. The Nuccios figured this put them close enough to the Narrows of the Straits of Yucatán. Armed with grenade launchers and their Uzis, they were prepared to intercept the *Brimstone.*

On the beaches of Cancun, the Nuccio Brothers enjoyed themselves while they waited for the signal from their radio operator. The brothers: Nick, George, Richard, and Danny looked on as their six bodyguards waxed their Scarabs at the docks north of Cancun Beach. The Brothers felt confident they could attack and board the *Brimstone* in a bold surprise attack.

Eventually, Frank began receiving calls from the other search aircraft. Each was calling to report no ship seen on present courses and would be returning to base. Their part in the search was over. Frank had chosen the middle heading and would soon land on the Mexican side of the Yucatán Straits. Now, the search would be up to them alone as they cruised on toward Cancun to re-fuel.

On board the *Brimstone,* the bodyguard for the Nuccio Brothers approached the radio operator. The bodyguard could see they were approaching land. They were currently sailing into a cove on the northern coast of Yucatán. It was Cape Catoche near the town of Chiquila. They would drop anchor to await a PBY Catalina seaplane to pick up the Lust Brothers and their bodyguards. They chose this type of plane for its long-range and amphibious landing capability. Their destination was the Isla Contadora, a relatively uninhabited island in the Gulf of Panama. Here, the Lust Brothers would set up their new cocaine trafficking operation headquarters.

The island was the largest of an archipelago, the Perlas Islands. In the 1500s, it was used by the Spaniards as a counting house for plentiful pearl harvests. Long ago, the pearls died out from an aquatic disease. But the name Perlas easily remained fitting for this chain of tropical hideaways. Fifty miles away, Panama City would suffice for modern conveniences and worldwide communication and, especially, accommodating international banks. In other words, it was a safe place for drug money.

20

Just after takeoff, Curtis spotted three fast boats heading north along the coast. Just out of curiosity, Curtis trained his binoculars on the three boats.

Focusing in on them, he shook his head speaking out loud, "I don't believe it! Frank, you might think I'm seeing things, but I just spotted Nick Nuccio in one of those fast boats."

Frank was shocked. "Well, if that's them, they can't be far from the Lust Brothers."

"We should follow them Frank. I think things should get pretty interesting very soon."

"Roger that, boss."

Curtis winced as he continued peering through his binoculars.

"Yes, Frank, it's the whole family down there, and a few new faces."

"Curtis, I'm going to have to throttle back and take some slow 'S' turns to keep from overtaking them.

"Whatever it takes Frank. Just don't lose them."

"No worries on that, they're going flat out now. It's a good thing it's such a clear day I can see their wakes at a distance. I'll just loaf along behind them keeping above our stall speed."

Curtis said, "I wonder what their strategy is? After all, there are only three boats and one big tanker."

"A lot depends on what type of armaments they have on board. Maybe they've got rocket launchers or something heavier. I can't imagine anything larger than a launcher would be useful on a boat that small. Whatever they are planning, it won't take long to find out. I'm reaching the point where we'll be turning around the eastern point of the Yucatán Peninsula. Curtis, do you think we ought to… alert the authorities?"

"What will we say, Frank? Would we tell them we see three suspicious speedboats traveling along the Yucatán Peninsula?"

"I guess you're right. I suppose we should wait it out, 'til we see something else happen."

Frank steered the twin Bonanza around the very tip of the peninsula as they cleared a rise just over the point. They each beheld a beautiful sight. The bright white sandy beaches and aquamarine water made incredible sightseeing. Yet, each knew they were not in for any pleasure cruise.

"How far have we come from Cancun, Frank?"

"Oh, I'd say about 50 miles now."

"Then we should be within radio range of Cancun, right?"

"Yeah, boss, I'm sure of that. That is, unless we get down too low."

Curtis winced and said, "That shouldn't be a problem."

After gaining a clear view of the harbor and the cove, they could see right where the *Brimstone* was. She was surrounded by the three fast boats that throttled down to begin their attack. The *Brimstone* was situated between two other freighters in the small cove. Unable to maneuver, they were at the mercy of the fast boats. They were going in between the bigger boats firing inward at the *Brimstone.*

Nick Nuccio shouted at his crewmen.

"Use your grenade launchers. Aim for the radio mast. If the Brothers try to come off the boat, aim for them. If they don't, use the rocket launcher on their rudder."

Each time the boats sped by them, they launched grenades at the radio mast. On the second round, they finally knocked it out. Thus far, no one had appeared on the decks. It looked like that situation would continue. Now, Frank had something to radio in about. Calling the tower at Cancun, he reported the violence he was witnessing. Soon a PBY Catalina with the Mexican DEA was dispatched. They, in turn, dispatched a message to Frank telling him their type of aircraft and their expected ETA. With a trained team, the DEA's crew was always on alert. Considering their speed of 150 kn, they should be able to arrive over the scene in less than half an hour. Frank worried that may be too late. Both he and Curtis felt helpless as they crisscrossed the area overhead. From a distance, Frank spotted a PBY coming in low. He assumed it was the DEA plane. Instead, it was the aircraft the Lust Brothers hired.

"Curtis, I don't understand why the DEA plane is landing. Why don't they fly in low and shoot it out with these boats?"

"Maybe they just don't want to get hit, Frank."

As the boats completed one more pass, four men came out on deck with Uzis. This time, as the boats came by, it was a different story. As the Nuccios ducked low in their boats, two bodyguards were hit and fell overboard. Just when, Nick was considering calling the whole thing off. He spotted a boat being lowered into the water. The crew of the boat allowed the fast boats to pass them allowing time for all the Lust Brothers and two bodyguards to scramble aboard. The PBY hired by the Lusts was on the water now taxiing toward the *Brimstone*.

Curtis squinted his eyes in anger as the scene unfolded below. With each pass they made overhead, he cringed at the thought of them getting away. Just then, the real Mexican DEA plane arrived on the scene. Initially, there was some confusion as they mistook them for another DEA plane. Frank soon straightened that out over the radio and told them who the bad guys were. Now, they leveled out for a pass at the speedboats. Because they were more maneuverable, it was difficult for the gunners in the nose of the Mexican PBY to get a hit. They swept over low banking steeply, intending to come around for another go at it. By now, the boat with the Brothers aboard sped toward the PBY waiting to take them away.

"They're getting away, dammit!"

The Mexican PBY lined up for another pass. Its pilot questioned his co-pilot.

"What is this other vessel doing, the one that is going slower? Do you suppose that is some sort of rescue boat? The other fast boats appear to be lining up to fire upon them."

"I'm not sure Capt. I think we should be sure we don't hit any innocent civilians."

The captain continued his dive, then leveled off. Sweat was beading on his brow as a look of indecision was forming there. Suddenly, he ordered.

"Hold your fire!"

The PBY swept up into the air again making a tight 60° turn to sweep back in the other direction. This gave the Nuccios time to close in with all guns firing forward. The small transport vessel was at high speed now closing in toward the PBY waiting to carry the Brothers away to safety. There were now six men kneeling at the railing firing back at the Nuccios. One of the bullets struck Nick in the forehead, sending him flying off the boat. George looked back from his boat seeing his brother, Nick, tumbling in the violent wake of the fast boat. This was no time for regrets, only vengeance. The boats continued their relentless pursuit.

Frank went on his radio to the DEA plane. He couldn't control his anger. He shouted, "Don't you see? Now, the men in those boats are firing at each other. Those men are about to get away! They are escaped criminals from the U.S. They're all highly involved in drug trafficking. You must capture or kill these men!"

Now, the Lust Brothers were beginning to board the plane. The Nuccios were right behind them closing in with two boats splitting to the right and one to the left, firing all the time. They had used up their rocket-propelled grenades. Now, Uzis would have to do the job. A hail of bullets riddled the side of the venerable old PBY. It was built for combat; it could take it. But, the last two men who attempted to enter the hatch were shot in the back and killed. It would be a great loss for two of the Lust Brothers, who were their fathers. Now, there were only four of the Lust Brothers and two loyal sons scrambling to board the aircraft. Immediately, the pilot slammed forward the throttles on the twin-engine seaplane beginning its struggle to escape the ocean's grasp. The fast boats swept past the delivery boat, alongside peppering the plane with their Uzis. Before the large side hatch could be drug shut, Peter, the aggressive self-assured brother, leaned out making a last desperate play firing back to take another Nuccio life. Peter paid the price instead, taking several bullets in his chest.

The DEA plane's pilot was in a quandary now. Should he pursue the Lust Brothers' plane or should he stay and fight it out with the fast boats? Frank tried to persuade the pilot.

"Captain, there isn't much time. The plane is getting away. You saw for yourself these men are armed and dangerous narcotics traffickers. I can assure you, capturing them would be a far better service to your country."

The Mexican DEA Captain replied, *"Señor,* what is your interest in these men? Do you represent a law enforcement agency?"

"No, sir. My partner and I represent an international insurance investigation."

"Then, you are civilians from America?"

"Yes, sir. You know, I am the one who told you about this incident and where to find us."

"Yes, and we are grateful for your help. However, you are a civilian flying in our airspace. Obviously, you have no jurisdiction here. It is I who decides how my mission will be carried out. I choose to deal with the violent criminals here at the time. My country's authorities will have to deal with the civilians in the aircraft when they land. I will radio out a bulletin for our forces to be looking for them. Now, I must attend to my duties. Over and out, senior."

Frank slammed his fist on the dashboard.

"Hell, boss, where are we supposed to go from here?

With a determined look, Curtis spoke firmly.

"We're going to follow that plane, wherever it goes. If we can't keep up, we will report the last sighting we've made of them."

"But, boss, he's got the range on us. We'll never catch up."

Now, the look of determination turned to anger.

"Would you please not call me boss? You know how it bothers me."

"Sorry b— Ah, it won't happen again. Look, Curtis, I know you're angry, but we must look at this logically. There is no way in hell we'll catch up with that plane unless it lands. I'm looking at about three quarters of a tank right now. There's a lot of jungle out there and I'm not flying over it without a cushion. As your pilot, I strongly recommend we go back to Cancun get some rest and reshuffle the deck."

Curtis was silent for a long moment. Then, he decided Frank was right.

"Well at least we can go back and watch what the Mexican DEA does with those Mafia bastards."

"Now, that is an interesting thought. I'll turn back now."

Frank banked the B -50 in a steep 90° turn. Leveling out, they both had time to glimpse the DEA plane making another run at the remaining boats. When the nose gunner got lined up on their track, the boats began to weave to and fro. The gunner led all the boats with a stream of machine gun fire with back-and-forth motions. His 30-caliber gun sent incendiary shells into the boat, exploding it in seconds. The other two boats drove hard for the coast as the plane banked making another round. By the time he was near the coast, the pilot decided to pull up aborting the gun run. Not wanting to risk hitting any civilians, he had to break off the attack. Both boats throttled back and slid underneath one of the many docks along the coast.

Curtis and Frank were glad to see one boat explode. Anyone could see, there would be no survivors from that one. Yet, it was a bittersweet victory seeing the other two escape. Curtis felt sure they would meet again, hopefully, on his own turf. At least, he could take solace in knowing the Mafia helped him do his job. Frank turned the plane southward leaving behind the aquamarine waters of Cape Catoché behind where the Gulf of Mexico and the Caribbean meet. On the return flight, Curtis had time to cool down reflecting on the whole matter.

"You know, Frank, you got a great idea. We should spend more time relaxing here in Cancun. Can Sandy come?"

"I'll try to arrange it, Curtis."

"I hope you can. I think we all need a break. It may be a relatively new tourist destination, but I hear it's becoming a world-class resort brighter and bigger than Acapulco."

"Well, I hope you're right, Curtis. After probing the core of the cocaine trade, I'm sure we could all use some rest."

The place chosen was once a deserted sand split off the eastern shore near a little fishing village called Quarto. The old Mayan name meant, Place of the Snakes. Of course, in modern touristas Mayan language it translated to Cancun. At first, there was nothing but jungle and mosquitoes. A road had to be built through dense jungle even to reach the eastern part of the Yucatán Peninsula. Cancun was the largest project this part of the country had ever seen. Now, it was one of the world's largest and most visited vacation resorts with everything one would expect from a world-class resort.

"What will we do next, Curtis?"

"When we land, I'd like to top off our tanks and put the bird in a safe hangar."

"Are we going out on the town tonight, Curtis?"

"All things considered, Frank, I feel it is appropriate. But first, call your wife and invite her down."

I went to the hangar phone right away. It was late in the day and I was lucky to get her after she came back from her shift.

"Hey, honey. It's your handsome pilot calling."

"He's not here right now, so what would you like?"

"Thanks, honey. That's real funny. It's not your style, though. Listen, I got some good news. Frank and I are here in Cancun and we'd like you to be with us. We're taking some time off for R&R."

Suddenly, there was still was on the other end. Then, Sandy's voice spoke, "Well, I must say, this has never happened before."

"Sure, it has. You know, I take you to Sanibel and fishing all the time."

"Sure, all the time," she said sarcastically.

"All right, honey. But, this is for real. We've got time and we'd like to have you come. There will be a ticket waiting for you when you get to the counter. You can take American Airlines to Merida Yucatán. I'll fly out tomorrow and get you there. I'll call you from the hotel we're staying in later tonight. Are you excited?'

"What will I wear?"

"Wear whatever you like. I'll buy you more clothes when you get here. So, travel light, okay?"

"Well, all right, honey. I'm flabbergasted! I don't know what else to say. Except, I guess, I could say a surprise vacation is the best kind of all. Don't forget to call me and tell me where you're staying, that is, before you get to partying too much."

"Don't you worry, honey. I'll call. Goodbye."

Now, I had to go to the hangar office and arrange for tomorrow's flight. I would get the weather just before I left and should make it up the coast in a little less than two hours. Now, it was up to Curtis and me to find decent lodgings. He and I talked it over and agreed we didn't want some fancy wild splash hotel. We preferred a more low profile Spanish-style if we could find one. We took a stroll along the beach where there was a wide boardwalk. Then, I spotted something across the street that looked interesting.

"Look over there, Curtis. That three-story building over there looks like a hacienda style hotel."

"Yes, I believe it does, Frank. Let's cross the street and check it out."

Curtis stepped off the curb and was immediately almost struck by a taxicab. I leapt forward grabbing his arm, yanking him back up on the curb.

"I need to remind *you,* boss, in Mexico the pedestrian does *not* have the right-of-way."

I noticed he was so shook up he forgot to wince. The lights of the Hotel Papa Gueyo were only neon trim around the doors in the front of the building. The rest was relatively dark. However, there was a neon vacancy sign. When we entered the lobby, we noticed there was a quaint outdoor courtyard style patio.

"I think we found our place, don't you. Curtis?"

"Yes, this is it. I believe Sandy will find this romantic and close enough to the beach."

After we checked in, I made my call to Sandy. Then, we were free to sample the nightlife. It was easy to see Cancun was mainly one large long strip down the coast. There were nightclubs and hotels and casinos lined far down the walk. So, we began our walk. We came across one place that was particularly bright and inviting. They were offering fajitas featured on their menu, so we dropped in there for our first experience of the evening. We were shown to our table and the waiter offered us a drink. Curtis ordered a margarita keeping in the spirit of things, while I ordered just a tame Jack Daniels-black and Diet Coke.

The waiter leaned over saying to me, "For future orders, *señor,* we call that a Slim Black Jack."

There were dancing girls on stage dressed in costumes decorated in various colored plumes of feathers. It was interesting, to say the least. When our drinks arrived, I toasted Curtis as his piercing blue eyes looked across at me. I could see he looked tired. Obviously, he had been under a strain ever since we lost the Lust Brothers in Tampa. I was sure happy we were in a place where we could relax. We enjoyed our fajitas. The friendly sizzling platter was quite filling and delightful. I could see Curtis began to loosen up as the night went on and he suggested another place. They were all the same to both of us, so we felt we couldn't miss. By the third bar, we thought we ought to be turning around and heading back on the boardwalk. I was glad we decided to return to base, as I found the sandals I had bought were catching between the boards, occasionally. I had to catch myself from stumbling.

It reminded me of a time long ago. I was stationed in lovely Ubon Thailand as a guest of the Royal Thai Air Force. It was one of those days that turned into one of those nights. Leaving the Officers Club, after my share of libation, I was heading back. It was raining, which in Thailand, was as normal as saying, "Hey, there's a tree over there in that forest."

Because it was raining, I was hurrying along to get to my hooch when I made one of the most fantastic swan dives onto the wooden matting we used to keep us above flood level. After slamming my face into the wooden slats, I ripped off half of my so-called bulletproof mustache. My pride was wounded. When I had the choice of appearing with half a mustache, or starting all over again, the choice was obvious. But, the emotional pain of the experience was never forgotten.

I was extra careful walking back to our hotel. We spent the night peacefully after a few revelers expended their fireworks. The next day dawned clear and the rising sun on the horizon streaking through pink clouds made for a beautiful site through our third-floor window. The beach was relatively quiet. I surmised most people here wouldn't awake until after noon, anyway.

I was prepared to take the trip to Merida to pick up Sandy alone. Yet, Curtis insisted he go along. Of course, I agreed. Yet, when he appeared after his shower, he was dressed in a tropical shirt and sandals. I felt I had to make some changes for safety sake.

"Curtis, I appreciate your style, but I suggest when you fly never wear sandals or short pants. Especially, in the jungle, you never know where you're going to land."

"I'll be right back."

In a few moments, he reappeared in khaki slacks and a nice pair of low quarter boots.

"Now, how do I look?"

"You look fantastic, Curtis, ready to fly."

I did admire the way he kept fit. With his broad shoulders and narrow waist, he always seemed to be on the go, but I could never see him exercise. I guess some people are lucky that way. It's their metabolism, I suppose. Just then, I heard the maid at the door. We were ready to leave, anyway, so we stepped out passing her in the doorway.

It was nearly 9 a.m. now. I knew we could slip though, since Sandy's plane would not arrive until 11 a.m. We pre-flighted the plane, taxied to the runway, and received our clearance for takeoff. The plane was flying beautifully; all the systems were in the green. We enjoyed the flight to Merida. We waited in a terminal coffee shop until we saw Sandy's plane arriving.

As she came down the steps, I waved. Then scooped her up in my arms and gave her a kiss I'd been waiting for. She seemed to glow and was very happy to be on vacation. The return trip was uneventful. We took two rooms at the same hotel. The following morning, we enjoyed our breakfast on a balcony facing the courtyard below. After three glorious days in the surf and the sand, Curtis felt the need to get back to Tampa. Sandy and I were reluctant, but duty called. We left the beaches of Cancun with a fond farewell.

The flight back to Tampa would be close to 800 miles. The fact that it was all over open water, made it a little more interesting. My navigation had to be spot on, as our range was only 1000 miles. Not much of a margin, if you're lost over the Gulf of Mexico. Although I'd flown long stretches over water while in the military, I always took strict precautions. My navigational charts were all updated. I'd received the latest weather from Merida and, for the time being, it looked clear out in the Gulf. Visibility was about 10 miles.

I decided not to put us on oxygen and chose an altitude of around 12,000. This way, just in case there might be visible landmarks along our flight path to use, if dead reckoning navigation was required. Along the way, we encountered some pods of whales. So, I dove down low enough for all to get a good view. It was a good flight and we arrived just before dusk. We were all happy to be home safely and we said our goodbyes to Curtis on the field. Once we were home, I told Sandy all about our encounter with the Lusts and Nuccios. She seemed worried for me, but I guess the vacation helped to ease her mind about my work. Anyway, my main concern was her safety. My next consideration was how to deal with the situation we were facing now. With the Lust Brothers living incognito and the rest of the Nuccio Brothers still on the loose, we had to devise a new plan.

21

Sometimes events create a plan. Those events can create a direction which all will follow. In this case, Curtis and I were left to follow. It was Fourth of July and Curtis was putting on one hell of a party at Pilot's Cove. All who work for Curtis were invited. The parking lot at the Cove was full that day. Curtis went all out, making sure we had a good time. Even tents were put up outside with extra chairs and tables for the overflow that was sure to occur in the Cove.

Sandy and I were tucked away in a corner at a table near the bar with our backs toward the wall. This way we could observe the activities without being stepped over by the crowd. Surely a good time was being had by all, and the noise level was getting near intolerable, when the band started playing. So, there was dancing and drinking and celebrating. In general, even the mechanics and the hangar personnel were invited and were getting a bit rowdy. One mechanic held a lit sparkler in our faces and almost singed Sandy's hair. I stood up and grabbed his arm spun him around.

"Take it outside, George."

"Aw, hell, Frank. I was just having a little fun. I didn't burn your tail feathers, did I?"

"I mean it, George take that thing outside. It's not safe in here."

At that, he began waving it back and forth in the air walking through the crowd. I stood up and got behind him grabbing him by the shoulder, escorting him out the door. I stood there talking to him for a while until he got more sensible.

I said, "Just stay outside here in the fresh air, George."

I helped him settle into a chair. It was then I noticed, looking over his shoulder, that the hangar doors were closed. Then, I remembered Curtis had scheduled fireworks for the evening. I thought closing the doors was only a precaution, so I put it out of my mind and returned to the party. Curtis approached Sandy and me at our table.

"Are you two having a good time?"

We each raised our glasses in salute, nodding our heads and smiling, as it was hard to be heard over the music. He came closer to me, so we could be heard.

"Enjoy yourselves, this evening. I hope you can watch the fireworks with us."

"Yes, we'll be there. We brought a blanket. We'll be looking forward to it over the tarmac."

"Frank, the day after tomorrow, I'm going to need you to fly up to Jacksonville for some aircraft parts we ordered."

"All right, that's no problem. What time you want me to leave?"

"I don't mind, about 10 a.m., I guess, there's really no hurry."

"I'll see to it, boss. No problem."

He must've been in a very good mood. He didn't wince that time. Sandy and I stayed on for the whole fireworks show. It ended at 9 p.m. They really did a great job preparing it. I'm sure a good time was had by all, judging from the mess left behind. I knew one thing, for sure — you couldn't say these party pilots were slackers. They picked up where everyone left off. When Sandy and I left the party, I was picking up again. We enjoyed a quiet day at home after the party. I just stayed around the house trying to fix this, that, and the other. Anything Sandy included on my "honey do list" were my orders for the day.

The following day, I arose around 9 a.m. I prepared myself for work, while I watched Sandy lovingly prepare me a breakfast of waffles and bacon. Then, it was off to the airport-pretty much routine. I figured to be back home at least by noon, so I said my goodbyes to Sandy, while she stood on the steps. She held her hand up as if she were holding the checkered flag when I came down the drive. She would sweep it by me. It was a little joke between us.

As I drove to the airport, I could see the weather was not ideal. It was partly cloudy and when I crossed the bridge there were whitecaps telling me it could be a windy takeoff. When I reached the hangar, I called Flight Service Station and got the true whether. It wasn't exactly good and might bring flight conditions below minimums, so I prepared to fly IFR to Jacksonville. Although it wasn't a long trip, it might be a bumpy one. As I was standing in the hangar, Curtis showed up.

"I'm glad you haven't left yet. I want to take a ride up with you to see someone in distribution. I want to see if I can work out a deal about free delivery next time. This is getting pretty expensive."

"Well, you know, you can always ship it by rail."

"No, I thought about that, but I want to get the parts in here faster."

I said with a smile, "Then I'm the fastest you got, Curtis."

"Yes, I suppose that's true, but I need you elsewhere."

We both settled into the cockpit going through our preflight check-list. Everything checked out, so I called the tower for taxi instructions. He directed me to runway 35. The winds were reported at 15 kn gusting to 20, though they were right down the runway. We taxied to the active runway, finished our run-up, and were given permission to take off with a straight-out departure. I eased the throttles forward slowly with Curtis's hand hovering just above them. This way, if anything got bumped or happened suddenly, there would be two hands at the throttles. We began our takeoff roll. Everything was normal. I peered ahead through our small slanted windshield. Clouds on the horizon were beginning to coalesce. There was no getting around the fact; it was going to be a good day for ducks. With the nose at a high angle of attack, I was climbing out when I reached approximately 500 feet. I heard a loud bang and felt a push from my right. Then the nose started coming down with a strong pull to my left. I tried compensating with right rudder, while instinctively scanning all my instruments to find what went wrong. Despite my efforts to pull up the nose, it would not come out of the turning dive.

I immediately told Curtis, "Get on the yoke, I need more back pressure. Look out your window to the right and back!"

"Can you see anything, Curtis?"

"I can't see anything from here. I'm going to unbuckle and go back and have a look!"

"Never mind, stay here. I need your help holding these runners. My instruments tell me we lost number one engine. We're losing altitude rapidly. We have to try to get back to the runway. I think we can keep the nose up long enough to get back on the runway. Keep an eye on our altitude, Curtis. I am going to try to make a slow 180° turn."

As I did so, the nose altitude began slipping even more. Seconds later, I was nose down losing altitude rapidly. With all power increased to maximum on the right engine, I could still barely keep the nose from dropping further. There was still a lot of drag coming from the right side of the plane, too. I kept easing back on the yoke trying to keep the nose near level. It was no use; it continued to drop. Suddenly, the stall warning light and alarm came on simultaneously.

"We're losing it, Curtis. We're going down!"

Instantly, the wing stalled. The aircraft was plummeting straight down.

"Brace yourself, Curtis. This is it!"

The last thing I remember was seeing the ocean filling up my view through the windshield. We plummeted 200 feet into the bay short of the runway by at least 200 yards. I put my arm up over my face as I felt the crushing impact as our aircraft thudded into the shallow waters of the bay. By the time I came to, there was water rushing in the cabin through our shattered windows. Air/sea rescue had already been dispatched. It was our luck that St. Petersburg/Clearwater International Airport was also a Coast Guard Air/Sea Rescue Station.

In minutes, they were hovering above us with a Coast Guard helicopter. My trouble, in the meantime, was I could not pull Curtis out of his seat. He was unconscious. In the murky waters, I could not see that his seatbelt was still attached. For several moments, I yanked on his upper body to no avail. With the last remaining gulps of air in the cockpit, I filled my lungs and went down to see what was keeping him in his seat. As my hands raced over his belts, I discovered to my horror, the latch was still attached. Quickly, I hit the button and released him. Then I placed my arms under his shoulders and pushed him through the small opening in our windshield. I followed, thereafter, coming to the surface with my arms under his shoulders. It was all I could do to paddle my legs and keep us both afloat. Thank God, there was a rescue cable harness dangling above us as we bobbed along in the shallow waters. A rescue crewman was now in the water with us. He grabbed Curtis first, recognizing his condition. He pulled his arms through the rescue sling and they immediately started reeling him into the chopper. I had to wait a little longer, but I didn't mind now. My main concern was seeing Curtis get help. Three minutes later, I was aboard the rescue helicopter heading back to its base. The attendants on board managed to revive Curtis, amidst a bout of coughing and spluttering.

Some personnel on the ground at our hangar witnessed the explosion of our right engine, after takeoff at low altitude. There was no doubt about the fact that the engine was stricken. The entire turbo fan engine pod on the right side had blown off completely, leaving a gaping hole in the rear of our fuselage. The added drag, coupled with no thrust, accounted for the strong pull to the left overcoming our number one engine's ability to deal with the drag. At such low altitude, there was no time to recover from a stall. So, our plane pancaked into the bay.

I re-awoke in the hospital, after noon of that same day. I could see Sandy sitting in a chair beside my bed. Curtis was in the same room with me. He had been knocked out when his head hit the window post in the cockpit. Although he suffered lacerations about the face and upper chest, and despite a concussion, his breathing was normal and his vital signs were coming back close to normal. I received much the same treatment. A good knock on the head had given me a concussion, as well. In addition, I suffered lacerations about the face and arms when I tried passing through the jagged Plexiglas in our cockpit.

Investigations of our crash began immediately. Unfortunately, rescuing the remains of the aircraft in the water made it more difficult. Because the aircraft was deluged for hours, it would tend to hamper some of the investigation efforts in finding evidence for the cause of the crash. Naturally, all the agencies would be involved. The National Transportation Safety Board would have first crack at the job, then the FAA and the Civil Aeronautics Board would also play a part. Because there were witnesses, there was no doubt the immediate cause of the crash was the exploding right engine. This happening to a Rolls-Royce Spey Turbofan engine was highly unlikely. This engine was one of the most reliable in the industry.

Once all the wreckage could be assembled on the hangar floor, the experts would go about determining what the probable cause was for such a catastrophe. Like a giant jigsaw puzzle, every piece recovered would be painstakingly put together. Once this task had been accomplished, the investigators determined it was an explosion near the right engine pod. Aside from the obvious, the investigation determined conclusively from the way the metal was bent outward, that the explosion could not have occurred inside the engine itself, but rather from something placed near the engine that was not part of the engine design. In other words, the explosion came from a bomb placed there before takeoff.

During my recovery, I learned something about my wife. Aside from her kind loving care as a nurse, she had another side when it came to attempts on the life of her loved one and it showed. It was a toughness I had never seen in her. When I was coming around and feeling better, she would sit by my side daily after work. Once, when she was holding my hand, I felt her squeezing it. I awoke smiling and began to speak with her. In the middle of our conversation, she suddenly stopped and looked at me with a steely look in her eyes.

"Frank, I can feel compassion for the sick and injured. But, when it comes to those who specifically set out to destroy you, I lose all kindness. When they find out who did this to you and Curtis, and they will, I want you track them down, and if necessary, put them down. The look of resolve in her eyes gave me a chill. I knew then she was deadly serious.

When Curtis and I were released from the hospital, we started our own investigation. We had a very good idea who would do such a thing to us. What we needed was a plan to flush out the rest of the Nuccios and deal with them.

Curtis came up with one, but it was risky. For the first time, we would go out of the bounds of insurance investigators. To deal with them, we would have to reach them on their level. This would, also, mean taking the law into our own hands. Because my life had been targeted, it made it easier for Sandy to accept. Though Curtis always acted within the bounds of the law, when his life was threatened he, too, found it easier.

Days later, after a full recovery, Curtis and I were sitting at Pilot's Cove.

"Curtis, you appear far too contemplative to do that Scotch any justice."

"It's just that I've got this idea knocking around in my head. I just gotta try and figure the details. Frank, I'm thinking I've got some imitation diamonds I procured in one of my fraud cases. In the business, they are known as cubic zirconia. That's the center of my plan. I know where the Nuccios hang out. They spend most of their leisure time at the Tropics Steakhouse on Dale Mabry Highway. I'm thinking, if I can get someone we really trust, that the Nuccios wouldn't know, we could have that someone approach one of the Brothers about a hot diamond deal. Now, that's something they could hardly resist. We could be waiting there and, if we're lucky, all three brothers would be, too. Once the deal starts to go down, we could step in with weapons, just in case, and hold them until the authorities arrived. I could arrange for one of the waitresses I know to call the cops, just before we spring the deal. Of course, there are a few loose ends, but basically that's the plan."

"That sounds pretty risky, Curtis, if you asked me. What if something goes wrong? For instance, what if they recognize one of us? Somebody could get shot. Also, who are we gonna get to make this diamond exchange for money?"

Suddenly, it was like a bolt from the blue. That certain someone just came to mind. *It could be, none other than, Howie Gardenes. He was old, unassuming, the perfect match for someone who could plausibly live in that shadowy world of stolen jewelry. His age could easily place them at ease.*

When I explained to Curtis what I was thinking, he thought it was an excellent idea and suggested we go see him right away.

On the way, it occurred to me, if we allowed Howie to draw them in on the diamond sale, the subsequent arrests would not hold in court. We would be knowingly trying to entrap them. If there were arrests made, once their lawyers got a hold of the case, it would be thrown out because of that entrapment. I put that before Curtis immediately.

"Yes, I know, I thought of that, too, Frank. But the diamonds won't be Howie's, their mine."

"You see, Frank, the diamonds won't be real and the arrest won't stick, but it will bring them in long enough for the police to listen to our case accusing them of attempted murder. At least, they can hold them 48-hours to investigate that more. Hopefully, in the meantime, they'll find something else from the aircraft wreckage to pin on them. At the very least, we can put them through a whole lot of discomfort."

"All right, I'll go along, but I still think it's plenty risky."

When we reached Howie's house, he was out back hosing down his boat. His little black and tan miniature dachshund, Jack, was there on the dock. He was running about between his legs and enjoying Howie spraying him down.

"Hello, Howie. I got someone I want you to meet."

"Well, how the hell are you, Frank? I haven't seen you in a while. Where you been?"

"Oh, I been here and about. Howie, this is Curtis Selway. He's my boss."

Curtis winced and stepped forward offering his hand.

"Hello. Howie. I've heard some good things about you."

Howie said, "I'd be careful, if I were you. Someone must've been leading you down the primrose path of deception. Anyway, let's not stand out here in the heat, debating. Would you fellas like a beer?"

We sat down in his trailer over beers and I explained why we were there.

"Howie, I've got a little job for you. I think it's right up your alley."

"Well, Frank, it seems to me the last time you were off on a job you came home and I got my trailer all shot up. Not to mention, you and I were in it at the time."

"Howie, would you like some get back from that?"

"Well, if it's not too dangerous. If it involves, guns I can't carry one. Nothing too serious, but let's just say they don't want me carrying a gun."

"You won't have to Howie. You just have to be your old natural self."

"Well, who is it that I have to lie, cheat, and steal from?"

Curtis explained the details of the diamond deal and where it would all take place. Howie was still up for it, so we agreed to meet at the Tropics Restaurant, so we could familiarize ourselves with the place. Howie would act as a down and out jewel thief. He would approach the booth where the Nuccios always sat. After making his pitch, we all would have to play it by ear from there. If they took the bait, Curtis could signal the waitress to make her call to the police. I leaned forward over the table where we sat and I spoke to Curtis.

"What if there are bodyguards, Curtis? What then?"

"The way I see it, the whole deal should go off quietly. Usually, the bodyguards stay in the back where the kitchen is. However, if there is any sign of real danger, we should fold the plan immediately. Once you see the interior of the lounge where they stay, Howie, you'll see that there is an exit door halfway down the length of the lounge. It leads to the parking lot outside. That will be your escape route."

"This all sounds pretty serious, Curtis. I hope they keep the beer cold there."

Curtis winced behind his steel rimmed glasses.

"Now, let's go over this plan again. Then, I'd like to set a time for us to visit the Tropics Restaurant."

I thought about Howie. He was going on 73. I found myself hoping his heart could take it. But when I saw his eyes light up when I told him how he could get back at the people that tried to kill him, I figured he deserved the chance. There's something about when people try to kill you that makes you change your mind about some things. I'm sure we all had that same mindset. It made me feel better to think I could stir up their nest for a change. We planned to meet at the Tropics on a Monday, when it wouldn't be so crowded. The actual day we chose for the deal would be the following Saturday. Having a crowd there would help us move about discreetly.

When we arrived at the Tropics Restaurant on Monday, Howie and I entered the lounge that was on one side of the building. Curtis went over to the restaurant side to meet his waitress friend. We sat at the far end of the bar from the intended booth. The Nuccios were not there, and we were not surprised. It was only late afternoon.

When we first entered, I discovered a distinctive aroma. It was a specialty of the restaurant. They kept freshly baked onion bread in a warming cabinet in the kitchen. This cabinet allowed that fresh aroma to permeate the lounge. Naturally, my senses told me I had to order some. It came to us on a plate with butter that Howie and I shared. Before me, there was a hot plate with butter and four steaming onion rolls. When I pulled the bread apart, the scent reached my nose. My taste buds moistened at the thought of consuming something so deli-cious. Howie loved it, too. He ordered a bowl of French Onion Soup to go with it. We sat looking about everywhere familiarizing ourselves with everything we could and enjoying every crumb. Curtis soon arrived at the bar to join us. He, too, could not pass up the restaurant's delicacy.

"Well, gentlemen, are you quite familiar with the interior?"

Howie remarked, "I could stand some more of these onion rolls."

"Yes, Howie, I can agree to that. What I really want to know is do you have any questions?"

Howie grinned, "No, not really. I think I'm ready to be your little jewel thief as long as the beer holds out."

As we drove home in Curtis' Bentley, I almost thought I was begin-ning to like this work. At least, no one was shooting at me. Curtis dropped me off at home, so I had a chance to be with Sandy for a while. After a couple of beers, I was ready for an intimate evening with her. She did not disappoint. She had wine chilled. We enjoyed some Chardonnay and I grilled some of those Snook we caught near Sanibel. The night seemed to last forever, as we went on together to bed. We spent the whole night tickling each other's fancy. The week together was a very positive stress alignment. I even learned that stressed spelled backwards is desserts. I couldn't help feeling the Nuccios were going to get their just desserts.

When Sandy entered my room on Friday evening, she knew the fun and games were over when she found me cleaning my gun. She did not ask what or where or even when. I know she understood. I could tell she was determined to let this one go. I guess everyone's tempted by get back sometime. I packed my bag and stood on the front step sharing a lingering kiss with Sandy.

I arrived at Pilots Cove at 7 p.m., as Curtis requested. I could see Howie's old station wagon was already there. When I entered, I found them both at the bar?

Hey, fellas, if this is gonna be a night of drinking, you can leave me out.

Curtis said, "Relax, Frank, were just having one beer."

Howie left the bar to relieve himself. Curtis leaned over and whispered to me.

When he got here, Frank, he seemed a little jittery, so I thought a beer might calm him down.

"Just be careful with him. You don't want to get him started, if you know what I mean."

"I do, let's get started."

We arrived at the Tropics at about 7:30 p.m. We each took up our places in the lounge. We didn't have too long to wait. At 8 o'clock, on the dot, Danny, George, and Richard showed up. It was still light outside, so we waited, communicating with hand gestures. We were getting used to the ebb and flow of customers and the rhythm of the lounge with its tinkling glasses and the low murmuring voices.

Curtis and I sat several booths apart without facing the Nuccios. I sat with my back toward, watching Howie. He was nursing his beer, waiting for what might seem an opportune time to approach George. He was their natural leader now, being the oldest. I could see, Howie was beginning to get nervous. His hands were twitching. He could hardly hold a match up to his cigarette when he lit it.

Finally, he got up the courage and slid off the barstool. When he reached the large booth, George was sitting in the middle between Danny and Richard. Howie approached George with his head bent down, almost solemnly.

"Mr. Nuccio, you don't know me, but my name is Howie. One of my friends here tells me that you might be interested in something I have for sale."

George said, "Yeah, what might that be?"

Howie didn't say anything; he just reached in his right coat pocket and produced a small rectangular jewelry box. Curtis had coached him to say there was $250,000 worth of jewelry in the box. When George looked in the box, he looked back up at Howie.

"Who told you I was looking for something like this?"

"Oh, Mr. Nuccio, I wouldn't want to have to tell you that. I promised I would keep that a secret."

George was a stout man, 5 feet 10 about 200 pounds. He was wearing a black silk suit that night, as usual, with matching Italian loafers. In fact, all the brothers were dressed in black. George had a penchant for diamonds and wore three on one hand and two on the other. He didn't ask Howie any more questions, but continued to poke the would-be diamonds around in the box with his stubby finger.

Finally, he said, "Let's go in the back. Howie was shaking now almost uncontrollably. From where Curtis was seated, he could tell. So far, no one had really taken notice of us. Howie and George left for the back. As they did, they walked through the kitchen. When they reached the very back of the building, there was an office next to the exit door. Standing by the door was a hulk of a man. Howie presumed correctly, he was a bodyguard.

"Wait here, I'll be right back."

Inside the office, George knelt and opened a safe. Aside from the stacks of $100 bills, there were several trays with diamonds in them. Also, there was a jeweler's magnifying eyepiece. He took it out and placed it in his right eye and stared down at the gems in the box that Howie delivered. He examined the stones in the box very carefully. When he was sure, he raised his head put away the ocular device and stood up looking very disgusted. He had unveiled the ruse. With his expertise, he had discovered they were not diamonds, but, in fact, what they really were. Now, he stepped out of the office and whispered in his bodyguard's ear.

"Take him out back. This guy's toast."

When the guard grabbed Howie by both arms he lifted on his toes. The man was so overpowering there was nothing Howie could do as his hand went up over his mouth. By now, Curtis had lost patience and walked briskly over to Frank.

"I've got to get to that waitress and have her make that call. This thing is going all wrong, Frank."

"I agree. I'm going to go out the exit here and make it around the back of the building."

"Okay, Frank. I'll go around the other side of the building."

Meanwhile, behind the Tropics Restaurant, George held a blackjack and slugged Howie over the head. He ordered his bodyguard to take Howie and roll him up in a rubber doormat just inside the back door.

"Now, go get the car. I don't want you to waste him until you have him in the trunk."

Once the bodyguard had pulled the long black Mercedes around, he popped the trunk. He picked up Howie and placed his rolled-up body in the trunk.

George ordered the bodyguard, "Put your suppressor on your gun and put two behind his ears."

Just as George uttered those words, I appeared from the opposite side of the building. My gun was already drawn when the bodyguard saw me. The bodyguard quickly pulled his weapon around and leveled it, but it was too late. My bullet already left the chamber. As he slumped down over the edge of the trunk, George dashed inside.

At that moment, three police cars arrived in the back parking lot. Two were at the front. After seeing George run in, Danny and Richard ran to cover the back door. Richard wanted to get to the safe, while Danny covered him. When the police saw one body draped over the trunk, the other man ran. Danny was their only target. Danny drew too late. One of the officers fired and took Danny down. Richard peeked around the corner for the last time. The police took him down, too.

I quickly put my gun back in its holster, before somebody targeted me. Then, I heard the squealing of tires from the side parking lot. George had abducted a woman in the lounge and made a break for it in her car. Two police cars gave pursuit. There was a high-speed chase on Dale Mabry that resulted in George over handling the wheel on a turn and flipping the car over the median. Both passengers were okay. George was taken into custody. Finally, it was all over.

Come what may, the whys and the wherefores had to be investigated, so the police invited Curtis and me downtown for a little chat. It took Curtis' lawyers and a whole lot of talking to get us out of this one. But, the common denominator remained. Three mafia bosses, known criminals, guilty of attempted murder, abduction and kidnapping, even grand theft auto, were taken down in one night. With two dead and one incarcerated, Tampa would be a cleaner town for some time to come. Also, George was accused of accessory to attempted murder of Curtis, Howie, and me, which should put him away for a long time.

The following night, Curtis held a party at Pilot's Cove. All our friends were there. We left Howie in charge of making sure the beer was cold enough. The following day, we formed a fishing party and sailed across Safety Harbor. Sandy and I were in each other's arms as the boat rocked back and forth in the sunset. Truly, it was a time of celebration. I didn't care if I caught a fish or not.

I held up my beer in a toast to my loved ones and friends.

"You know it's always the big ones that getaway. But, if I know Curtis, they won't get away for long, right boss?"

Curtis winced and replied, "You know, Frank, I very much look forward to that."

Sandy said, "Yes, me, too."

IN MEMORY OF
TOM RICHMOND

Thomas E. Richmond, proud Floridian and author of 9 books, left his earthly home behind on October 5, 2018. Tom loved writing and his books were written about things that needed to be said through historical fiction. He was an historian and believed it was important to keep history alive for his readers and students.

Tom was a U. S. Air Force Veteran of the Vietnam War. There he was a fighter pilot and flew nearly 100 missions. He remained an avid aviation enthusiast throughout his life. Fans of his books, no doubt, noticed this when reading his stories. In civilian life, he held a private pilot's license and was a developer and supporter of the Prairie Aviation Museum in Bloomington, Illinois. He felt the museum was a place for people of all ages to learn about aviation history and to see planes from other eras.

Tom enjoyed traveling and visited the Caribbean basin, Panama, and all fifty states, as well as many other parts of the world. These travels and experiences colored many details of his written works.

In 2018, Tom received four President's Awards from the Florida Authors and Publishers Association: a Gold Medal for *Five beneath Philly* (with co-author, Susan Bandy) in the Adult Fiction Genre, Historical Category for Writing; a Bronze Medal for *Hollow Vengeance* in the Adult Fiction Genre, Historical Category for Writing; and Silver Medals for *Five beneath Philly* and *The Winnower* (both with co-author Susan Bandy) for Cover Design, Small Book Format Category. Recognition and receipt of these awards acknowledging his work and writing ranked as one of the greatest thrills of his writing life.

Tom Richmond's contributions to historical fiction and writing will be greatly missed by his many readers.

He rode upon a cherub, and did fly: yea,
he did fly upon the wings of the wind.

— Psalms XVIII, 10